She wouldn't cower before him.

The rulers of the empire devoured the weak. She waited until he came forward to pull the curtain aside with a sweep of his arm. The tiniest of concessions.

'Tell me, Governor.' She ran a fingertip across her own cheek. 'How did you get that scar?'

His eyes narrowed. 'A woman,' he said after a pause.

Her lips teased into a smile. 'Fascinating.'

His hand tightened on the curtain, the material clenched between his fingers. At once his pupils darkened, his breathing grew deep. The signs were there and she could read them like lines of poetry. How else was a woman to protect herself in the world of men? Li Tao, for all of his supposed cunning, was just another man.

'You do not disappoint,' he said in a low voice.

He dropped into the familiar form of address. The spark in his eyes showed the first hint of any heat beneath the cold exterior.

For a dark moment she was caught in the call of his gaze. They were close, nearly touching. She had provoked him on purpose, but regretted it as an alarming awareness unfurled itself within her, prickling just beneath her skin. The regiment of soldiers surrounding them faded. There was only one man here she had any fear of.

'And here I had thought the game was over for me,' she murmured.

THE DRAGON
AND THE PEARL

Jeannie Lin

First published in Great Britain 2012
by Mills & Boon, an imprint of Harlequin (UK) Limited.
Harlequin (UK) Limited, Eton House, 18-24 Paradise Road,
Richmond, Surrey TW9 1SR

© Jeannie Lin 2011

ISBN: 978 0 263 22910 3

Harlequin (UK) policy is to use papers that are natural,
renewable and recyclable products and made from wood grown in
sustainable forests. The logging and manufacturing process conform
to the legal environmental regulations of the country of origin.

Printed and bound in Great Britain
by CPI Antony Rowe, Chippenham, Wiltshire

Jeannie Lin grew up fascinated with stories of Western epic fantasy and Eastern martial arts adventures. When her best friend introduced her to romance novels in middle school the stage was set. Jeannie started writing her first romance while working as a high school science teacher in South Central Los Angeles. After four years of trying to break into publishing with an Asian-set historical, her 2009 Golden Heart®–winning manuscript, BUTTERFLY SWORDS, was sold to Harlequin Mills & Boon.

As a technical consultant, backpacker, and vacation junkie, she's travelled all over the United States as well as Europe, South Korea, Japan, China, and Vietnam. She's now happily settled in St Louis, with her wonderfully supportive husband, and continues to journey to exotic locations in her stories.

You can visit Jeannie Lin online at: www.jeannielin.com

A previous novel from this author:

BUTTERFLY SWORDS

THE DRAGON AND THE PEARL
features characters you will have already met
in BUTTERFLY SWORDS

**Available in Mills & Boon Historical *Undone!*
ebooks:**

THE TAMING OF MEI LIN
THE LADY'S SCANDALOUS NIGHT

**Did you know that these novels are also available
as ebooks? Visit www.millsandboon.co.uk**

Acknowledgements:

In the process of writing, this story both evolved and changed, yet it always stayed true to its original heart and spirit and emerged an even stronger tale than the one I envisioned. I have to thank my talented and dedicated editor, Anna Boatman, for her guidance. Thank you to my agent, Gail Fortune, for always being a protective lioness. Also a special acknowledgement to three talented writers: Bria Quinlan, Inez Kelley and my sister Nam, for always being there with a keen eye or a sympathetic ear—whichever was needed at the time.

AUTHOR NOTE

In BUTTERFLY SWORDS my hero and heroine spent the first part of the story wondering about the warlord Li Tao—a man they would eventually have to confront. In truth, I spent half of that book wondering about him myself. What kind of villain would he be? Would he be self-serving and power-hungry?

By the time Li Tao finally did stride onto the page he emerged as someone completely unexpected. I knew before BUTTERFLY SWORDS was finished that I would have to write another story featuring this cold-hearted and calculating warrior, if only to answer for myself how a man who has set himself up against an empire, and has done so without apology, could ever find redemption. More importantly, what woman would be his match in love and war?

The later eighth century was a time of political upheaval in China. Military governors called *jiedushi* grew in power enough to challenge the imperial throne. THE DRAGON AND THE PEARL allowed me to imagine and explore the underworld of spies and assassins as well as the art of war in the fall of the Golden Age. The characters are not based on any specific persons from history—rather they're drawn from the spirit of the many colourful and larger-than-life figures of the Tang Dynasty. I hope you enjoy the journey and find the

Chapter One

Tang Dynasty, China—ad 759

Lady Ling Suyin waited in the parlour at the edge of the Snake hour, her house rendered silent except for the buzz of dragonflies outside. The tea before her had long gone cold. The last servant had brought it that morning before fleeing.

The boldest of them had begged her to join them, but the warlord who was coming for her would burn every village along the river to find her. She wouldn't add to her growing collection of debt. Another stone on the scale.

She straightened at the crunch of boots over leaves at the front of the house. They were steady and deliberate. Her heart pounded harder with each impending step. He'd come alone. Her breath caught as the imposing figure appeared in the doorway, every bit the demon they spoke of in the imperial court. Black robe, dark hair cut short, an impassive expression that revealed nothing to her. That meant she had nothing over him.

'Ling *Guifei*.' His voice rang deep as he greeted her by title.

'I am no one's Precious Consort any longer, Governor Li.'

Suyin remained seated and let the military governor approach. If she stood, her legs might fail her. The prominence of his features added to her fear. This was a face that could never be overlooked.

All sun-darkened skin and sharp angles. A scar cut below his left eye, ruining his stark symmetry. That was new.

The first and only time she had seen Li Tao, he'd stood before the imperial court as a young man being commended for his valour. The restless energy that once had radiated from him was constrained behind a wall of discipline. Time had honed him to razor sharpness. Time had not left her untouched either.

'This humble servant is here to offer himself as the lady's escort.'

All the civility in the world could not take the edge off him.

Her stomach fluttered in warning, but she breathed through it. She propped an elbow on to the table and made her tone as light as possible. All the while, her heart pounded so hard she could barely hear her words.

'A thousand apologies, my lord, but I have no plans for travel.'

'This place is no longer safe for you.'

As if she could be safe with him. There was nowhere safe for her any longer, no allies left to protect her. Would the late Emperor's enforcer come for her after so many years? She had thought her secrets long buried.

Suyin dug her nails into the edge of the table as he stepped closer. She had been left alone to fend for herself before, but she had been young and defenceless. An accomplished courtesan should be able to command her fear. She should be able to command the man in front of her.

Li Tao halted two strides from her and she spied the silhouette of a weapon inside the drape of his sleeve. An assassin's blade. She lifted the cup and took a sip to cover her shock. Cold, bitter tea slid over her tongue. Experience allowed her to keep from trembling, but she had no control over the way her heart raced or how her palms grew damp as he loomed over her.

She managed to keep her hand steady as she set the cup down. Her next words came out in the melodic, careless tone she had perfected. 'Since my lord has come so far for this task, we should not waste any more time. Shall I gather my belongings?'

'There is nothing the lady needs.'

The warlord addressed her as if she were his superior. It wasn't much, but there had to be some way to use it. She caught the trailing edge of her shawl and draped it over her shoulders. She stood straight and paused before gliding past him.

He made no move toward her, but he was watching. All men did.

She stepped through the empty house, listening to his purposeful stride on the floorboards behind her. He was too close. By the time she emerged outside, her fingers were numb from being clenched so tight.

A palanquin awaited her by the side of the single dusty road leading from her manor. A regiment of soldiers outfitted in black and red assembled around the litter. The military governors, the *jiedushi*, commanded their own regional forces independent of the Emperor's army. No one challenged them within their own domains, but this stretch of the forest was clearly under imperial jurisdiction. This was an affront the Emperor would not overlook.

Li Tao followed her like a gathering storm to the sedan and the urge to flee nearly overwhelmed her. If she ran, it would only remind him that he was a hunter, a warrior, a killer. As it was, some part of him thought he was a gentleman.

'Where are we going?'

'South.'

That was all he'd grant her. With a heaviness in her chest, she looked back. The August Emperor had built this home for her before his death. The manor itself meant nothing to her. Her gaze drifted to the river beyond, a rolling canvas on which the sunlight danced. She breathed deep to take in the scent of the river, of the surrounding moss and earth. This was what she would miss.

It had been too much to wish that she could be hidden away and forgotten. Perhaps she had always known someone would come for her. Debts had to be repaid in this life or the next.

She stopped before the palanquin and turned to find herself face to face with the most ruthless of the *jiedushi*. He was a tower of lean strength and corded muscle up close. And he was still assessing her with that penetrating gaze.

She wouldn't cower before him. The rulers of the empire

devoured the weak. She waited until he came forwards to pull the curtain aside with a sweep of his arm. The tiniest of concessions.

'Tell me, Governor…' she ran a fingertip across her own cheek '…how did you get that scar?'

His eyes narrowed. 'A woman,' he said after a pause.

Her lips teased into a smile. 'Fascinating.'

His hand tightened on the curtain, the material clenched between his fingers. At once his pupils darkened, his breathing grew deep. The signs were there and she could read them like lines of poetry. How else was a woman to protect herself in the world of men? Li Tao, for all of his supposed cunning, was just another man.

'You do not disappoint,' he said in a low voice.

He dropped into the familiar form of address. The spark in his eyes showed the first hint of any heat beneath the cold exterior.

For a dark moment, she was caught in the call of his gaze. They were close, nearly touching. She had provoked him on purpose, but regretted it as an alarming awareness unfurled itself within her, prickling just beneath her skin. The regiment of soldiers surrounding them faded. There was only one man here she had any fear of.

'And here I had thought the game was over for me,' she murmured.

He didn't respond. Her shoulder brushed against his sleeve as she slipped inside the wooden transport. His black eyes remained on her as the curtain fell back across the opening.

The journey came to Suyin in fragments snatched through the window. She caught glimpses of thick vines growing over the trees, the reflection of sunlight off distant water. Li Tao rode at the front and his soldiers kept her surrounded at every moment. This must be Li Tao's infamous first battalion. They called themselves the Rising Guard and held the reputation of being the fiercest warriors in the empire.

The dense shade and the babble of her river gave way to a dirt road grooved with wheel tracks. They were going south, further away from the seat of imperial power. She no longer had a place in the new Emperor's court, but she clung to the illusion that the centre of the empire was a safe and civilised place. What lay beyond was lawless and unpredictable. That was why they had needed the *jiedushi*.

On the fourth day, they passed an armed barricade. Grim-faced soldiers patrolled the line and she ducked away from the window.

It was true. The regional armies were assembling. She had isolated herself from the capital city of Changan to escape from the unrest, but news had still drifted to her over the last year through her servants. They made weekly trips to the city markets while she remained shut away in her manor.

There was only one reason for a barricade in the interior of the empire. There was infighting among the military governors. They had been gaining in power for years and continued to seize control in the uncertainty of Emperor Shen's rule. Perhaps she should have gone into hiding with the servants after all.

With a shudder, she pulled her shawl tight around her shoulders. She was dressed in the same clothes she had worn when they had come for her, the only possessions Li Tao had allowed her to bring.

She hated this part. The going away. The earth element in her longed to remain grounded in one place. Travel never held good tidings. Abrupt change brought back memories of being uprooted and taken some place far and unknown. It always seemed to come to that, and she knew from experience there was never a way to return.

The survival instinct returned to her, encasing her like a second skin. She sharpened her senses and became aware of everything around her. Li Tao prepared for war with swords and soldiers. She had her own weapons.

Over the next days, the open road faded beneath the shadow of a mountain and the soil became dark and rich. They travelled into a verdant forest of bamboo. The stalks rose high overhead. They called it the bamboo sea, not for any vast stretch of water, but for the rhythmic sway of the bamboo and the rustle of the spear-tipped leaves in the breeze. The green canopy engulfed them on all sides. When she blinked away from the window, a red haze remained over her eyes, veiling the world in an unnatural glow.

Suyin peered out of the window of the sedan to search for Li Tao. He rode tall in the saddle with his back straight. His dark robe stood out against the forest green. Naturally, he became her main focal point. He had all the power and she had none.

He'd barely spoken to her except for the scant conversation they'd exchanged by the river. Why would he go beyond his barricades to take her captive? Her influence had died with the August Emperor. She was merely a relic now, faded and wrung free of any usefulness.

The caravan came to an abrupt stop and the curtain was swept aside. Once again, Li Tao stood before her. He extended his hand and she had no choice but to take it, pressing her fingers briefly over his before letting go. The fleeting warmth of the touch lingered on her skin and a disturbing awareness curled around her as she stood beside him. She knew how to identify influence and power, but had never been so recklessly drawn to it.

She redirected her attention to the mansion nestled among the towering bamboo. It was twice the size of her home and built in the same opulent style of imperial architecture. The silhouette invoked the elaborate pagodas of the palace with wooden beams and tiled rooftops. Its grand structure intruded upon the tranquil forest.

'Why am I here?'

'As I said, it was not safe for you by the river.'

Her head tilted to him in challenge. 'So the governor has appointed himself as my protector?'

His only reply was a wry twist of his lips before he gestured toward the front of the mansion. The man hoarded his words like gold coins. Every action was so controlled, she wondered if he ever lost himself in anger or passion. The last thought sent a shiver down her spine.

Li Tao remained behind her as they moved past the twin-lion statues that guarded the entrance. With every step, she became more aware of his dominance. His stride was confident and his authority complete. The illusion of deference he presented by allowing her to lead the way was laughable. How long would it be before he made his true demands known?

Household servants filed into the entrance hall one after another. Only seven of them, a small number for such a spacious compound. A grey-haired, round-faced woman headed the assembly. She gasped when Li Tao made the introduction.

'Ling *Guifei*!' The old woman bowed and bowed. The narrow bones of her shoulders protruded through the brown servant's robe.

'Jinmei, show Lady Ling to her apartments.' Li Tao cast a dismissive glance in Suyin's direction before turning to leave.

Insufferable. She flushed hot with anger as he disappeared down a corridor. He had treated her with the same indifference throughout the journey. She had been taken from her home under force of arms, yet he cast her aside as if she was of no importance at all. It was—it was worse than being interrogated and threatened. At least then she'd know what his plans were.

The head woman touched her arm gently. 'Come with Auntie Jinmei.'

The guards marched behind them as she led Suyin through the spacious hall.

'*Guifei* is more beautiful than they say,' Auntie cooed, using the revered title the August Emperor had bestowed upon Suyin. 'We are honoured and overjoyed for this visit.'

A pleasant visit indeed. Escorted by fifty armed men.

Auntie padded along in her slippers and led Suyin past the parlour to the interior rooms. The chambers stood silent and spacious with furnishings laid out in neat angles. Everything was meticulously dusted and nondescript, as unrevealing as the master of the house.

She followed Auntie outdoors through a central courtyard with a carefully arranged garden. The gardener brushed his wiry fingers over a hedge before cutting with his shears. His eyes neither focused on his hands or the sharp blades in front of him as he worked. When he addressed the lanky youth by the fish pond, his gaze remained vacant, stopping just short of fixing on his target.

The youth caught her eye as she passed. He looked to be sixteen, grasping at the edge of manhood. A clump of damp grass hung dripping from one hand while he watched her. His left arm hung rigidly against his side, the fingers of his hand withered and gnarled like a pigeon's claw. She tore her gaze away with sudden embarrassment.

Auntie beckoned her along. 'Master Li would want Ling *Guifei* to have the most luxurious of accommodations. We hope the lady will be pleased.'

The image of the blind gardener and his crippled assistant lingered. In the palace, even the lowliest of servants were chosen for physical beauty to perpetuate the illusion of perfection.

In the eastern section of the house, Auntie led Suyin up a staircase. Her assigned guard stayed outside the double doors as they entered the apartments.

'Good light. Positive energy from all directions.' Auntie walked in first, opening door after door. 'In the mornings Ling *Guifei* can watch the sun rise over the cliffs.'

The woman reminded her of the elder servants who had served in the palace for so long they nearly held rank. Their speech and manner might be subservient, but they possessed all the cunning in the world after the secrets their eyes had seen. In the palace, Suyin had learned never to underestimate the servants. She had formed alliances wherever she could.

Auntie took her through the sheer curtain on to the balcony. From there she could see the ridge of the grey cliffs in the distance. The clean, crisp air of the forest surrounded them. Gripping the wooden rail, Suyin peered at the yard below.

Li Tao had imprisoned her on the second floor. A vast gorge opened up beyond the edge of the stone tiles. The granite walls plunged sharply to disappear into oblivion. Even if she were brave enough to make the climb from the balcony, there was nowhere to run.

She had been through all of the possibilities. The warlord could be holding her hostage, which was unlikely as she no longer had any allies in the empire. His capture of her could be purely an act of defiance against imperial authority. More likely he thought she held some vital secret. There had been a time when she had had many secrets at her fingertips.

Suyin called out as Auntie started to sink behind the curtain, 'How long have you served the Governor?'

'Fifteen years, my lady.'

From the beginning, then. Suyin leaned once more over the rail and breathed deep, catching the scent of moss and dampened earth.

From the very first time anyone had ever heard of a man named Li Tao.

Chapter Two

Li Tao loosened the leather strap that secured the sheath against his arm. He was alone in his study, shut away from his soldiers, the servants, and from *her*. The illustrious Ling Suyin was deep within his stronghold and far from the grasp of his enemies. Now he had time and space to think. To consider.

He drew the thin blade concealed beneath his sleeve and set it across the desk amongst the folded letters. A pile of grey ash lay beside the candle, the remains of the note that had sent him beyond the barricade on a whim. The message had been unsigned and the language obscured. Deliberately so, no doubt, in order to make it impossible to gauge its significance. The report informed him that the military governor, Gao Shiming, had sent men to capture Ling Suyin, or Ling *Guifei* as she had been titled by the late August Emperor.

The former Precious Consort. A woman who should have meant nothing in the schemes of courts and men now that her benefactor was dead. She had been installed at an isolated river bend to live out the rest of her days in exile. What would Gao want with such a woman?

His instincts told him it was a ploy, but for once Li Tao ignored them. The cryptic message had held a warning, but also something else. Almost a promise. It insinuated he'd regret it if he didn't act quickly. The Precious Consort's name stood out among the characters. Ling Suyin.

At the height of her fame, gossip had streamed from the imperial city of Changan about her. She was a seductress, a fox spirit, the most beautiful woman in the empire. In the prosperity of the old regime, poets and courtiers could fixate on a single woman and make her into a goddess.

Li Tao had caught a single glimpse of her the first time he had been to the palace. The hunger that had gripped him had been immediate and all-consuming. He had been a young man then and had hungered for many things: acclaim, respect and power. The sight of her now, more than a decade later, stirred nothing but a faint echo of that forgotten desire.

At first, he had assumed the old wolf must have been obsessed with Lady Ling after seeing her on the Emperor's arm for so many years. Perhaps Gao wanted the unattainable beauty and glory she represented. But Li Tao had intercepted assassins stalking toward the river bend. Shadow men sent to kill swiftly.

The assassins had died before they could be interrogated. The last of them had fallen on to his own blade to avoid being taken alive. It required money and influence to hire men with that level of dedication. Lady Ling apparently still held some value. A rival warlord wanted her dead, someone else wanted her alive, and he had been lured into the centre of it.

He sat down behind the desk and pinched the space between his eyes, trying to ease the gathering tension. A pile of papers lay stacked before him. A summons demanding his presence in the court at Changan lay on top. Below that, more proclamations stamped with imperial seals.

Over the past years, the imperial forces had diminished while the border armies under control of the *jiedushi* had grown stronger. The imbalance frightened the ministers in the court enough to try to limit the power of the military governors. As if crippling a strong limb would mask the weak one.

Li Tao ignored the decrees and edicts. His duty was to protect this domain, as the late Emperor had decreed. He'd do it even if it meant defying Emperor Shen and his meddling court. He had kept the borders secure and maintained peace within his district, putting down potential uprisings and keeping his captains in line. And he'd built up his army.

Gao had accused him of treason for these actions. The coward had made his claim a thousand *li* away before the imperial court. Li Tao needed to switch tactics to face such an enemy. He needed to use subterfuge and artfulness. He needed someone like Ling Suyin. That must have been why he'd been compelled to bring her here.

It was a lie. He shoved the proclamations aside. Lady Ling was here because she had been alone when he found her. She'd been abandoned. She'd been pale with fear when she'd seen him, yet the courtesan had regarded him with elegant resolve, as if she still held the empire in her thrall. He could have interrogated her by the river. He could have left her at the provincial seat in Chengdu. He could have simply ignored the cryptic warning. Instead he had taken her with him into his domain, to the place he'd worked so hard to keep away from outsiders.

He'd placed her in the south wing in the same room where his once-intended bride had stayed. The arranged marriage to the Emperor's daughter had collapsed before they'd ever set eyes upon each other. How Gao must have delighted in that failure. In the last year, he had been visited by nothing but disaster and now Lady Ling had materialised like another ill omen.

This agitation of his senses was nothing more than the draw of any male to an alluring female. Yang to yin. But he would never make the mistake of thinking of Ling Suyin as a mere woman. She was a seductress and a shrewd manipulator. A she-demon in the guise of a beautiful woman.

Her treatment was extravagant for a prisoner. Auntie brought tea and ordered a wooden tub brought to her apartments. The bath water had to be heated in cauldrons in the courtyard and hefted up the stairs in buckets, but the guardsmen performed the task without complaint.

Suyin was left alone to soak in the steaming bath, but her muscles remained knotted and anxious. What could Li Tao possibly want from her? She considered all the possibilities, even the blandly obvious one: desire. But a powerful warlord wouldn't seek a courtesan nearing her autumn years, or go across barricades to do so. Not when there were younger, more easily attained comforts within his borders.

In the imperial harem, a concubine who had not caught the Emperor's eye by the age of thirty would be cast out to a convent or given to a lower minister for marriage if she was fortunate. She was nearing that age now. Besides, Li Tao didn't look at her the way her admirers always did—with lust and yearning. Perhaps a touch of awe. Men couldn't hide it, not even before the August Emperor. She would catch it in their heated stares before they looked away.

They were never truly looking at her.

There was no such shame in the warlord's eyes. His gaze fixed on her so intensely, as if trying to pierce into her and pry her secrets loose. He'd find nothing there. She could fill the shell of her body with whatever spirit she needed.

The cooling water told her that her mind had wandered. She rose and dried herself without calling for Auntie. With her hair still damp, she pulled on the pale sleeping shift and crawled into the alcove of the bed, succumbing to the exhaustion of the journey.

Her body didn't care that she was trapped in a tiger's den, though her mind churned throughout the night. It ran with no destination.

When morning came, a shuffle of movement in the outer chamber awakened her. Her muscles ached from the restless slumber.

She sat up and eased her feet into a pair of slippers before going out into the outer chamber. 'Auntie, what is all of this?'

The sitting room resembled a flower bed with a dress in every colour draped over the chairs and tables. Auntie lifted an armful of rose-coloured silk, vibrant and layered like the petals of an orchid.

'The lady will look very beautiful in this.'

Suyin found an empty space among the wardrobe to seat herself. The gowns were as exquisite as the ones she had worn in the palace. Trade had dwindled in the marketplaces over the past year. Checkpoints and barricades had been erected between the provinces, stifling trade. Such finery was unseen outside of the twin capitals of Changan and Luoyang.

Strange that Li Tao would have such a collection waiting for her. She thought again of her initial suspicion, but nothing about his behavior indicated he wanted her in that way—excerpt for that one, brief flash of heat by the river.

She could never be another man's mistress—even if she outlived the late Emperor by a hundred years she would belong to him only. It was imperial law.

'Auntie must think the Governor and I are already lovers,' she prodded.

The old woman pursed her lips as she laid a gown carefully over the painted screen in the corner.

'Your master didn't tell you that I was coming, did he?'

The loyal servant wouldn't answer. 'Which would the lady prefer?' Auntie asked.

The old woman's eyes flickered over the sea of colours. Auntie had been a young girl once. That part of her must still long for delicate, pretty things.

'It would be quite a scandal, a former concubine and a military governor,' Suyin went on.

With a sniff, Auntie moved to draw the curtains open. Her laboured footsteps scuffed against the rug on the floor. 'Master Li wishes to speak to the lady this morning.'

Sunlight streamed in a wide band through the centre of the room. Suyin curled her legs up beneath her and watched Auntie as she returned to the sitting area.

'What if I told Auntie that the governor has brought me here as his prisoner?'

'The lady asks too many questions. She must get dressed before Master Li leaves.'

Apparently, Li Tao was not one to care about scandal and Suyin could do nothing to penetrate Auntie's unquestioning acceptance of her master's actions.

She selected the rose-coloured silk and followed Auntie behind the dressing screen. Auntie's hands were slow as she tied on the embroidered bodice and pulled the outer robe over it. When Auntie bent to smooth out the layers of the skirt, Suyin wanted to urge her not to make such a fuss. There were no younger girls in the household staff to help with the task. No wife, no family. The mansion was so empty that one could hear every creak of the floorboards.

Much like her own home by the river.

Auntie evened out the ends of the crimson sash and tied it around Suyin's waist, leaving the ends trailing down. Then the old woman beckoned her before the mirror.

'The lady's hair is thick and black as ink.' Auntie ran a brush through in long strokes. 'She is fortunate.'

One day she might live to be grey and bent like Auntie. Her skin would wither and she would be unrecognisable. Perhaps then the empire would grant her peace.

'Auntie should know I am not the Governor Li's mistress. I only met him a week ago. We've never spoken.' She tried to catch the old woman's eye through the reflection in the glass, but Auntie's head remained bent at her task. 'I am loyal to the memory of the August Emperor.'

Auntie sniffed again. 'Master has always been loyal to the August Emperor.'

'But not to Emperor Shen.'

Suyin winced as Auntie tugged at her hair to wrestle it into a knot. The point of the ivory hairpin jabbed into her scalp. She would have no ally here.

The claws of the familiar game were closing in, the one she had mastered in the imperial court. Who could she trust? Who would help? She had played it ever since being taken away from her home as a child, bought for the bride price of a hundred copper coins.

Watching Lady Ling was like watching a well-crafted opera. She sat before him in the parlour, shoulders lifted in elegant repose, a peach blossom against the colourless walls. The curve of her lips as she sipped her tea was too perfect to be unpractised.

'I have been thinking.' She glanced at him over the rim of the cup. 'It's not me you want.'

'What is it that I want?' he asked.

'I'm nothing but a symbol. Capturing me must be as significant as—' she looked at him with a sideways glance '—capturing a flag. Why else would a warlord have any interest in a lowly concubine?'

'Lowly,' he mused.

He leaned back against his chair to study her. Suyin was undeniably beautiful. So much so that it was both hard to look at her and hard to look away. Soft, sensual mouth and skillfuly expressive eyes wide. The ivory-pale skin at her throat alone made his fingers itch.

'You were once a courtesan in the pleasure district of Luoyang,' he remarked.

'A long, long time ago, Governor.'

'Many secrets flowed through Luoyang.'

She smiled at him. For him. 'Wine and music and all sorts of secrets.'

The words carried the lilt of laughter, but when her gaze fixed on him he caught the cold flash of calculation. There was much more to her lure than seduction. Her every gesture spoke of possibilities. Her every movement enticed him to relax his guard, while her defences were most certainly in place. He had no patience for such ruses.

'I have no need of a mistress.'

His words fell impassively, yet his stomach knotted at the thought of this woman in his bed. Merely a twinge before it was gone.

Her lips pressed tight. She set her teacup down with a distinct clank against the wooden table. 'I wasn't offering.'

Never directly. The unspoken was always so much more tempting. He could continue to let her tease and beguile or he could set the terms.

'They say you can bring a man to his knees with a single look,' he said.

She propped her chin on to her hands with wicked interest, well aware of the picture she presented. 'They also say I seduced the Emperor and brought down the empire.'

'Nonsense.' He found his pulse increasing to the rhythm of their exchange. His body warmed and he almost liked it. 'I know what will bring down this empire and it has nothing to do with one man's obsessive love for his precious concubine.'

'The Emperor never loved me.'

The abruptness of her denial surprised him. Looking downwards, Suyin traced a fingertip absently over her teacup. A ripple of sadness crossed her face. The imperfection heightened her allure and disappeared so quickly he wondered if she had put it there for his benefit. He would go mad trying to decipher her.

'They say things about you as well.' She was no longer trying to charm him. Her voice sharpened to a dagger's point. 'About all the men you've killed.'

'At the Emperor's command,' he replied evenly.

'And they were all at his request?'

'No.'

The lady carried herself admirably. It was only after his prolonged silence that she blinked away.

'The Emperor died of illness in his bed, Governor Li. I had nothing to do with it, despite what the rumours may say. If…' She faltered, staring at the dragon ring on his second finger. 'If that is why you've come for me.'

There had been rumours that the August Emperor's sudden death had been due to poisoning. She hid her hands beneath the table, but not before he caught the tremor in them. Deliberately, he folded his fingers over the insignia, hiding the ring from view.

'You had the most to lose from his death. The Emperor was your protector.'

'Emperor Li Ming was a great man,' she declared, looking more vulnerable than he'd ever seen her.

'Li Ming was a great man,' he echoed.

It was best he think of her as another man's woman, even if that man was already dead. It was best not to think of her as a woman at all. He let his gaze slide over her face, assessing her as he would an opponent. By cleverness or coincidence she invoked the name of one of the few men he respected. One of the two men to whom he had ever sworn allegiance. He had betrayed one for the other.

'You said you knew what would bring down the empire,' she continued in a more conversational tone. 'What would that be?'

'The empire will bring itself down. The imperial court has become removed from the reality of governing.' The answer came easily. He'd seen the decay from within for too long.

'And the warlords can smell the blood,' she countered.

The Precious Consort had done much more than pour wine and play music during her reign in court. He watched her with more care.

'Men who are accustomed to war find themselves restless during times of peace,' he goaded. 'They crave that taste of battle, the feel of death hanging over them.'

The barest of creases appeared between those pretty eyes. He found he liked catching her unaware.

'How you must miss all those plots and schemes, Lady Ling.'

'Miss them?' The melodic quality of her voice sharpened. 'I fought for my life every day in the palace.'

She tilted her gaze at him and he detected the steel beneath her elegant demeanour. A flash of armour amidst the softest silk. Endlessly elusive. No wonder men tried to capture her in paintings and flowery words. He, for reasons he couldn't clearly discern, had simply captured her.

It was his eyes, she decided. That was why his adversaries feared him. Endless and black and set deep in a face devoid of any hint of kindness. The eyes of a man who was capable of anything. The cut of the scar across his features added to the sinister aura.

How appropriate that he spoke of battle. She could sense him circling, reading her the same way she tried to read him. The look he gave her now wasn't warm...but it wasn't cold. She could feel the blood rise up her neck. The low throb of her heart beat at her defences. Why did her body respond like this now? Why this man, when she needed her wits about her to survive?

He leaned closer. 'Living with danger for so long changes you.'

Something about the remark felt ominously personal. A ghost of a smile lit his face, more in his eyes than his mouth. She traced a fingertip nervously over the tabletop. His eyes attended to her every move.

'I don't miss the danger. I was happy on the river.' Or she had been, once.

'Alone and abandoned? The beautiful Ling *Guifei* was not meant to fade into obscurity.'

'Don't call me that.'

Precious Consort Ling. Li Tao's comment wounded her more than it should have. In the Emperor's court even a pet name was elevated to an official rank. She was set apart from the world and would be for the rest of her life. It had been a long time since she'd had a conversation such as this one. She welcomed it, even as jagged and treacherous as it was.

She had resigned herself to exile with its loneliness and empty days. At least she had been free. Suddenly she was tired of crossing words with Li Tao, tired of guarding every look.

'For as long as I can remember, every man I have met has wanted to bed me or kill me,' she said bitterly. 'Tell me which one you are so I know which face to wear.'

He straightened, incited by her directness. 'Which sort of man is Gao?'

She frowned. 'Gao Shiming?' The sound of his name after all these years still made her go cold with fear. This was worse than she could have imagined.

'What does Gao want from you?'

'I don't know. I'm nothing to him.' She burned beneath Li Tao's steady gaze and wondered if he had ever interrogated the men he'd been sent after. Or had he simply served as executioner under the Emperor's orders?

'So it is you and Old Gao challenging each other for the dragon throne,' she said with forced casualness.

'You sound bored.'

'In the imperial court, every man is a conspirator.'

'I have no interest in the imperial throne,' he declared.

'But I'm so rarely wrong.'

He smiled at her banter, but his expression intensified. 'The empire is falling into ruin because it clings to the idea of one king-dom and one ruler. The Son of Heaven lording over the Middle Kingdom. That dream is over.'

She stiffened at his cynicism. 'That sounds suspiciously close to treason.'

Speaking out against the Emperor with such scorn was enough to be deemed treason, but Li Tao also had an army at his com-mand. He stood and she noticed he hadn't touched the tea or any of the food. Cautious, even in his own home. She stared down at her own plate, recalling days in the palace when any bite could be her last.

'Not close to treason,' he replied. He moved behind her. A shiver travelled down her spine. 'It is treason.'

His long fingers curled around the back of the chair, exerting his dominance. The skin of her neck burned. She was afraid to look at him. Afraid of what she'd see. His presence overshadowed her. The surrounding space closed in and she was trapped.

'Emperor Shen has declared that we limit the strength of the provincial armies.' His voice was cold and quiet.

'And you refused?'

'I will not let him cripple me. Our enemies are waiting to attack. All they need is a sign of weakness.'

She breathed with relief as he stepped away. The *jiedushi* had become too strong. Men like Li Tao and Gao Shiming listened only to their own ambitions. She wanted no part of it any more. Let the warlords fight their battle. All she wanted was to go home and be left in peace, but she was no longer safe there. Her past had come for her.

With Li Tao standing so close, his presence caging her in, she couldn't help but consider the obvious solution. She could become Li Tao's lover. From the way he devoured her with his eyes, she knew he wouldn't refuse. She had yet to touch any part of him, but she could imagine how he would feel. Steel and fire. He would demand complete devotion, but he would be a fearsome protec-tor. The idea sent a disturbing anticipation through her that she couldn't comprehend.

But she had been bartered away too many times in her life. She would not sell herself again. Not when she had finally tasted freedom. She turned to him, but never had the chance to speak.

One of his guardsmen approached and stood a respectful distance away. Li Tao looked to him, and then left her with nothing more than a brief nod. One moment he was an overwhelming, overbearing force behind her. The next he was gone again as if she were too insignificant to be dismissed.

She watched Li Tao's imposing figure as he left the courtyard. Her armed escort returned to her side. The soldier stood beside her, a pillar of unmovable rock as he waited patiently for her to stand. He would have probably waited until noon if she had decided to stay there.

Gao must be using her somehow to bait Li Tao. She needed information and Li Tao revealed so little. She needed to get away quickly. The two warlords were starting a civil war. It would pull the other warlords into the conflict as well the Emperor himself.

She stood and started back toward her chamber. The guardsman who followed her like a second shadow was perhaps a little beyond twenty years, not a veteran, but not a novice either. His face was by no means soft, but it was infinitely kinder than Li Tao's.

The gardens were empty in the second courtyard. Ah, not completely empty. The boy with the withered arm crouched in the corner, pulling at weeds. He was so slight and unassuming, she had nearly missed him. Once again, he caught her eye before looking away hastily. When one was weak and vulnerable, the only defence was to watch and listen and learn, much like a frightened rabbit sniffing the air for the wolf. She had been that rabbit all her life, but the key was never to show the fear.

The guardsman urged her to keep moving. He lifted his hand to gesture towards the stairs. How steadfast were Li Tao's people? Did they serve out of fear or loyalty?

'What do you call yourself?' she asked as she started up the steps.

'Yao Ru Shan.'

She listened to the deliberate fall of his footsteps as they climbed upwards.

'You must have accomplished great things to serve in such a trusted position,' she ventured.

Nothing. Silence. She longed to find someone in this household who was not so stingy with words.

As she reached the door to her apartments, she let the end of her shawl slip from her shoulders. The delicate cloth wound down her body as it fell to the floor. She paused, allowing Ru Shan enough time to bend to retrieve it. He caught her eye as he straightened and bowed stiffly. He had a broad face, square in shape. His emotions were clearly evident in every movement. Proper, righteous, loyal above all else.

She forced back a triumphant smile as she lifted the cloth from his hands.

'Thank you, Ru Shan.'

Loyalty could be shifted. She glanced at the soldier once more before pushing the doors open and slipping inside.

Of the servants she'd met, she wasn't yet sure who was strong enough to stand up to Li Tao, but she needed to work quickly. She knew how this would end. Emperor Shen and the other warlords would come for Li Tao. They would cut through his barricades and destroy his army. If he hadn't already fallen on his own sword, he would certainly hang.

Chapter Three

Li Tao's captains assembled in a half circle before him outside the mansion. The canyon opened wide behind them. He had summoned them from their posts to give their reports in person. He needed to look each man in the eye. Now more than ever before, loyalty was critical.

'Governor Li.'

Lady Ling's voice rang out over the expanse of stone, much like the floating beauties of Luoyang. They would coo and flirt from windows that overlooked the streets, but their entreaties were never for him. He kept his back to her pointedly.

'My lord, I have something to discuss with you,' she said, with the carelessness of a breeze. 'Oh, forgive me. You're occupied.'

Grey-haired Zhao glanced upwards. 'Ling *Guifei*?'

The other men seemed to lose focus at Zhao's breach of etiquette. Their gazes drifted past him to seek out the infamous beauty. Even the most seasoned of them could not remain disciplined.

'Gentlemen.'

A single, sharp reprimand brought all eyes back to him. The captains straightened with deliberate attention.

Suyin did nothing without a purpose. She'd chosen this moment for a display of will. By mid-morning, word of the Precious Consort would spread through the barracks along with the rumours.

What an enticing picture she must present overhead, elegantly poised over the balcony as she held his men in rapture. He didn't need to look upon her. He could see the furtive desire reflected in every man's face. Li Tao's blood simmered.

How had the August Emperor dealt with the knowledge that every man wanted his concubine? Of course, a sovereign was supposedly blessed by heaven and above such jealousy, while Li Tao was just a man.

And Suyin was not his concubine.

He listened to the rest of the reports and then dismissed the captains. He turned once the last man was gone. 'Yes, *Guifei*?'

Her gown was blue today, evoking cool air and sky. She leaned forwards with her hands braced against the rail, tapping a nail against the polished wood in agitation. 'I don't like being called that.'

'Lady Ling, then. What is it you need to discuss with me?'

'The artwork in this chamber.'

'There is no artwork there.'

'Precisely.'

Conversation with her was indeed an intricate dance. He waited.

'If I am to be held prisoner in this room, there should be something to look at besides these four walls,' she said.

'You are not being held prisoner.'

She stared down at him incredulously. 'I am not?'

'Go to the door.'

He was unable to resist a smirk as she disappeared through the curtain. In a heartbeat, she appeared around the side of the house. She aimed a line towards him, lifting her skirt out of the way of her feet. Ru Shan followed closely behind.

Li Tao assessed her quickly, not allowing his gaze to linger. Her hair was carefully pinned and her cheeks held a hint of colour. That was the essence of Ling Suyin. All she ever permitted was a hint.

She came up right beside him, close enough that she had to tilt her head to meet his eyes. 'Am I free to leave, then?'

He shook his head. 'The house, the gardens. Explore them as you wish.'

'But not beyond?'

'I cannot ensure that you are protected otherwise.'

She made a derisive sound. 'Protected.'

Even her indignation was somehow charming. He had always assumed a courtesan's power was in distraction, in idle conversation and empty flattery. Suyin was much more complicated.

She gestured at the now-empty area. 'Were those your notorious captains?'

'An interesting display you put on for them. If they were young and brash, one of them might consider putting a knife in my back to take possession of you.'

'Like a trophy,' she said with a sigh. 'The August Emperor always boasted about your soldiers, how fierce and disciplined they were. How does a new army gain such a formidable reputation?'

He shrugged away her attempt at flattery. 'Young men have something to prove.'

'Perhaps their leader has something to prove?'

'You can't truly be interested in this.'

She tilted her head in what wasn't an answer. When she turned away, he found himself following obligingly as she wandered toward the gorge. There must be a wisp of sorcery within her.

'This house looks like it's about to fall off the edge of the world.' She peered into the misted depths.

'The cliff provides a natural barrier. Easy to defend.'

'Have you ever seen the bottom?' She inched forwards until her toes touched against the emptiness beyond. A breeze stirred from the chasm.

'Stand back,' he cautioned. What he wanted to do was wrap an arm around her and drag her back to safety.

She took her time before complying. The silk of her gown rippled against him while he inhaled, then exhaled slowly. He hadn't moved, yet his heart was pumping fast. She was playing with him. He was...he was letting her.

'You know that bringing me here can be seen as an act of defiance.' The words were a warning, but her tone was one that stroked his skin. 'It would be best if you released me. What use could I be to you when you already have soldiers from the mountain to the sea?'

'Where would you go?' he asked. 'Old Gao was looking for you. He expected you to be alone.'

She swallowed. 'Gao again.'

'Gao sent assassins after you that day.' He stepped close, fighting the urge to touch her. 'It's not me you should be frightened of.'

'You stopped them? Why?'

Why? He didn't have to be a hero to want to save a lone woman from being destroyed senselessly.

'I'm grateful, then. All this time, I thought that I…that you…' She blinked up at him, looking confused and vulnerable.

'I don't want gratitude,' he spat out. 'All I want is answers.'

She flinched and the mask returned. Good. The seasoned courtesan was an easier adversary to deal with.

'What have you done to make an enemy of Gao?' he asked.

Her gaze became distant. 'Perhaps I do know a few things about Governor Gao Shiming.'

Suyin didn't know if it was the chasm at her back or Li Tao's imposing presence that had her heart beating so wildly. He was fearsome to behold up close, with nothing and no one between them to shield her.

'Everyone knows Gao wants that throne,' she said.

He threw her a look of mild impatience. 'I do not need to know what *everyone* knows, my lady.'

The strength of his face fascinated her. She had never seen anything like it. From his sun-darkened skin to the short crop of his hair, he looked nothing like the cultured ministers of the court. He was staring at her intently, willing her to reveal her secrets. There was an almost frightening beauty to his harsh features.

'Should I write you a list? Recall every plot he's orchestrated? Every man he's sent to the executioner? Gao has built his influence over the reign of three emperors.'

'Then what do you have that could possibly be a threat?'

She had to be careful. The secrets she kept were enough to cut her own throat. 'Do men like you need a reason?'

He grew very quiet. 'Men like me.'

He met her eyes with a look that took her breath. She had no answer. Li Tao had raised a strike force so fierce that no one dared to challenge him directly, not even Emperor Shen. But he had saved her life.

She would not play these men against each other. She had never used the art of secrets in that way. All she'd ever wanted was to stay alive. And, as single-minded as Li Tao was, she wasn't even certain he could be manipulated.

'Gao is cunning,' he continued when she said nothing. 'More clever than I. Probably cleverer than you. It could be that he planted you here, so conveniently in my hands.'

She'd had the same thought, but she denied it vehemently now. 'Gao is nothing to me. We haven't spoken in all these years.'

Her view of the house was suddenly blocked by the expanse of his shoulders. She tried to slip past, but the sharp drop of the gorge prevented her escape.

'You *have* been trying to seduce me from the moment we met,' he accused lightly.

'That would be foolish.' And dangerous.

'No? Then why are you looking at me like that?'

'I don't know what you mean.'

She had spent so many years presenting a face to the world. Beckoning glances and secret looks. Perhaps it had simply become a part of her.

He prowled a step closer and her mouth went dry. Every breath came with great effort. She shouldn't have allowed herself to be cornered. A predatory glint lighted his eyes.

'I might consider it.' His voice was a low strum in her ear. 'If the situation were different.'

Her cheeks flushed and she couldn't deny the dark thrill uncoiling within her. But this wasn't about desire. It was about control and Li Tao wielded it meticulously. She assessed the impenetrable fortress of a man before her.

'I might consider it as well,' she replied. 'If you were not on the brink of death.'

His expression darkened. There was too much risk becoming

involved with a man like Li Tao. A man who had no fear of consequences. His hand circled her arm as she attempted to move past him. His grip wasn't forceful, but she couldn't break free.

'Is this all an act?' he asked.

'Yes. All of it.' Her voice held steady, though her pulse jumped erratically.

She was used to being watched. Being admired no longer moved her, but Li Tao's black gaze penetrated despite her defences. The heat from his hand seeped through the thin material of her robe. Everything about him overwhelmed her with quiet power: his commanding height, the hard shape of his mouth as he regarded her. With just the pressure of his fingers, he drew her closer.

She expected the descent of his mouth, but never would have anticipated the gentleness of the kiss. Her lips parted as his explored hers. His fingertips lifted to her cheek in an undemanding, but undeniably possessive caress. She nearly allowed her eyes to fall closed. She almost yielded against the heat and pressure and the slow stir of his mouth. Instead she dug her nails sharply into the flesh of her palms. She fastened her eyes on to his, permitting the kiss, but never surrendering.

He lifted his head a mere inch, hovering close. His breath caressed over her as if the kiss hadn't yet ended. 'All deception?'

'I have been wooed by kings and poets, but you, only you, have ever touched my heart.'

She mocked him with a lover's whisper, but he smiled in response.

'I like the lie.'

The low roughness of his voice stroked down her spine. If she didn't remain focused on his face, she would stumble helplessly into the abyss. Li Tao was an impossible man to read. His gaze smouldered with desire; the scant space between them grew laden with it. But there was something else in his eyes, insurmountable control and calculation.

'With a face like this you must have had countless lovers.'

Surprisingly gentle fingers traced a line along her jaw and a fever rushed over her. She needed to free herself. He had her cornered in every way possible.

'You are mistaken,' she whispered. 'I choose my lovers very carefully.'

'I would never expect something for nothing. Especially not from you.'

'From what I have heard, you're not much for negotiation,' she said.

'Give me one night.'

Her retort caught in her throat. His suggestion, presented with such cutting clarity, shouldn't have caused a flood of heat in her stomach or the trail of yearning that slipped between her legs like a slow curl of smoke.

Li Tao himself seemed troubled by the proposal. 'You can't be surprised,' he taunted, but it came out hoarse, without his usual force behind it.

'I already told you, I am not on offer.'

For the first time, her feminine instincts failed her. She should have turned this negotiation to her advantage; instead she wondered how Li Tao would feel crushed against her, skin to heated skin. His kiss wouldn't be so controlled then.

But she knew what this was beneath the rise and fall of his chest, beneath the heat of his touch. It was only the desire of a powerful man pursuing an unattainable prize. The moment she gave him what he wanted, her appeal would fade.

He smiled faintly. 'The answer is no, then.'

'The answer is no.'

She brushed past, careful not to touch him. Her knees threatened to crumble with each step.

'If I had not come for you, you would be dead,' he reminded, catching up with her easily.

'Li Tao.' There was a misplaced intimacy in addressing him so directly. 'I know very well you were not acting out of kindness. Now show me the rest of this prison since it appears I might be here for a while.'

He walked beside her with his hands clasped behind his back. To anyone observing, they might even appear companionable. Between him and Gao, she was caught between an old cunning tiger and a young fierce one.

Chapter Four

Luoyang—ad 737
22 years earlier

The streets of Luoyang never slept. After the evening gong, the section gates would close, but the drinking and gambling within the wards would continue until dawn. All the harder to scratch out survival as a thief.

During the day, Tao could snatch a yam from a pedlar's basket and push his way into the web of alleys behind the shopfronts. He would tuck himself into a dingy corner and devour it raw, chewing through the coarse skin. When he was waist-high and stick-thin, he could hazard such recklessness and suffer only a beating if caught. The welts toughened him until he grew numb to the sting of a bamboo switch. Now that he was older, the archers upon the city wall would simply put an arrow through him before he could shove through the crowd. He had no choice but to wait for night-time when darkness provided cover. But the city remained active and the guard patrols stayed ever vigilant.

The gambling halls and pleasure quarters stood as palaces of the gutter world and the lords who ran them were brutal men who could not be crossed. There was always business brewing in their shadows, jobs for someone who knew the alleys of Luoyang better than the rats.

Feng, the head of the eastern street gangs, held out a knife to him in the alley behind the drinking house. A slant of light from the back door illuminated their meeting and the smell of roasting meat drifted from the kitchen. The greasy, rich aroma nearly brought tears to his eyes.

'Boy like you wouldn't have a good knife.' Feng's smile revealed uneven, yellowed teeth. 'Looks suspicious, if you're caught.'

The weapon was rusted near the handle. Tao closed his hand around the hilt. He didn't ask about the man Feng wanted killed. There was no need to know any more when he had decided this was the only way.

'Be sure to hit the heart.'

Feng poked a bony finger against his ribcage and Tao swallowed his anger at the indignity. He was little more than skin and bone, his shoulders just beginning to broaden.

'Follow through and shove the blade upwards,' Feng said with a final vicious jab. 'Even if you miss, he won't survive for long.'

Tao hid the knife close to his side and gripped it so hard his fingers stiffened around it. The roughened hilt melded to the flesh of his palm. He didn't have far to walk, only across the street into a dark corner where he could see the entrance to the drinking house. Laughter came from inside, floating down from the upper level where noblemen dined and whored, fat with food and wine. All he had to do was wait for the right one to come out.

His legs grew stiff with waiting. He dropped his shoulder against the mortared brick of the alley. Hour after hour, noblemen staggered out of the door, tripping over their ornate robes. Eventually, the laughter died down. The lanterns still glowed from the rafters, but the clink of cups had grown sparse.

The man wasn't in there. Feng had given him only this one night to do this deed and the man wasn't there. Or Tao had missed him in those moments when he had let his eyelids drop out of exhaustion. In desperation, he considered rushing the door and ploughing upstairs to find the man. How far would he get, an unwashed street urchin with his clothes worn threadbare?

Two men came stumbling through the beaded curtain over the

entrance. Tao straightened and his palm started to sweat around the knife.

Two. He hadn't anticipated that. Either of them could overpower him.

'One more!' The nobleman weaved back and forth in the blue robe that marked him as the target. 'One more for the road.'

His companion laughed beside him and dragged him upright. 'Not a drop left in the place, my friend.'

Now. He moved without taking the time to shake the stiffness from his limbs, without any thought as to how he would fight off both men. Only the companion saw Tao emerge on to the street. His expression sobered, but he didn't call out for help. He merely straightened and stepped away.

Tao stalked forwards like a tiger, like an arrow. He didn't look at the man's face. He focused in on the point between his ribs where Feng had directed him. The knife lifted and he shoved the blade with all his strength, punching through cloth and flesh, never stopping. This was the only way.

Hot, thick blood washed over his hand, the copper stink of it like the butcher shop. The man made a grunting, gurgling noise. Only then did Tao glimpse his face. He wished he hadn't. Rounded cheeks and weak chin with eyes wide in confusion. His careless drunkenness stopped cold.

The blade snapped and Tao staggered backwards, grasping only the hilt. He ran, shoving his way back into the shadows. At any moment, the outcry would rouse the city guards, and he would hear the twang of the archer's bow. The arrow would enter his back and pierce through his heart like the rusty blade had pierced the nobleman's chest.

It was the first time he had taken a life. He felt no joy in the killing, but he felt no remorse either. The truth was he felt nothing. None of the nervous exhilaration or hunger that came when snatching food from the marketplace.

He found Feng in another nest of alleyways at the designated spot. His decaying smile gleamed lurid in the dimness. Feng dropped three coins into Tao's palm.

Somehow Tao's feet took him back through the wards to the familiar hovel tucked in quieter streets. The sky was lightening in the stillness before the market gong. Auntie's window lay open. The old woman trusted no harm would come to her. From the doorstep, he could hear her stirring a pot of rice for the morning meal. The heat from her stove clung sweet and warm around him.

He stared down at the coins in his hand, a wicked hint of silver stained red. He rubbed the coins clean against his sleeve and dropped them just inside the window before turning to go.

Present day—ad 759

The rhythm and pattern of the household was an easy one to find once Li Tao released her from confinement. The mansion was arranged neatly in a double courtyard. Each morning, several servants could be seen sweeping along the bays. The clip of the gardener's shears sounded in the garden. The kitchen and all the meals were ruled over by a balding cook that everyone called 'Cook'. A regiment of soldiers patrolled the perimeter, but rarely set foot in the house. If she watched from the windows, she could measure the day by their rounds.

The routine was ordinary. Mundane enough to lure her into a false sense of security. Li Tao often rode out early in the morning before the house awoke. Late at night, she would see a candle burning in his study. It had taken only two days to realise she could see his window from the garden.

She waited each day for their next encounter. He had interrogated her, taunted her and kissed her. A kiss that was as inscrutable as he was. And then the contemptible proposition for a single night in her bed—but he hadn't sought her again after that.

Every morning, Auntie brought her a tray with tea and her morning meal along with news about the price of grain and what Cook was preparing for the midday meal. Today, the rice congee had settled into a cold paste and Auntie was oddly silent while she helped her dress.

'Be cautious today,' Auntie warned as she tied her sash. 'Today is an unfavourable day.'

Astrology was one of Auntie's pastimes. She would count the days off on her fingers and declare it a favourable day or a poor one. She had already divined that the year would be a difficult one for Suyin. An easy prediction considering she was being held prisoner by a rogue *jiedushi* and wanted dead by another one. Auntie deliberately overlooked the circumstances with happy ignorance like a frog in a well. Suyin wondered how much Li Tao had revealed to any of the servants.

Her morning stroll through the garden revealed an uncharacteristic silence. The servants were gathered in the front hall. They pressed against the entrance, craning their necks like a flock of geese to see over one another.

'It has happened again,' one of them murmured.

'Why is everyone whispering?' Suyin asked, coming up behind them.

'Superstitious peasants,' Auntie scoffed, but she too stood back.

The servants stepped aside for her as she peered out through the open doors. The clearing at the front of the mansion was empty except for the swaying shadows of the bamboo stalks.

'There's nothing there.' Suyin found that she too had dropped her voice to a hush. The press of the servants hovered at her back.

'Over there, between the lion statues.'

One of them pointed out the spot to her. A red parcel rested on the top step, a splash of jarring crimson against the white stone.

'It came in the night.'

'Same as last year.'

'Same as every year.'

She looked back at the servants. 'What is it?'

They all shook their heads while Auntie worried her hands together and said nothing. It was clear they were waiting for her to do something, deferring to her because of her perceived status.

She turned back to the silk-wrapped parcel. Her rational mind told her this air of mystery was unwarranted. Someone intended for this delivery to spark gossip. With a show of resolution, she squared her shoulders and stepped out beyond the portico.

'Lady Ling, wait!'

It was the first time Jun, the gardener's assistant, had spoken directly to her. Without thinking, he reached for her sleeve with his one good arm, but then shrank back embarrassed.

'Be careful,' he said.

She was touched by the display of gallantry.

'There is nothing to be afraid of,' she assured all of them, but her voice rang eerily in the still morning.

This endeavour had become a test of will. They were all petrified with a mixture of curiosity and fear and looked to her to take the lead. She couldn't give up the opportunity to establish authority. With a deep breath, she stepped past the threshold.

The guardsman Ru Shan walked protectively beside her as she made her way to the steps. He had become her constant shadow from the moment she set foot outside her apartments each day.

'Do you know?' she asked him.

He shook his head slowly and his gaze swept the bamboo forest surrounding them. As they neared the package, he moved a hand to his sword as if the box would lash out at them like a snake. What was this ominous delivery? And where was Li Tao while his servants cowered?

She knelt to pick up the package and straightened quickly. Nothing happened. She could feel the edges of a wooden box beneath the silk. Unable to resist, she tipped it this way and that to try to decipher the contents.

'Lady Ling!' Auntie called to her from the house, like a worried mother whose child had strayed too far. 'Come back inside.'

Suyin held the box close and spared one final glance out to the forest, glancing into the endless dance of bamboo. The click-clack of insects greeted them from the lush depths. Back inside the servants closed around her, staring at the silk-covered box in her hands. None of them dared ask her to open it.

'Where is Governor Li?' she asked.

Auntie nodded toward the first corridor that wound its way down the main bay. 'In his chamber.'

'His chamber?'

Li Tao usually emerged from his apartments before dawn. The curiosity in the front hall had grown thick. She couldn't help but imagine there was some hidden power in the box she held in her hands. It was wrapped in the style of wedding gifts and festival offerings. It made her heart beat faster, holding that little box that had the entire household in awe.

'I'll bring it to him,' she said.

The servants nodded, co-conspirators in this adventure. Auntie took a couple of steps alongside her before stepping away at the mouth of the corridor. From what she had seen, no one ever went down this corridor but Li Tao.

Ru Shan made no protest and let her take the lead. Day by day, he was relinquishing control to her. The changes were so small he couldn't notice, but she paid very close attention.

At the end of the walkway, a Taoist mirror hung over a set of double doors to ward off evil. This must have been Auntie's doing. Li Tao didn't appear to be a believer in mystic symbols.

She knocked against the door. 'Governor Li?'

'*Guifei?*' His deep voice sounded from inside, raised in surprise.

Why did he insist on calling her that? That title didn't mean anything anymore.

'A delivery has arrived for you.'

There was silence, followed by a furtive shifting within.

'Enter,' he said finally.

She pushed the door open with two fingers. Li Tao sat with his chair propped against the opposite wall, dressed in his usual dark robe. Light filtered through the waxed panes of the window behind him, casting his face in shadow. To one side, set within an alcove, was his bed.

When she had first thought of it, there was something wickedly bold about approaching Li Tao in his private chambers. She suddenly regretted her recklessness.

'I have something for you.'

He stared at the parcel in her hands. 'Come inside and close the door.'

She hovered in the doorway, too astonished to comply. Ru Shan tensed beside her in the hall. His growing protectiveness could be of use, but a direct confrontation with Li Tao would prove deadly. Hastily, she slipped into the room and shut the door behind her.

Once again, she was alone with the warlord. The mystery of the box was suddenly overpowered by a more primal instinct. She edged along the wall, keeping her distance.

'It's been days since I've seen you,' he said.

'You know exactly where I am, Governor. I can hardly hide from you,' she teased in an attempt to conceal her growing unease. He still hadn't moved from his seat.

'You've been busy,' she continued.

'Yes.'

'This…this was left at the house last night.'

She hated the desperation of her one-sided conversation. Every time they engaged one another, she seemed to have lost any ground she'd gained previously. The last time they had spoken, he'd kissed her—though it was more a challenge than a lover's kiss.

He had scandalously proposed she spend one night in his bed. Her thoughts wandered back to it every night while she slept far away from his chamber, but now that she was here, the proposal came back to her with a sharpness that stole her breath.

Swallowing past the sudden knot in her throat, she held out the box. 'Is this a gift?'

'Open it.'

The ribbon pulled free easily and she let the tail of it run from her fingers as she unwound the silk wrapping to reveal a rosewood box inlaid with a circle of jade on the lid.

'Look inside.' His voice pulled tight around each word.

Slowly, she lifted the brass clasp and nearly dropped the box when she caught the gleam of the blade. It was a dagger, the triangular blade thick and wickedly tapered. She set the case on to the table with trembling hands and backed away quickly.

'Flattering that the old man should send such a pretty weapon,' he said.

His attention focused singularly on to her, his icy demeanour vastly different from the man who had pressed his lips to hers so seductively. A thin, shadowed object lay across his palm.

'I always knew he had people hidden close to the heart of the empire.'

Her stomach lurched. It was a knife in his hand. He twirled the weapon carelessly between his fingers.

She backed away from the box one step at a time. 'You're mistaken. I had nothing to do with this.'

It was useless to beg. That was his reputation, wasn't it? When Li Tao came for you, your pleas fell upon deaf ears. The blood drained from her face while her mind fumbled for an escape.

'Did he also find you in Luoyang?' he asked.

His question caught her off guard. He rose to his feet and she stumbled back, her shoulders coming up against the alcove of the bed.

'He would see how your beauty could be used.'

'Gao?' Had he somehow guessed her connection to the old warlord?

She flinched when he took hold of her chin and forced her to meet his eyes. 'The rulers of this empire are so drawn to beauty.'

There was no compliment in his words. The knife remained poised lightly in his free hand. The threat of it brought her to another time and place. The same haze of fear had choked her then. The men who had come for her had looked at her with cold eyes as they'd held out two choices, a knife or poison.

'Gao doesn't own me.' Whatever ploy this was, she knew nothing about it. She'd been snared in it somehow and she had to convince him.

'No, not Gao.'

Faster than a serpent's strike, he had her arms pinned against the bed frame. He still held the knife. She gasped as the bone handle dug into her wrist.

'Did Lao Sou send you?' he demanded.

'Who?'

'Did the old man send you?'

'I don't know any old man. No one sent me.'

'Someone wanted you here. With me.'

His face was a rigid mask above her, jaw taut, his mouth a harsh line. If she called for help, Ru Shan would come storming in, but then Li Tao would kill them both. He held her pinned and there was nothing she could offer, nothing she could bargain with. She had never felt so helpless.

She was only alive at his whim. Nothing could sway him. Not vulnerability or tears or lies. Her desperate plea came out in a flood of words.

'You think anyone would send me to kill you? That I would walk in and do it while you were watching? You took me from my home. All I want is to go back.'

He had her caged against the bed, overpowered by his size and strength. A glimmer alighted in his eyes, a spark of passion amidst the blind anger. His hold loosened enough for her to slip her arms free.

She thought he would kiss her again. He was so close, the heat of his body enveloping her. Wildly, she realised she wanted him to. It would be no gentle caress this time. Not with the tension that vibrated through him. She needed something to penetrate this terrifying coldness.

'You know who sent that box.' Her breath came in shallow pulls. 'Someone who sends it every year.'

'I have powerful enemies.'

He was still watching her, a sharp line etched between his brows. She was afraid to move, afraid to invoke the demon caged inside him. His chest rose and fell, the pulse in his throat jumping beneath the tanned skin as the tension transformed to desire. There was an answering call within her. It was always this way between them, though she couldn't understand why.

'What does it mean?' she asked.

Her mention of the dagger broke the thrall over him. He glanced once at the open box.

'Leave.'

Chapter Five

As soon as Li Tao freed her, she fled from the room and stumbled through the corridor. She could still feel the bruising pressure of his hands pinning her, holding her captive.

Auntie waited at the end of the corridor, her expression twisted with worry.

'Lady Ling?'

Suyin tore past the old woman and left the servants in the entrance hall.

'My lady, what happened?'

Auntie insisted on following her into the garden. Struggling for breath, Suyin sank on to one of the flattened boulders lying in the soft grass. She needed to escape from here. Her captor was not only ruthless, he was likely mad.

'Unfavourable day, indeed,' Suyin snapped. 'You knew what would happen, didn't you?'

The old woman stood several steps away, her hands clasped before her demurely. Suyin clutched at the smooth stone below her, trying to steady the pounding of her heart. It always came to this, a knife at her throat, men coming to silence her. When she'd left the palace, she had vowed that she would no longer be used in the schemes of powerful men. She had been brought here by someone's design, she was certain of it.

'Auntie was hoping the lady could convince Master Li.'

'Convince him of what?'

The old woman shrank back at her anger, but Suyin couldn't find it within her to feel any remorse. Li Tao had held a blade to her. He had never directly threatened her with it, but that didn't matter. What frightened her even more was what had happened afterwards. She had fought to keep herself safe from men like him all her life, only to be drawn to Li Tao despite every survival instinct within her. They called it the seduction of power. She hadn't fully believed in it until now.

'What could I possibly convince him to do?' She raised herself to her feet. 'I am a prisoner, brought here against my will.'

A commotion rose from the depths of the front hall. The sound of Li Tao's strident voice resonated against the walls followed by the stamp of his footsteps. She was relieved to have some distance between them as he left.

'Master Li is a good man.' Auntie ventured forwards to grasp her sleeve. 'You are the only one he will listen to.'

'He listens to no one.'

'That is not true! Master spends more time here now. He enquires about your welfare constantly.'

He had asked Auntie about her? Most likely he was trying to discover her secrets.

Suyin pulled away in agitation. 'If he didn't make everyone out to be an enemy, he wouldn't need to live in constant fear.'

She didn't realise the truth of it until she spoke the words aloud. Li Tao had been afraid, as she was afraid. It was apparent that Auntie worried for him as well. Auntie trusted her and she needed to find a way to use that to her advantage. It was her best chance for escape.

'Auntie, the governor speaks constantly of defiance and rebellion.' She lowered her tone cautiously. 'I'm afraid it will destroy him.'

'Master is not a traitor. He's a good man.'

Suyin watched guiltily as tears gathered in the old woman's eyes.

'The box is a warning, isn't it?' Suyin asked.

Auntie started to respond, but then clamped her mouth shut and glanced furtively towards the house.

'Governor Li is gone,' Suyin assured. 'What does the box mean? Has your master ever mentioned an old man?'

Li Tao had interrogated her about an old man, Lao Sou, when he'd had her pinned.

'Old man? Cook is old…'

Suyin sighed impatiently. 'Not Cook.'

'The box is a reminder.' Auntie whispered even though the others were too far away to hear. 'Master doesn't think I know, but Auntie remembers everything. Once it was a sign of favour. Now it is a warning.'

'Favour?'

'From the August Emperor.'

'The August Emperor is dead. He has been dead for two years.'

'I know that!' Auntie snapped. The old woman wasn't completely intimidated. 'The Emperor would send Master Li a gift every year in honour of his service. Since his death, someone else must be sending the gift to remind him of his loyalty to the empire.'

Suyin bit back her cynical response. It was either Gao or some other rival who was sending the dagger to provoke Li Tao, but Auntie would think the best of him no matter what the circumstances.

She needed to bend Auntie's fear and loyalty to her advantage. She took hold of Auntie's thinning shoulders and spoke in a grave tone.

'Li Tao has refused to swear loyalty to the throne. How long before Emperor Shen publicly denounces him?'

Auntie paled, but she could only nod in agreement. If Auntie knew about the armies and the barricades, then she must know that Li Tao's days were numbered.

'The lady must convince him to reconsider. He hangs on your every word. He is so taken with you that he is afraid to blink when you are near for fear of losing sight of you.'

If only some measure of her reputation were true. Men didn't fall at her feet in adoration as the stories claimed. It was all careful observation and planning. And Li Tao was endlessly unpredictable, more so than anyone she had ever met. He wanted nothing from her but one night. A conquest. Very far from being in her thrall.

'Your master's pride will not allow it,' Suyin argued. 'But I may have some sway with Emperor Shen.'

Auntie's eyes brightened with hope, never questioning the lie. Former consorts had no power at all, especially after the scandals and rebellions that had followed the August Emperor's death. She had been fortunate that Emperor Shen had allowed her to leave the palace with her freedom and her life.

'If I can send a letter to Changan, I will speak on your master's behalf,' she pressed.

'But who will deliver the message?'

Her gaze shifted to Ru Shan at the other end of the garden. Li Tao had chosen an honourable man to guard her, but such honour could be adapted to her advantage. Auntie would go along, as well. The dear old woman cared for Li Tao. No one had ever fought so hard to save her. She had always been on her own, even while supposedly under the August Emperor's protection.

The imperial court had forgotten she had ever existed. But the Emperor Shen was a just ruler. When he found out that Li Tao had taken her, he would demand her return. She would be gone from this house before Li Tao's many enemies closed in on him.

When they returned to the house, the plan was already in place. Auntie herded the servants away before beckoning Suyin down the corridor. Ru Shan followed silently behind. He was easy to turn to their cause. Protecting a defenceless woman against a warlord appealed to his warrior's code.

Needles of guilt pricked at her heart. It had been too easy for her to manipulate an old woman's trust and a soldier's loyalty to her advantage. She was nothing but lies wrapped upon lies and she always had been. She had no choice. No one could save Li Tao. He had already declared his fate by defying the throne. Still, she hoped she would be released without bloodshed. Li Tao wouldn't risk his position to keep her captive. And when she was free, perhaps she would be able to speak on his behalf.

What did she care what became of Li Tao. Already she was losing her sense of purpose. She needed to concentrate.

Auntie padded hurriedly down the hall, stopping before a set of doors opposite the bed chamber. Even while Li Tao was gone, his foreboding presence lingered.

'No one is allowed inside the master's study,' Auntie told her as she slipped a key into the door. 'Be quick!'

Li Tao trusted Auntie and no one else. It made her wonder about the true relationship between the two of them.

Auntie pushed the door open, but would not enter. She poked her head inside to search about as if fearing Li Tao might have returned. When she was satisfied, she waved Suyin in.

'Master remembers where he puts everything,' Auntie warned before shutting her inside.

The wooden desk was arranged below an aperture in the roof to allow for light. Suyin hurried to the desk and peeled a blank sheet of paper free from the stack and folded it into her sleeve. She hoped he didn't go so far as to count them. A spare ink stick and brush quickly followed. They would need to return these items to their exact locations. She couldn't resist a quick scan of the desk, but Li Tao had left no communications in sight.

She turned to go, but curiosity overwhelmed her like an insistent itch. The study was as simple and austere as the rest of the house, the walls were bare. How could Li Tao stand to stare at blank walls day after day? Did he do nothing but plan his battles?

A single cabinet spanned the far wall next to a shelf of books. There had to be something inside that would give her a hint of who Li Tao was. Even though she would soon be gone, she needed to know.

In case there was some way to use the information, she told herself.

Like Auntie, she looked once more over her shoulder, searching the corners of the room with unreasonable caution. She imagined Li Tao sitting alone in the dark at his desk with a single lamp burning beside him.

Be assured of your success and you cannot fail. Madame from the pleasure quarters used to say that. Suyin said it to herself now.

She pulled on the handle and found the cabinet unlocked. The oiled hinges swung wide to reveal a set of identical daggers to the one in the box. The blades were crafted from blackened steel and they fanned out against the inner wall in a grand display. She held her breath as she counted them. There were fifteen.

By the next morning, Suyin feared that Auntie would worry her fingers to the bone with how often she wrung them together. Suyin sat her down and poured the tea for both of them.

'Auntie does not look well,' she suggested mildly.

'The lady is kind, but Auntie is fine—'

'Perhaps Auntie should stay in bed for the day,' she interrupted pointedly. 'Let someone else tend to the governor.'

Li Tao would hear Auntie's nervous rambling and know immediately that something was out of place. Suyin's plan was already in motion and all she had to do was wait. Hopefully Auntie's ability to present a good face would strengthen with time.

Auntie spilled her tea over the table when a knock sounded on the door. Suyin left Auntie to answer it herself.

Jun stood in the hallway, averting his eyes from her face. Her heart went out to the boy when she saw how he tried to hide his withered arm, angling his left side away.

'Master Li wishes to see you. He is in the garden,' Jun said shyly.

She breathed with relief. They would be outside in full view of the servants. After the way Li Tao had threatened her, she couldn't risk being trapped alone with him. Auntie stood back in the sitting area, her forehead creased in a nest of lines. This was how honest people reacted to deception. She gave Auntie a reassuring nod before stepping outside.

Jun fell into step behind her. He was tall with the lanky awkwardness of youth. From what she could see, Li Tao provided for his servants, yet Jun retained a lean wiriness that came from a childhood of scarcity. She had seen it in her village and in the streets of Luoyang.

'How long have you served the governor?' she asked.

She strained to hear his mumbled answer.

'Eight years, Lady Ling.'

Li Tao presented a confusing picture. He was an efficient military governor. His men were disciplined and loyal, and he was known for promoting men through the ranks based on skill rather than social standing, much like the August Emperor. Yet the warlord surrounded himself with such an incongruous crew of servants.

'Where did you live before?' she asked to distract herself as they descended the stairs to the second courtyard.

'At a monastery…an orphanage,' Jun corrected himself. 'Auntie asked for Master Li to take me in.'

'That was generous of him.' So he was capable of kindness. He also seemed to be obliging and respectful of Auntie.

Jun stopped abruptly at the edge of the courtyard. 'Lady Ling?'

'Yes?'

He bowed his head. 'You are very beautiful.'

Despite her jaded nature, his sincerity warmed her. This unassuming boy, innocent and hopeful, expected nothing in return for his flattery.

'Thank you for your kind words, Master Jun,' she said with a smile.

He blushed furiously at that and couldn't look at her for the rest of the walk to the garden.

They emerged through the circled archway and her attention centred on to Li Tao. He stood beneath the shade of the cedarwood pavilion. Stood rather than sat. He never paced, never made any unnecessary movements. He turned and studied her as she approached. His feral side was held in restraint; at least she hoped so. Her pulse quickened.

'Lady Ling.'

He invited her to sit with an outstretched hand, but she stopped short of the pavilion and refused to come any closer. Jun stood by her side, looking confused.

'It is difficult to be gracious when you held a knife to me the last time we met.'

Li Tao's steely expression transformed into a frown. He dismissed Jun with a wave of his hand and the boy backed away, kneeling to some task behind the shrubbery.

'I frightened you,' Li Tao said. 'I apologise. Please sit.'

His façade of civility didn't reassure her. She ascended the wooden steps into the pavilion and noticed the faint shadow over his jaw as she glanced up at him. He looked unkempt, as if he'd just come from the road. She moved past him to take her seat on the stone bench.

It wasn't only fear that caused her heart to race. His nearness stirred her blood, urging her to tempt fate. That made him more dangerous than Gao and all of the other interlopers who had ever plotted against her. When he seated himself across the table, she was grateful for the barrier between them.

'Ru Shan is away,' he said. 'I will need to assign another guardsman to your care.'

She smoothed out her sleeves and folded her hands together on the surface of the table, using the casual gesture to mask her nervousness. She knew exactly why Ru Shan was away. He had used the ruse of visiting his ailing father.

'Are you afraid I'll escape, Governor Li? I would lose myself in this bamboo sea before I found the road.'

'You shouldn't be left alone. Not after what happened.'

What happened? 'I wasn't in any danger from anyone besides you.'

He didn't answer for a long stretch; she was afraid she'd been too bold.

'Accept a peace offering, then,' he said finally.

He lifted a bundle wrapped in canvas on to the table. She stared at him in surprise as he beckoned for her to open it. Theirs was the oddest of acquaintances. She couldn't decipher what Li Tao was to her. Adversary, protector, companion. Madman.

Perhaps she was mad as well. Why else would she be tempted to accept the tainted protection he offered? She could hide away in the cover of the bamboo forest.

Her message to the Emperor was already travelling toward the capital. Even if Li Tao wasn't so unpredictable, she couldn't stay. When Emperor Shen came for him, she could be implicated as a co-conspirator even though she had been brought there against her will. Or worse, they would come with swords and arrows with no pause to sort out who was who.

She reached for the bindings, but hesitated, remembering another package she'd opened in his presence.

'It's not a trap,' he replied when she looked to him.

The image of the fifteen daggers haunted her. She was afraid to ask about the strange delivery, as if the mystery would hold her captive if she uncovered it.

She untied the knots while Li Tao leaned back to watch her. His offering was somewhat awkward given the circumstances, yet oddly earnest because of it. The canvas peeled away to reveal a lacquered case inlaid with abalone shell. She gasped when she lifted the lid and saw the musical instrument inside. The arrangement of the silk strings over wooden bridges sent a flutter of delight through her. She'd left her *qin* by the river with the rest of her abandoned belongings.

'It's beautiful.'

'The instrument maker told me this was his finest work,' Li Tao said. 'But I have no eye for such things.'

She ran her fingers over the polished surface board, teasing the strings. The clear notes rose in the air with a sense of freedom.

'You're glowing.' His tone held its own hint of pleasure.

She looked to him and wished that she hadn't seen the quiet satisfaction in his eyes. He was focused on her. Always on her.

'Did you ever hear me play, Governor?'

'I never had that honour.'

'Madame Ling taught me. She taught me everything.' She lifted the instrument from its case and set it carefully on to the carved legs. 'In Luoyang, I would play in the front room for an hour each night,' she said, bubbling with excitement as she adjusted the tuning knobs. 'Only one hour, nothing more. I would close my eyes and play and all of those men would fall madly in love with me.'

His mouth curved the tiniest bit upwards. 'Every single one?'

'Every single one.'

In the entertainment district of Luoyang, she would sit behind a sheer curtain to build an aura of mystery. Wealthy patrons struggled to catch a glimpse of her through the gauze. Some would offer to pay for just a look.

Unless the offer was exorbitantly high, Madame usually refused, laughing at her own cleverness. 'The picture of you they have formed in their minds is more beautiful than you could ever be.'

Her parents had forfeited her in name and body, thinking she would be betrothed to some merchant. They hadn't known the well-dressed servants were actually kidnappers who supplied the entertainment quarters. Her den mother, Madame Ling, had given her the surname that would later become known throughout the empire.

Li Tao settled comfortably in his seat as she positioned her fingers over the strings. Suyin attached the ivory guards over her fingers and plucked out three notes, letting herself sink into the sound and vibration.

'What song would you like to hear?' she asked.

'I don't know any.'

The way he watched her made her heart ache with anticipation. He folded his hands before him, his demeanor relaxed and indulgent for once. The intimacy of the moment struck her—to be playing for him for pleasure with nothing between them. No curtain and none of the artifice of Luoyang.

Except there would always be deception between them. She was plotting her escape and he was looking for some way to use her.

'You'll like this one,' she promised. She looked down to the strings as if that was enough hide the lies. 'It's about a battle.'

Lady Ling had the most exquisite hands. They moved in waves over the strings, one hand pulling at the silk strings to test them, the other adjusting the wooden bridges. The scattered notes floated through the air, not yet forming music. Her expression took on a tranquil look. She tilted her head to listen to nuances of tone that were beyond his ears. Maybe that was how she read people so well, catching the subtle meanings hidden in voice and inflection.

Finally she straightened her shoulders and poised her fingers over the span of the strings. She inhaled, gathering herself, and began to play.

The legend was that Ling *Guifei* had charmed the August Emperor with her music. She commanded the universe when she played, the trees and the stars. That part was poetic nonsense, but the music pulled at him inside and out. The rhythm sent his blood rushing through his veins.

She played with her eyes closed. He closed his own eyes, joining her in the darkness. She had said the song depicted a battle, but nothing of the sort came to mind, no lofty images of horses and banners waving or battalions clashing over hills. Only darkness and a pure sound that filled him, creeping into spaces he hadn't known were empty.

Desire flooded his body, the dull throb building to an acute pain that would not let go. His hand tightened on the arm of the chair.

Ling Suyin was exactly the sort of person Lao Sou would have recruited: talented, resourceful and cunning. He wanted her regardless—the warmth of her skin, the reluctant willingness of her mouth. He even wanted her detachment and her defiance. Would the Old Man have predicted that as well?

As the final notes struck, he opened his eyes.

'Did you enjoy it?' She played on. The second song flowed over his mind like cool water, but did nothing to ease the ache in his body.

'You play well.'

'Such ardent praise,' she reprimanded lightly. Her fingers continued to walk along the strings gently.

'Don't you tire of compliments? Look at Jun over there. He won't blink for fear of losing the sight of you.'

She laughed and the sound puffed up his chest. At the other end of the courtyard, Jun slinked further behind the shrubbery, realising he had been caught. Li Tao couldn't fault the boy. Greater men had found themselves helpless at this woman's feet. The music lulled him into the first sense of peace he had allowed himself in long time. He wanted to sink into the dream and accept where it took him.

'Where do you go every day?' she asked in a tone of disinterest.

'Nowhere you would find entertaining.'

This must be how she was able to pry secrets from the most powerful men in the empire. He had no skill for filling silence with conversation, but he found himself wanting to do so. To reciprocate the moment she had created.

'I received another imperial summons to appear before Emperor Shen in Changan,' he stated. Nothing secret about that, it being an imperial proclamation.

The gentle music faltered before continuing. The notes took on a hint of shrillness beneath the soft warmth.

'Then you must go and make peace with Emperor Shen.' Suyin stared down at the instrument.

Was that concern he detected?

'Once they have me in Changan, it'll be the death of me.'

'If you don't go, they'll hang you as a traitor.'

'They behead traitors, Ling *Guifei*,' he replied mildly.

She flattened the strings with her hand to stop the sound. 'Why do you insist on calling me that?'

'To remind myself that you are not mine.'

Silence hung between them.

'But you don't want me,' she said, her tone cutting. 'Other than for one night.'

'One night can last a very long time.'

The blush in her cheeks caught him off guard. He had assumed such flirtation was second nature to a seasoned courtesan.

'I don't wish to see you hanged…or beheaded.'

'Not without a fight,' he promised.

'War and death. That's all men like you know.' She pushed the instrument aside and sank back as if it no longer held any joy for her.

'This summons is an ambush. The imperial court has all the

power in Changan. I'll face whoever comes for me here, on my own terms.'

Suyin fell silent. She tapped her fingertips thoughtfully against the tabletop as she struggled with her next words.

'Please reconsider,' she said finally.

'There's nothing to consider. Gao has the court in his palm,' he said.

She made an impatient sound. 'I told Auntie you wouldn't listen to anyone.'

That left them at a standstill, staring at each other across the field of battle. But she wasn't quite the enemy. He traced the shape of her mouth and the curve of her throat. Suyin's breathing quickened in response. No one else dared to suggest that he back down. Certainly no one had counselled him regarding his own welfare.

She was beautiful.

She was complicated.

There wasn't a thread of trust between them, yet he still wanted her. Discipline and caution meant nothing when she was near.

'Tell me one thing,' she said. 'What does the dagger mean?'

'It's a reminder.'

'Of what?'

'Shibao.'

'The siege against Tibet.'

Of course she knew the history. She had been Emperor Li Ming's consort for fifteen years. She'd shared the sovereign's bed. Resentment flowed like poison through Li Tao's veins. Jealous of a dead man. There wasn't a more worthless emotion.

'One of the worst defeats of the empire,' he said.

'But you were commended for your bravery. Everyone knew your name after that battle.'

'It was undeserved.' He wasn't being humble. If she meant to appeal to his sense of honour and duty, it didn't exist. 'In the end, all debts must be paid. The message of the dagger is that no one can be careful for ever.'

If only she knew the truth behind the legends. He was no hero. He was tempted to tell her everything, but with the old empire falling to ruin around them, it made no difference any longer.

Chapter Six

Shibao, Tibet—ad 745
14 years earlier

Facing death on the battlefield was different from facing death in the dingy corners of the city. In battle, the sheer crush of bodies made survival unpredictable. Skill meant nothing in the thick of it. Planning, valour, strength…nothing. That was what made this task all the more challenging. He could come out alive or he could succeed in his mission. One or the other, but not both.

By now, Li Tao knew what the eve of battle felt like, knew the taste of it in the air. He'd been inserted into the growing forces of the imperial army for the last five years. In his first battle, he hadn't even been issued a sword, but the Emperor's continued excursions into foreign lands to gain territory had given Li Tao plenty of opportunity to climb the ranks. Today, he lined up shoulder to shoulder among the first battalion, stationed near the dragon banner on the fields of Shibao. In the distance, the flags of the Tibetan kingdom waved in challenge.

The August Emperor himself walked the line. This was no fattened monarch who watched over the battle from a hilltop in the distance. The Emperor would ride where the battle was thickest, urging men forwards with his will. To all who witnessed it, he was truly invincible, the Son of Heaven.

Li Tao had to admit the Emperor was a natural leader of men. He was at his best amidst the stamp of horses' hooves and the clash of swords. His detractors scorned that he was far more comfortable on a saddle than on the throne. Several attempts on his life had been made in the imperial palace, but all had failed. His death today would be a kindness, a warrior's death.

Like every other man, Li Tao bowed low as the Emperor passed by. Inexplicably, the Emperor halted. His face displayed weary lines from sleeping in the same tents as his men and eating by the same cooking fires. The studded bands of his armour were dulled with dust and blood.

'What is your name, swordsman?'

He straightened. 'Li Tao, Imperial Majesty.'

This seemed to please the Emperor. 'We share our family name. Perhaps a hundred years ago, our ancestors were kinsmen.'

Li Tao raised his fist humbly to his chest. 'This soldier can only hope to bring honour to our name today.'

As he expected, the corners of the Emperor's eyes creased in a rare moment of good humour before battle. The ruling classes were slaves to lofty ideals of honour and glory. He could spout empty words and lure them like gulls.

Li Tao wasn't even his true name.

'May you wield your blade with honour today.'

The Emperor spoke the blessing and reached over to grip Li Tao's shoulder. His fingers tightened briefly. With a nod, the Emperor continued down the line.

Li Tao followed the view of the Emperor's back until the sovereign disappeared in a sea of leather and steel. An ill-fated twinge settled in his chest. The unwelcome gesture had been almost fatherly.

ad 759—Present day

Li Tao emerged through the pass with his sentry at his flank. In the shadow of the ridge, the bamboo stalks shot up through the loamy earth to form a corridor. The drift of the green canopy beckoned his return.

The bamboo sea had cloaked the troops he had amassed and trained over the years. This hidden army could very well be seen as a sign of treason, though the other *jiedushi* had done the same. They could anticipate the unrest that would follow the fall of a great Emperor. Men like Gao Shiming sought to capitalise on the instability to gain power while Li Tao fought to maintain order, even if he had to defy Changan.

Cool forest air surrounded him like a long, drawn-out sigh. His thoughts shifted from the tension of the barricades back to his infamous guest. Before he realised it, he was urging his horse into a gallop over the final stretch of road winding up to the mansion.

A constant restlessness had taken root within him. At night, he would lie on a pile of rugs in the nagging darkness of the barracks and conjure up a swirl of coloured silk beneath his eyelids. In the silent stretch before dawn, he imagined Suyin's voice and the elusive scent of her perfume. All trace of her would disappear by the time the troops assembled in the morning and he would issue his commands without any thought to her. Then night would come again.

He needed to be rid of her. The temptation was too great.

He needed to keep her close. The temptation was too great.

At the house, he dismounted and strode through the side entrance. The stillness of the interior pricked his awareness, the absence of footsteps or the murmur of voices. No one came to greet him in the front hall. Even on the slowest of days, he expected a measure of activity in the late afternoon as the servants completed their chores.

The minute jump in his pulse was followed by a chilling calm. He slipped the blade from beneath his sleeve and stepped soundlessly through the main salon, his weight shifting on to the balls of his feet. He searched the corners and scanned each dim corridor. At the portico, the lilt of a familiar voice floated to him.

'Was that the sound of riders?'

With a deep breath, he slid the weapon back into its sheath and adjusted his sleeve with a sharp tug before moving out into the open air. The doors of the sitting room had been propped open to provide a view into the gardens. The last of the tension drained from him when he saw the layers of yellow silk wrapped in pink. Suyin glowed like a vibrant flame among the sombre guardsmen who lined along the walkway.

'Governor Li.' A sewing needle gleamed between her first and second fingers.

He had to be mistaken about the brightness in her tone. 'Where is Jinmei?' he asked.

'Auntie has gone to Rongzhou for the spring festival. Everyone went with her except for the gardener, who is too blind to see the lanterns, and Cook because this worthless woman cannot even boil rice to feed herself.'

He started to ask her why she hadn't gone with them, momentarily forgetting his strict orders to keep her in the house and guarded at all times.

He stepped through the garden doors to come up beside her. A swathe of dark cloth hung from her hands.

'What are you doing?'

'Mending, for Auntie. I am making use of the daylight while I still have it.'

She bent to her task. The silver needle darted in and out of the cloth, guided by her skilful fingers. He was surprised to see it was one of his tunics. She continued chirping away while she worked.

'Auntie told me she used to be a seamstress. She is much slower now than she used to be. Her joints are swollen and her eyesight is not as keen as it once was.'

'You do not need to do that.'

The elegant Ling *Guifei* shouldn't be bent over such a menial task.

'I am nearly finished,' she protested. 'It is not so different from embroidery… There.'

She pulled the end of the thread taut and bit through it in a tiny flash of teeth. His stomach tightened involuntarily at the careless gesture. He lowered himself on to the seat beside her.

Her gaze raked disapprovingly over the dust that covered his clothes. 'You were gone for three days this time.'

'There were urgent matters I needed to attend to.'

'These urgent matters are keeping you longer and longer.'

Questioning him as if she were the mistress of the house seemed to put her in oddly good spirits. She perched over the arm of her chair and waited expectantly for an answer. She was becoming more comfortable in his presence while he was more on edge every time he saw her.

'Did the August Emperor confess all his secrets to you like this?' he asked.

'Yes,' she replied impetuously. She ran her finger along the sleek, polished wood. 'Tell me all your troubles and I will nod and sigh until they float away.'

She demonstrated with a wordless, gentle murmuring in the back of her throat that caressed over him. He laughed and shook his head at her display.

All a lie, he reminded himself. A very pretty lie and he was charmed in spite of it.

'Gao's army is moving south,' he began.

He watched her face as he continued. It remained a careful mask, clean of any emotion.

'As well as the Emperor's,' he added.

Her lightheartedness faded. 'You say this so calmly.'

'This was inevitable.'

'Is this what you wanted?'

'No.' That one word of confession was more than he had spoken to anyone about the inevitable battle before him. He passed a hand over his temples and the weariness poured into him as if the dam had cracked open. 'I seem to want to tell you things I shouldn't.'

'Then keep the secrets you need to keep,' she said gently. 'Tell me the rest.'

It could be a ruse. It most likely was a ruse, but it sounded like kindness.

'Emperor Shen wants to control the *jiedushi* out of fear of rebellion,' he began. The tension wound tight around his chest like iron chains. 'But without our armies, the borders will crumble.'

'Yet you weaken the empire by challenging Shen.'

'So a sovereign should never be challenged?'

She considered his answer for a long time, but said nothing.

'There was a time when Shen might have listened to me, but now...' He closed his eyes and laid his head back.

'What of the other warlords?' she asked.

'Too shrewd to take sides, but Gao is forcing the issue.'

A lesser man might attack the weaker positions first, but Gao didn't want a drawn-out struggle. He'd take out the strongest first and watch the others fall in line with him. The old wolf had even managed to find a way to do it under the guise of serving the Emperor.

'Gao has always known how to manipulate the court. With a thousand servants inside the palace, all he needed were a few under his control.'

He opened his eyes to see Suyin stabbing the needle into a pincushion. She folded the tunic into a neat square in her lap, smoothing out the corners fastidiously.

There was no need to ensnare her into the trap he was caught in. He could return her to her home by the river and wash his hands clean of her, but Gao still wanted her dead. She needed his protection whether she desired it or not.

'Do you know there will be a full moon tonight?' Her tone lightened deliberately. She set the folded square of cloth aside and sat back, looking out over the courtyard, past the rooftops. 'Auntie tells me the household goes to Rongzhou for the festival every year.'

He nodded. 'They stay for days until the celebration is over.'

'You never go with them?'

He supposed he never had.

'We would celebrate in the palace with elaborate lanterns,' she went on when he didn't answer. 'And eat sweet sticky dumplings.'

She was making a valiant effort to distract him, but idle conversation wasn't an art he had mastered. He followed her gaze to the darkening sky even though there was no moon yet to see.

'I miss the lantern festival in Luoyang the most. The lanterns would be strung from balcony to balcony.' She traced an imaginary line in the air with her hand. 'Everyone would be out in the streets, packed close together.'

Her face lit with an unrestrained energy and he couldn't help but recall the scene she described. How many times had he pushed his way through the crush of the crowd as a boy in Luoyang? He had craned his neck to watch the paper lanterns swinging overhead. All the colours glowing against the black sky.

'The lanterns would burn all night in Luoyang,' he said.

'Have you been to the eastern capital?' she asked.

She flashed a genuine smile at him. Her hand dangled over the arm of the chair and he was stricken by the urge to lace his fingers through hers. But if he did, he might frighten away the hopeful, bright-eyed girl who had emerged and the artful courtesan would return.

He stood abruptly. 'Do you ride?'

'I don't know how.'

She stared at him, startled, but she took his hand when he held it out. For once she didn't ask any questions and simply let him lead.

They were soaring through the forest, jostled and tossed at the whim of the black beast beneath them. Li Tao had his arms about her while she clutched at the front of his robe. Silk whipped about her legs. She held on as the earth pounded by. She prayed.

Li Tao had foregone the palanquin to set her on to the saddle in front of him, pulled up against the cradle of his hard thighs. Embarrassment was quickly replaced by abject terror as the horse surged forwards. An escort of ten soldiers rode along with them and the combined thundering of their mounts around her added to her disorientation.

'Please slow down,' she begged, then shouted it again when he couldn't hear her over the pound of hooves.

He spoke over the top of her head. 'You won't fall.'

Impassive and stone-faced as always as if he could command away her fear. He handled the reins with ease as he leaned forwards, absorbing the impact of the ride. He must be revelling in the way she cowered against him.

'Governor Li.' She dug her nails into his chest until she connected with taut flesh beneath the rumpled cloth.

'The town is close,' he assured.

It was *not* close. She buried her face against his shoulder and squeezed her eyes shut to escape the roar of the wind. The steady pulse of his heart sounded beneath her ear in contrast to the frantic hammering of hers. He threw a rough arm around her to steady her, a matter of necessity rather than any show of concern, she decided. She was going to be sick.

Finally they reached their destination and he pulled the horse to a stop. He dismounted first and closed his hands around her waist to lift her from the saddle. Her legs trembled like saplings as she settled on to the ground. They stood by wooden gates with a cluster of buildings before them and a babble of voices floated from the streets.

'Rongzhou is too far, but there is a smaller festival here,' he said.

She ventured ahead, the harrowing ride soon forgotten. The sound of drumbeats came from the centre of town accompanied by flutes and the crash of cymbals.

A dozen armed soldiers would not be a common sight for a town of this size. At the main square, the crowd parted hastily for Li Tao and his retinue, but the celebration continued around them. She was brought to the front to watch as a troupe of musicians performed in the centre of the clearing.

An uncommon happiness swelled within her with the cadence of the music. Such a change from her solitary days bent over calligraphy or embroidery. The lanterns hung from the rooftops just like they had in Luoyang—cages of light folded from waxed paper with candles flickering inside.

Li Tao stood close behind her. She jumped at the first snap of the firecrackers and grabbed on to him. His arm remained wooden beneath her hand, but he permitted the touch.

When she tried to speak to him, he shook his head, unable to hear above the noise. He bent down and she had to lift herself on to her toes to reach his ear.

'Over there!'

She wanted to be in the thick of the crowd and absorb the celebration before returning to the long silences of his mansion. Li Tao indulged her, guiding her through the gathering with his hand secured at the small of her back. All the while he scanned the crowd. His men fanned around them protectively.

She had done this so many times as a girl in Luoyang. Every year, she had watched the lights and people and listened as the matchmakers roamed the streets bestowing fortunes upon young couples late into the evening. The blessings were all fantasies: longevity, marriage, all that you desire. The night would always end for her at Madame Ling's, but out in the festival crowd she would hope to catch a young man's eye. A scholar with a kind face. Someone to walk alongside for the evening.

The childish dream returned to her so vividly amidst the sulphur smoke and the scraps of red paper littered at her feet from spent firecrackers. She looked up to find Li Tao gazing toward the sky. The moon had risen full overhead, large enough to touch. The sturdy lines of his profile stood out distinctly against the heavens.

He looked down at her then. She still held on to him and he tensed beneath her touch.

'Governor Li,' she said. There was nothing after that. She had nothing else to say.

'Lady Ling.'

His voice resonated deep enough to cut through the firecrackers and the music and the applause of the crowd. It penetrated her, leaving her weightless. He was nothing like the boy, the man she had once dreamed about. She had wished for someone thoughtful and doting, who would touch her hand and gently kiss her in the shadow of some corner.

Her chest grew unbearably tight. Li Tao was a cold, severe, unyielding sort of man. But she almost wanted him to kiss her anyway. They were both clothed in secrets, but they didn't have to pretend around each other.

'Buy me a lantern,' she implored.

'Which one?' He looked up again, searching through the coloured shapes that swung above the crowd.

Her gaze settled on a sun-yellow orb with an emerald dragon painted across it. 'That one.'

He gestured to a man in the crowd. Before long, the merchant was reaching above with a wooden pole to unhook the lantern. He brought it before her and she stared at the dance of candlelight. Her dragon flickered to life with glowing eyes and a swish of scales.

'Yes, that one,' she said with satisfaction, resisting the urge to grasp it in her hands. Her lantern was merely a wick of flame inside delicate paper, easily destroyed if she wasn't careful.

Li Tao paid for it and handed the hook over to one of his men as they continued through the streets. At a corner stand, he bought her candy made from a nest of spun sugar wound around and around a stick. The fine threads melted against her tongue, warm and golden.

The town was a small one, but for the moment, it was the world. She was sorry when they reached the edge of it. The drums were still beating and the moon was climbing to its highest point.

They returned to the horses at the outskirts of town. The men untied the reins from the post and started readying the mounts for the return home. She blew out the candle inside the lantern, folded it carefully along the spines and then paused to look at the moon away from the lights of the festival. Li Tao stood beside her until his guards began to pace.

Once again, he touched his hand to her back, fingers curving around her waist. This time there was no excuse for it other than that he wanted to. She could barely breathe.

She wanted to tell him then that he was fighting a losing battle. That death wasn't the only way. He needed to swallow his damned pride and find a way to compromise with the Emperor. But Suyin had already chosen her course. Her message would reach Emperor Shen before long. She had done what she needed to save herself as long as Ru Shan wasn't discovered. As long as Emperor Shen felt honour bound to respond to her plea.

'We need to return,' he said. 'The roads will be dark.'

To her regret, Li Tao removed his hand, letting it fall away. He stood like a dark tower over her, barely illuminated by the light of the moon. She passed the tip of her tongue over her lips. The taste of burnt sugar lingered. Ling *Guifei* was never without words, but it was the hundredth time that night she had found it hard to speak.

He swung up into the saddle and lowered his hand to help her up. Her temple rested against the heated skin of his neck and she could feel his pulse beating as she pressed close.

'Ride slower this time,' she admonished.

He was nothing but shadow. A solid shape in the night. She wound her arms about his waist and he tensed before exhaling slowly.

'I will,' he said.

Chapter Seven

The three days of the celebration came and went, but Suyin tried to hold on to the warmth and the laughter. The dragon lantern remained on her dresser, lifeless without the fire inside.

Time became muddled in the circular routine of the household. Her existence had whittled down to the long wait. There were days she even found herself waiting for the sound of Li Tao's footsteps in the front hall or the glow of a lamp in his study. She hadn't seen him since the night of the festival.

Only because his presence disrupted the rhythm, she told herself. When he was there, she had to change herself, act differently, think differently.

She caught the pungent scents floating from the kitchen during her morning stroll through the gardens. When she wandered inside, the scene that greeted her brought back a lost splinter of time from another kitchen: a cramped, dingy corner of her family home by the river. A place that no longer existed.

The stove radiated an oppressive heat. Even with all the windows and the door thrown open, the air in the kitchen boiled to a swelter as the midday meal neared. Cook admonished her the moment she set foot inside.

'Be careful, everything is hot!' he said. 'This is no place for Lady Ling.'

He tried to shoo her away, telling her food would be brought as soon as it was ready. There was more affection in his scolding than all of the compliments bestowed on her in Changan. She convinced him to let her stay by begging him to put her to work.

Cook had several pots boiling over the wood stove. A wispy steam rose from the baskets stacked beside her while she dug into the bundle of flour. This lumpy concoction had no resemblance to steam buns that she could see.

Cook tried to show her the technique with his hands in the air. 'Roll and knead it.'

In the corner, Jun leaned against the wall to hide his arm away from sight. He managed a smirk, but wasn't yet bold enough to laugh outright at her. The servants came by to glance in the kitchen and greet her, before ducking away with smiles on their faces. Li Tao's household appeared to be a harmonious one, though their master seemed removed from it.

'What are Governor Li's favourite dishes?' she asked.

Cook grunted in response. 'Master has no care for good food. He eats whatever is in the kitchen when he returns. Salted pork, old rice.'

The thought of Li Tao dining alone every night brought on an unexpected twinge of sadness. He was so isolated, constantly building up his defences. She'd sensed that loneliness at the festival while he stood beside her, looking up at the lights. The imperial court believed him a traitor and death threats appeared at his door. Even she conspired to free herself from him.

A shudder ran down her spine despite the heat of the kitchen. She turned back to the dough. 'Show me again, Cook. This doesn't feel right.'

The cook took two steps, his bamboo sandals clacking against the tiled floor. 'Dear girl! Heaven and earth,' he scolded. 'Stir the soup pot if you want to help.'

He pried the stringy dough from her, dropped it on to the board and began to work it in circles with the heels of his palms. The bare spot on the top of his head glistened as he bent to his task.

'Strong hands,' he mumbled. 'You need to have strong hands.'

Suyin passed her forearm over her brow, avoiding her flour-caked fingers. The silk gown clung to her skin and her hair fell in loose strands about her face. Jun offered her a kitchen rag for her hands and received a quick swat from Cook for his gallantry.

'Lazy! Go get me a chicken.' He started to form rounded buns to place into the steam basket. 'The lady likes chicken ginseng soup.'

'Lady Ling!'

Auntie's frantic cry from outside interrupted the hectic comfort of the kitchen. The old woman came through the open door and grabbed onto Suyin's sleeve, decorum forgotten in her haste.

'The death of me!' she wailed. 'Come quick.'

Goddess of Mercy. Suyin's stomach twisted as she stumbled after Auntie. Emperor Shen's response had finally come. Or Li Tao had been harmed in some way. She passed through the archway to the second courtyard and saw that the situation was much, much worse.

Li Tao stood black as night, sword drawn, his jaw clenched with rage. Kneeling on the grey stone at his feet was Ru Shan with his arms bound behind him.

'My fault!' Auntie ran forwards and collapsed on to her knees before them. 'All my fault. Master Li, be merciful.'

Suyin rushed to Auntie's side and tried to lift her sagging body from the ground. 'Auntie, you're making it worse,' she whispered.

Auntie fought against her, too distraught to listen. The old woman grasped for Li Tao's arm, oblivious to the sword he held.

'Tao-tao,' she pleaded. 'Do not do this.'

He flung Auntie away and reached into his robe, pulling out a pale square of folded paper. The look he gave Suyin froze her blood. Slowly, Auntie dragged herself to her feet and stood to the side, weeping.

Li Tao's grip tightened on the letter. The glowing festival lanterns had lied to her. There was no warmth there.

Suyin straightened defiantly. 'This was my doing. Only me.'

Cook, Jun and the rest of the household gathered at the edges of the courtyard. A foreboding row of soldiers stood at attention along the walkway. Their presence sent everyone into a muted state.

'You knew you were bringing a fox into your home,' she said, though she trembled like a child inside. She needed Li Tao to direct his anger towards her, not at the honest people implicated in her schemes.

His eyes narrowed and his grip tightened on his sword until his knuckles grew white. 'I will not suffer treachery.'

Ru Shan lurched to his feet, but before he was upright, Li Tao struck him across the face and sent him sprawling. A stunned murmur snaked through the crowd. Auntie clenched her fist and pressed it against her mouth to force back her sobs. Suyin watched helplessly, numb with fear. She'd brought his wrath on all of them.

She forced herself into the space between Ru Shan and Li Tao, standing as tall as she could to face off against the warlord.

'I acted on my own!' Ru Shan sputtered from behind her.

Li Tao towered over them both. The blade gleamed wickedly and she forced her gaze away from it to stare at his face. She couldn't back down. She couldn't bear any more bloodshed, another debt to weigh on her soul.

'Your servants believed everything I told them,' she taunted. 'I am quite convincing.'

Li Tao's mouth twisted grimly. She'd pushed him too far. Her breath caught as Li Tao raised his sword, but he jammed it back into the sheath. He snatched her wrist into an iron grip and dragged her through the interior hallway. Her feet stumbled against the floorboards and she tried to look back on the others, but he yanked her forwards cruelly.

He threw open the doors of the front parlour and shoved her inside. She stumbled before swinging around to face him. Her heart beat uncontrollably. She couldn't breathe, couldn't think. Her entire body trembled with fear, with anger. She could no longer tell.

'You're an animal!'

'And you're a sorceress.'

He slammed the doors shut and swung around. Survival instinct took over. She scrambled away from him as he came towards her. Her eyes circled the room for a weapon, anything to defend herself with. Her foot caught the edge of a divan. She fell to the floor, but he hauled her up against him.

'What did you offer Ru Shan?' he demanded through clenched teeth.

He brought her face close to his, forcing her to look at him. His hand gripped the back of her neck and she felt the first stinging threat of tears. But even now, shaking in his grasp, she refused to show him that surrender.

'Did you offer him your body?'

She clawed at his hands, needing to free herself and get as far away from him as possible. He was dangerously strong, unpredictable in his wrath.

'What man wouldn't fall to you, honour be damned?'

The heat of his body surrounded her, overwhelming her. Suddenly his hold on her shifted. One arm captured her waist to drag her against his chest before his mouth descended on hers.

Heat and pleasure coursed through her at once, fierce and wild and uncompromising. She fell boneless against him, winding her arms around his neck dizzily, drinking in the salted taste of his mouth. His desire reached through to feed on the kiss, but the anger remained. His arms wrapped around her.

No. Not like this. Her mind fought even though her body surrendered. Not in this thoughtless, desolate hunger.

She sank her teeth into his lower lip and didn't let go until she tasted blood. He tore away from her with a curse.

'Fox demon.'

'I am not a whore,' she seethed.

She stumbled back on to the padded *chaise*, her legs weak with desire. Blindly, she fumbled for the vase on the end table and succeeded in knocking it over before grabbing on to it and launching it at him. He swatted it away, sending it crashing to the floor.

'No, not a whore.' He stalked towards her and all she could do was double up and press back against the seat. 'A seductress and a liar.'

He braced one knee against the seat. She grabbed one of the embroidered pillows and held it in front of her like a shield.

'Get away.'

'I am not going to force you.' His lip was swollen and a trickle of blood welled from it. He swiped it off with the back of his hand. 'I have never forced a woman.'

They stayed at opposite ends of the *chaise*. She pushed herself as far away as she could, her shoulder blades coming up against the armrest. Desire still pulsed through her, hot and swimming in her blood, mixing with the fear. Her thighs grew weak, her sex damp with wanting. She would never understand how her body, how every inch of her skin, yearned for this man. It went against everything she ever knew.

'Did you give yourself to Ru Shan?' His voice ground against her shattered nerves. The sharpest edge of his anger had dulled, but the threat remained.

Only now did she fully understand what fueled his rage. It was jealousy. Raw, primal jealousy.

'I gave him nothing.'

'Nothing? A loyal man shuns his duty for the mere privilege of serving you?'

It was difficult to have him this close when she was still flushed from the onslaught of his mouth. She hated this weakness.

'I'll do anything in my power to escape.'

'You have them all in your hands, bewitched and bent to your will.' He cast a sideways glance at her. 'I underestimated you.'

Moving ever so slowly, he took hold of her ankle above the edge of her slipper. Not forcefully, but with a firm, sensual touch against her bare skin. Heat radiated from him to course throughout her body.

She froze, but couldn't pull away. Not even when he rose and angled himself over her until he had a hand braced on either side of her. Her back pushed against the seat while he looked down at her as if he would devour her. Her chest rose and fell erratically, her entire body straining to get closer to him as he held himself above her, solid and masculine and powerful.

With a long, drawn breath he seemed to come to a decision. 'Ling Suyin, you can tempt any man.'

'I am tired of compliments,' she retorted.

He lowered himself on to her and his mouth captured her lips. Heat, so much heat. She flushed beneath the anchor of his body. There was no reason to it.

His eyes found hers. The pupils were opaque and unreadable. His breathing was forced. She clasped the pillow between them reflexively, but he tore it from her hands and tossed it aside. Immediately he returned to deepen the kiss, sliding roughened fingers along her bodice and dipping below the embroidered edge. Her breasts swelled at the caress, pushing into his hands as he stroked her nipple.

She was lost in the cascade of pleasure. Li Tao was roughly skilled. Unrelenting. Her arms circled around his neck to pull him closer. The sumptuous weight of his body pinned her to the cushions. He ground the hard ridge of his sex between her thighs.

A moaned escaped her lips. She might have moaned his name.

'Give me one night so we can be done with this,' he demanded. It was at once a command and a plea.

His mention of this bargain cut through the haze of pleasure he had woven around her. He wanted boundaries. Terms. Control.

'You'll hardly find one night to be enough,' she snapped.

His black eyes narrowed at the challenge. Deftly, with unerring confidence, his hand slid over the drape of silk that covered her leg before slipping beneath.

She cried out as he found her sex. All the defiance in the world couldn't keep her back from arching or her eyes from squeezing shut in tortured delight. He slipped a hard, calloused finger just inside her, claiming her.

'What will it take, Lady Ling?' His fingertip circled the tiny pearl of her flesh, sending shocks of light and fire through her.

His seduction was as unforgiving as the rest of him. The pressure of his hand on her was too much to bear. Her vision blurred as he explored.

'Or maybe it won't take much at all,' he ground out cruelly.

His fingers were slick with her dew. Her breath came in shallow pants. Li Tao would never let himself fall prey to anyone. One night was all he wanted. One night, but he offered the universe for it. His fingers stroked and stroked sensation into her until her body throbbed with need.

She was ready to give him anything he wanted, ready to beg for it. But Li Tao kept up the pretence that this was a negotiation. Maybe she needed it to be that way as well.

'My freedom,' she gasped. His fingers flicked over her sex and she bit down hard against her lip, digging her nails into his arm. 'One night and—'

Her voice cut off as he bent his head to her throat, kissing softly before scraping his teeth against her delicate skin. She cried out sharply, every sense heightening.

Gentle, then rough. Generous, then cruel. It was always like that with Li Tao. Soon she wouldn't be able to ask for anything but him, all of him. With all of her will, she took hold of his hand and dragged him away from her body, twining her fingers tight into his to trap them. Finally, she saw what touching her was doing to him. His eyes were clouded, every muscle in his face drawn tight.

'One night and then you take me home,' she said. He tried to kiss her, but she ducked away. 'Those are my terms.'

His eyes sparked. 'Agreed.'

Once again he tried to kiss her. Again, she avoided him and his eyebrows drew together perilously.

She met his challenge without flinching. 'It's not yet dark outside.'

After a pause, he smiled. A slow, wicked smile that made her melt beneath him. His body remained taut over her.

'Ling Suyin.'

The world was contained in the way he spoke her name. Lust, frustration, admiration and something else. Something she didn't dare to guess. He raised himself from the seat. A quick glance between his legs explained the slowness of his movements.

'Come to me tonight.'

She swallowed. Her heart would burst if this continued. It was already pounding desperately. 'Take me home tomorrow.'

Twisting away, she sat up and tugged at the silk bodice, trying to cover herself. Li Tao combed his fingers through his dark hair, not looking at her. The unsteady cadence of his breathing punctuated the abrupt silence.

She wanted to be done with it. She needed an end to the temptation and the fear and wanting him despite all of it. Their bargain was her final escape route. She could survive one night and all the pleasure he promised. One night and nothing more meant her heart was safe. And she'd have what she wanted. Her freedom.

Neither of them spoke until he had put some distance between them. His hand was poised on the door.

'You didn't beg for your lover's life,' he remarked.

She threw him a look over her shoulder. 'He was never my lover. And if I had spoken for him, you would certainly have had him killed.'

Li Tao could still smell her perfume. He marched his prisoner through the forest to the edge of the bamboo sea while the scent of Suyin's skin lingered.

He'd spilled his troubles to her in a careless moment. They'd stood side by side, looking up at lanterns. She'd seen it as weakness and she'd decided to strike. Clever, beautiful, *calculating* Ling Suyin.

Ru Shan walked in silence, flanked on either side by his former comrades. The fallen soldier knew better than to plead for his life. The soldiers forced Ru Shan to his knees. This was what needed to be done and Li Tao took no pleasure it. Deserters and traitors could not be spared. It corrupted the discipline of the troops.

Ru Shan threw his chin up in defiance, baring his throat to the sword. Love would do that to a man, fill him with false courage and render him a fool.

'Do it,' Ru Shan choked out.

'Did you hope that if you rescued her, she would give her heart to you?'

The soldier's jaw clenched proudly, his eyes focused inwards, on some remote corner of his mind. Likely thinking of Lady Ling as he prepared to give his life for her.

Anger knifed through him, forcing the air from his lungs. She had worked her wiles on many men, he reminded himself. The most influential men of the empire. In a way, he pitied the young man. What chance did an idealist like Ru Shan have against an experienced courtesan like Ling Suyin? She wouldn't need to promise him anything. Every look was an unspoken promise.

In a single, swift motion, he unsheathed his sword. He should do the deed himself. Ru Shan deserved that much.

'You were a worthy soldier,' he said, lifting the weapon.

'Spare her.'

The blade halted mid-air. That Ru Shan would even beg for anything at this moment caught him off guard. The younger man looked up at him squarely. A sheen of sweat beaded on his forehead, but he spoke through the fear.

'We swore our lives to your service, but Lady Ling has not. She should not suffer for your treachery.'

So this was what his followers thought. That he was leading them to certain death. Ru Shan had never spoken so many words to him. The soldier had never faltered in his duties, yet he had harboured this belief inside him. And Suyin was able to delve deep enough to exploit it.

His sword hung heavy in his hand. What a waste. Lady Ling had not turned a weak-hearted man. Ru Shan had a strong spirit and was well respected, a brother to these men. In time, he might have risen through the ranks.

'Let him go,' he ordered, turning away.

The other men stared at him. This act of mercy shook the foundations of the code they all fought by. It was a long stretch of time before one of them dared to come forwards with a knife to cut Ru Shan's bonds.

'Never let me see your face again,' Li Tao warned.

Ru Shan stayed kneeling. He bowed, touching his head once to the ground. 'This is for the honourable man who once was. But you will destroy Lady Ling along with everything you have created.'

Ru Shan rose then and walked away, weaving through the bamboo.

Li Tao waited for the lone figure to disappear into the green. It was a mistake to let him go. Ru Shan was a young man pining for the love of a complicated woman. He was also a fighter and a soldier, dangerous in his exuberance.

People like Lady Ling were incapable of love. They were both alike in that way. The imperial palace was as cutthroat as the winding streets of Luoyang. She would never allow anyone to possess her just as he answered to no master. There were no illusions between them. Perhaps that was the lure. Desire without emotion, cold and clean.

When she met his eyes, it was always with challenge. She understood the tooth-and-claw struggle for survival deep within her bones. Desire meant nothing in the face of that struggle, except for a few stolen moments.

They could forget for one night. Perhaps her passion was feigned, another ploy. He didn't care. That night he'd take his fill of her. Suyin's lure would fade when she no longer danced like smoke in his head, when she became flesh and blood and silken skin beneath him. Then he'd send her away as she so desperately wanted. Let her face Gao on her own. She was more than capable.

Suyin could take whatever secrets she held with her. He didn't need them and didn't need her for anything more than what she could give him that night.

Chapter Eight

Suyin stepped into the garden, fighting to steady herself after the intensity of the confrontation with Li Tao. The soldiers remained hovering at the passages, but the warlord was gone. She could tell from the silence of the house and the listless way the servants milled about the edges of the courtyard. There was always an inexplicable sense of emptiness when he wasn't there.

'Go,' she urged gently. 'Continue with your duties as usual.'

The servants responded to her as if she were the mistress of the house. One by one, they moved away. She knew they would gather in a distant corner to mull and gossip. Jun and Cook were the last to leave. The boy held a brown-feathered chicken by its feet as he trudged towards the kitchen. She managed a weak smile for him before he departed.

Auntie came to her. 'Master Li has taken Ru Shan! In his anger, he might…' She swiped at her nose with a handkerchief, her eyes red and swollen.

'None of you will suffer for this. I swear it.'

Auntie was intent on fretting. 'But Tao—Master Li will not tolerate disloyalty.'

'The Governor knows this is my doing,' Suyin replied, sounding more confident than she felt. It was clear that she had no control over him, or herself, when they were alone.

Li Tao was foremost a warlord and warrior. A man of discipline.

He wanted complete control of everything, even over what would pass between them that night. Especially over that.

She shouldn't have pulled Auntie into her schemes. Not when she knew how ruthless Li Tao was. He had the entire household cowering under his fury. Then he had kissed her and tormented her until she was clinging to him. She folded her arms tight around herself. Every part of her felt swollen, awakened and raw with sensation.

One night was all he wanted from her in the end. She should be relieved. When the lust and physical need were cold and done, he would have no reason to keep her. Madame had taught her that.

A strand of hair fell over her eyes and she pushed it back. No wonder they all stared at her so fearfully in her disarray. The sun was starting to sink in the sky. She didn't have much time left before dark.

She let Auntie take her arm and lead her back up to her room as if she were a doll. The stairs seemed to stretch on endlessly. Her feet fell heavily on each step. The surge of emotion had left her drained.

They returned together to her quarters. Suyin sank into a chair in the sitting room and began working her hair loose from its knot. Auntie rushed to help her, pulling the pins to lower her hair with a gentle, careful hand. The tenderness of it made her throat tighten. Of all of them, she would miss Auntie the most once she was gone, but she couldn't stay. She had to think of survival. That was her one true talent. Her ability to bend men to her will was only a myth.

'My lady must know Master Li would never hurt her,' Auntie said, squeezing her hand.

'Auntie is too trusting.'

'Tao will have to seek atonement in the next life, but he would never harm a defenceless woman.'

Suyin stifled a bitter laugh. 'Defenceless?'

Auntie was blind when it came to Li Tao, but the old woman was mistaken about her as well. She had caused enough harm in her life without ever holding a weapon in her hand. Hadn't she sent Ru Shan to his death? Li Tao's eyes had been flat, reflecting nothing as he'd held his sword over the soldier. It was a killing look.

But he hadn't acted yet.

Auntie disappeared momentarily and returned from the dressing room with a comb. Suyin took it from her hands. 'Please go check on Ru Shan. Don't let Governor Li know that I asked.'

Li Tao had accused her of turning his servants against him. She couldn't bear the thought of what he would do to Auntie and the others if he suspected any more disloyalty.

The old woman nodded and hurried away. The hinges creaked as she closed the doors behind her. As soon as she was alone, Suyin doubled over in her chair, eyes closed, hand pressed against her midsection to steady her breath. A wave of fear, nervousness and excitement rushed through her all at once until her head swam.

This is what Emperor Li Ming had taught her to do in the palace. Everything shown in public had to be controlled. Once hidden away, she could feel everything.

She squeezed her eyes shut, but that only made the hard press of Li Tao's mouth against hers come back to her tenfold. What had she agreed to?

This merging of anger and desire was more dangerous than any threat of violence. His discipline had broken in the parlour and she had been caught up in it, welcoming the danger and demanding more. But she had prevailed. He was going to release her. They'd both have what they wanted. She'd have her freedom, he'd have his precious control.

They had been dancing around each other for weeks. She needed the fear and the temptation to be done with. She wanted Li Tao despite his rebelliousness—wanted him because of it. She was supposed to belong to no one but the Emperor, but Li Tao didn't care about imperial law. He brought out emotions she thought she'd never experience again. When she was close to him, Suyin longed for him to touch her. When he did touch her, desire overwhelmed her and she was lost. She'd fought against this feeling of powerlessness all her life.

And she loved it now.

Was Li Tao right about her? Had she lived with danger for so long, she craved it?

After tonight she would be free in more ways than one. Her dangerous fascination with Li Tao would end once she was no longer trapped in his house. Even Auntie and Cook's kindness couldn't make her forget that Li Tao was doomed. She would find a place to disappear along her river and forget. She had always been able to move on to another place and weave a cocoon of safety around herself. Gao might seek her out once Li Tao no longer protected her, but she'd avoided the old wolf on her own for years.

The comb was still clenched in her hand, the teeth biting into the palm. It slipped through her nerveless fingers as she lifted it to her hair.

All of this was supposed to be second nature. Yin and yang and the ways of sensual fulfilment. Yet she was shaking hard as she had the first night she'd been summoned to the Emperor's chamber.

Li Tao wouldn't be a gentle lover, but his hands had stroked her with exquisite knowledge. He knew how to pleasure a woman. She had no doubt of that. Her skin tingled from his caress, her body aroused and searching. He would expect the same knowledge of her.

The extent of her reputation was laughable. How could imperial concubines be expected to be goddesses in the bedchamber when they were trained to please only one man, the Emperor?

Auntie returned and wordlessly picked up the fallen comb. 'Master Li took Ru Shan. No one knows where,' she reported in a hush.

Suyin stared ahead, her mask of control slipping back in place. 'No harm will come to him yet.'

'Are you certain?'

'I'm certain.'

Li Tao wouldn't come to her that night with blood on his hands. Her willingness was important to him. She didn't understand what rules of honour he lived by, but he treated her with a semblance of civility, even protectiveness. At least, until she provoked him.

'Lady Ling, you look pale.'

'We need to fix that.' Her thoughts were far away.

Auntie regarded her questioningly.

She would need a bath. Her hair needed to be pinned, her skin perfumed. She couldn't appear as anything less than ravishing for Li Tao. She took wicked satisfaction in how her beauty confused him. This was a different allure from the one she projected to the court. With Li Tao, she was a woman for once, something more than a pretty illusion.

The door to the study opened into darkness. Suyin placed her hand against the wall to guide herself. The lamps inside had been extinguished. The lantern in the hallway provided the only light.

Li Tao was there. She could sense him. The darkness magnified his presence. He was nothing but a silhouette. Unknown and tempting.

His hands curved over her shoulders. Li Tao pressed her flat against the wall as their gazes locked. He was breathing hard, his chest rising and falling. She couldn't find her next breath no matter how hard she tried. With his eyes on her the entire time, he reached out to push the door shut.

His mouth found hers and pried her lips roughly apart. Before her eyes could adjust to the darkness, he was kissing her with his hard body strained against her, hip to hip. He trapped her in a fierce embrace. Everything all at once. No time to form any thought.

Better like this. She moaned in surrender as his tongue invaded her mouth. Ribbons of heat curled through her limbs and she hooked her arms around his neck. Better like this, without a word. She couldn't trust herself not to challenge and confound him the moment she spoke. This way, she could just feel.

She let herself be swept into the hunger between them. Her eyes closed as her head fell back and the darkness surrounded her. She pressed against Li Tao, feeling his tension through every muscle.

One of his hands dug into her hair as the other pulled at the sash at her waist. The hairpins fell away haphazardly. He cared nothing for her efforts over the last hours. He pulled at the layers of her dress and slipped them from her shoulders. A faint tearing sound broke through the silence. The cadence of his breathing filled her ears, the sound of it urgent, desperate.

She reached for his robe, but he was much faster, more efficient. In a few short motions, he tugged his clothing away and dropped the material beside the pool of her dress. Only the embroidered bodice remained tied over her breasts. Soon that was gone too. He was bare before her as well, sculpted and powerful. She had no time to look before his hands were on her, curving over her breasts, her hips. He was flying and she couldn't catch him, didn't know what to do with her hands or her body. His calloused palms scraped over her sensitised flesh and his mouth invaded hers again, stealing away her breath. She had never been so exposed, so vulnerable.

With insistent purpose, he lowered her to the floor until she lay on the discarded layers of her gown. He bent his head to take her breast. *Heaven and earth.* His mouth was searing hot on her skin and unrelenting. Her head fell back against the wooden planks as her arms stole around his waist to hold on.

Whenever she had imagined this, her dream lovers had always been gentle and caring. She was wrong; this was what it should be. His teeth scraped her nipple and she let out a startled cry. The shock of pleasure through her was unbearable. He did it again, biting against tender flesh already sensitive beyond thought. A flood of dampness gathered between her legs. She dug her nails into him, demanding more.

He had planned this. She had stayed in her room as the sun fell and darkness descended and when he didn't come, when he didn't send for her, she had gone to search for him. All the while Li Tao had been waiting, letting her desire build into a summer storm.

She had to stop herself from thinking like this. There was no plan, no meaning layered upon meaning here. She blinked, trying to focus on him. When he finally pulled away the rest of his clothing to lie skin to skin on top of her, no warmth had ever felt so complete.

He opened her legs and watched her face as he slid a finger purposefully along her folds. It was the first moment of quiet he had allowed her and it was only to tease her, letting the sensation build and build within her until she gasped out his name.

She reached for his face, tracing the stark ridges of his cheek-bones. Her fingertips soothed against the edge of his scar and an odd tenderness seized her. He was beautiful with the awe of lightning storms and tigers.

Flinching, he snatched her hand away from his face. Sentiment wasn't what he wanted from her. He guided her hands between his thighs. His hips thrust the hard, naked length of him against her palm. He swelled even more against her touch, pulsing and rigid. He parted her legs on the wooden planks of the floor and her muscles tensed.

It was going to happen. She held her breath. He centred himself before sliding down and into her in one steady thrust, pushing to the hilt.

She tore inside. Her body wrenched tight around him and she bit down against her lip to stifle her scream. Li Tao went still above her, the fevered energy of his passion stopped.

Madame had always said there would be a moment of pain, but once again she had lied. The unbearable sensation of being penetrated and stretched continued as her body struggled to adjust to the new invasion of a man's body inside her. She closed her eyes, hoping to dull the sensation. When she finally opened them, Li Tao glared down at her.

'How?'

She shook her head. His hands clenched into fists on either side of her shoulders. Her arms were still around him. His hips shifted inadvertently and her breath caught. She could see the indecision in his eyes. Then he squeezed them shut and shook his head helplessly. Jaw clenched, he lifted slowly and then pushed back into her, trying to keep his movements slow, but it didn't matter. She could feel every inch of him within her, stretching her, the sensation intensified.

Eventually her tight walls grew damp, yielding only slightly. He rocked himself into her, sliding in and out, unable to deny himself.

Through the pain, she held on to him, fingers digging into sweat-dampened skin. A current of distant pleasure rose to combine with the pain as his thrusts deepened. His rhythm became erratic. He pulsed once, twice, then his entire body wound tight as his essence spilled into her.

He pounded his fist against the floorboards in frustration and she flinched at the impact. With a curse, he lifted his body away from her.

'How is this possible?' he demanded, his voice thick.

She gathered the discarded silk around her shoulders and sat up, hissing at the unexpected ache. Li Tao's coupling had left her sore and filled with an acute loneliness. She had been naïve to believe there would be a long night of seduction once the great lie had been revealed.

'Many concubines live their lives untouched in the inner court, forgotten.' Her attempt to appear dispassionate failed when her voice broke.

Every muscle in him pulled tight. 'Not you.'

She leaned back against the wall for support as he faced her, his knees braced against the floor, his nakedness forgotten. Her response angered him further, but maybe she wanted it that way.

'You know the answer,' she said.

'I don't know anything.'

If he thought hard enough, she was certain he would discover what the August Emperor had fought to hide for so many years. But Li Tao didn't care about the secrets of the imperial court. His eyes burned through her.

'Why didn't you tell me?'

Her lips parted in silence. There was no answer to that. Who would believe that Ling *Guifei*, the great seductress, had never been possessed by a man? Her eyes burned from sudden tears that she hoped the darkness would hide.

He swiped his robe from the floor in a violent motion, but then threw it aside. His chiselled body rippled with shadows as he stormed from the room, leaving her stranded amidst the tattered silk.

* * *

Li Tao threw the chamber door shut behind him. He shoved his hands through his hair, denying the satisfied flush of his body. The scent of jasmine clung to his skin. Visions of sensual eyes, pale skin and her perfect mouth swam before him. He grabbed a pair of trousers from the wardrobe and pulled them on impatiently.

Lies. Everything about Ling Suyin was a pretty, unfathomable lie. The score of her nails down his back and the exquisite tightness of her flesh around him had given way to the shocking breach of her maidenhead. The empire's symbol of beauty and feminine sensuality was an untouched virgin.

He'd taken her quickly as a defence, the only defence left to him. There were stories about Ling Suyin being discovered in the pleasure dens of Luoyang. She had bewitched the Emperor with a single look. After a night with her, Emperor Li Ming had forsaken all others.

Hadn't she lured him with every word and every sensual glance? Had her restraint been coyness or innocence? Up to the moment Li Tao sank himself into her, she had responded with an unrestrained passion he had attributed to experience. He sank on to the edge of the bed and rubbed his hand over his temples.

He needed to take apart everything he knew about Lady Ling. She hadn't seduced Ru Shan, not with her body. The thought gave him a moment of relief, followed by a surge of anger. She didn't belong to him, but his thoughts would not release her. She had yielded to him. No other man but him.

When he'd left her, there had been genuine sadness in her eyes. At that moment, he no longer knew what was real. He would never know her. The moment he had her in his grasp, she slipped away as if to spite him.

Chapter Nine

Suyin stayed on the cold floor for a long time after the door slammed shut. Li Tao had left, but the ghost of his fury hovered, bearing down on her. Slowly, she retied the laces of the bodice and gathered the robe around her shoulders.

Li Tao had believed the stories and the rumours like everyone else. How could anyone not be disappointed? Even a goddess could not measure up to her legendary reputation.

She wanted to curl back on to the floor. The great burden was finally lifted. The August Emperor was long gone and she was free, but her relief was tainted by a sense of emptiness and loss she couldn't place.

Her legs trembled when she tried to stand. She steadied herself with a hand against the wall. Long ago, she'd resigned herself to never knowing a lover's touch. An insignificant sacrifice for a life of luxury and security. As secure as she could be in the imperial court. She had buried the yearning and the hope inside until Li Tao had kindled her desire. Suddenly, she wanted it all, the clouds and the rain and the entire universe hidden within the touch of their bodies. Everything the poems and pillow books had spoken of. All the emotions the other girls had whispered about to each other in the darkness.

This mystery between male and female—there was nothing earth shattering to it. The waiting and wanting were greater than the act itself. Madame Ling had always said as much. Why, then, did she still long for him? She knew about the physical pain that came with the first coupling, but she hadn't expected the feel of Li Tao inside her to reach so deep it made her heart ache. He had pierced through the loneliness she had hidden away for so long.

Outside, the corridor was empty and she stared down the shadowed passage, waiting. She didn't want to face Li Tao when her emotions were scattered within her. The mystery was done with. She could go on with her life.

With every step, the dull ache between her legs reminded her of Li Tao's uninhibited lovemaking. He had not been gentle with her, but his rough caresses had been far from unwelcome. The shock of his entry had filled her with fear, joy and an unanswered promise. The intrusion was almost unbearable, overwhelming her with sensation. The only part she regretted was the deception. Li Tao hadn't been able to stand the sight of her when he stormed out.

The garden was unlit except for a single lantern at the entrance. A wave of desolation swept in. She couldn't bear to stay another moment. The guards shouted, but she ignored them. She slipped out to the back of the house and halted at the edge of the gorge, trapped. The guards clamoured after her.

'Leave me alone,' she snapped.

In the night, the chasm spread out like a gaping abyss. The chilled breeze tugged at the edges of her dress and stung across her face. When she left the bamboo forest, there was nothing waiting for her but solitude, a string of silent days.

For once, she let the tears fall. They slid down her cheeks and blurred the night around her. Li Tao had awakened a longing within her that went beyond physical desire. She had been bought and traded all her life. She had thought it would be enough to return to her river, to belong to herself and no one else. To be safe. But it wasn't enough any more. Maybe it had never been enough.

Beneath the howl of the wind, she heard the pad of footsteps.

'Ling *Guifei*.' It was Li Tao.

'Do *not* call me that.'

She brushed away the tears with a harsh swipe of her knuckles and turned on him. Li Tao was dressed only in his underclothes.

His feet were bare on the cold stone and his pale tunic stood out against the darkness. The soldiers behind him looked on uncomfortably and kept their distance.

'You have nothing to worry about, Governor. I have nowhere to run.'

Only the moon lit his face. The anger she remembered had melted away. 'Come back inside.'

He held himself away from her, his body rigid. He appeared worried, almost fearful, but she must have misread his expression. Li Tao feared nothing, not all the demons in hell.

'Are you here to demand the rest of your night?' she asked cynically.

Her chest grew painfully tight. She swung away from the sight of him to stare into the endless gorge. He let out a sharp breath behind her.

'Please, come back.' The words rasped in his throat. 'I'll leave you alone. I won't touch you.'

She didn't want to be left alone. She'd been alone for too long. Li Tao held out his hand, his expression full of concern. Why couldn't he simply be the ruthless warlord? She knew how to handle men like that.

Tenuously, she took a step towards him. His arms closed around her and she couldn't stop herself from sinking against his chest. His heart tapped out an erratic beat and he held her so tightly it was nearly painful. She didn't understand his reaction now after he had abandoned her so brusquely back in the study.

'Are you hurt?' he murmured against her hair.

She tried to shake her head, but the movement was lost against the crush of their bodies. With a sigh, she hid her face against his neck, secured in the nook between his chin and shoulder. This was so, so strange. She expected some challenge or accusation, but it never came. The heat of his skin warmed her against the evening air and she floated in the darkness, hanging on to him.

'Governor.' The title sounded stiff on her lips. 'You are not even dressed.'

Her hair was unbound and her robe dishevelled. What a picture of scandal they presented. Li Tao remained oblivious to everyone else. He tucked her close to his side as he led her into the house. They retreated to his chamber and she didn't protest when he guided her to the alcove of the bed and seated her on the edge.

He stroked two fingers lightly against her cheek. 'You are not hurt?' he asked again.

She closed her eyes to savour the careful way he touched her, too overwhelmed to understand what any of this meant. She feared that if she questioned it, the moment would shatter.

'You were never the August Emperor's lover,' he said.

'So the secret is revealed.'

'How?' he asked again, calmer this time.

'You know the answer. The Battle of Shibao.'

He straightened, his brow creased in a frown. The slit of his tunic revealed a swathe of muscled chest, a keen reminder of how his powerful body had angled over her before he slid into her. She shuddered, the ache below her hips a faded memory of the exquisite swirl of pain and pleasure.

'Emperor Li was nearly killed in that siege,' he said.

'Some of his wounds never healed.'

The explanation was simple, but the people believed the Emperor to be god-like, his childlessness a curse from heaven. And she, a temptress who had lured him into an obsessive, fruitless union that had led to his downfall. Legends captured the imagination much quicker than the truth. The ploy had allowed Li Ming to rule for only a little longer, long enough to try to stabilise the empire.

'That must have been lonely for you,' Li Tao said finally.

The gentleness of his tone startled her. Flustered, she fussed with her hair, trying to smooth it back. 'Well, one can hardly miss what one doesn't know.'

'I meant keeping this secret for so long.'

His mouth quirked with ironic humour and blood rushed to her face. It was easier to feign sexual superiority when she'd been ignorant. She gathered the edges of her dress tight over her breasts and fought the ridiculous urge to hide beneath the blankets.

Li Tao's smile faded as he watched her. 'Lady Ling, you would not do anything...' He hesitated before continuing, 'Anything to harm yourself?'

Did he think that she would throw herself from the cliff because he had bedded her? She was inexperienced, but far from an innocent virgin fearing shame and ruin.

'I have spent too much time fighting for my life,' she assured. 'You can put your guilt to rest.'

'You should have told me.'

'Would it have changed anything?'

He paused as he considered his answer. 'I would have been more careful.'

His voice rumbled deep within his chest, reigniting the longing that hummed beneath her skin. How her body remembered him. The inexorable way he parted her to prepare for his entry and the way his gaze had fixed on to her as if he'd never let her go. Her face burned even hotter.

'It doesn't matter.' She needed to get away from his bed and the memories that were too fresh in her mind. 'We had an agreement.'

'I remember,' he said.

In the morning, he would take her home. She would be free, but free to do what? To hide from Gao alone and unprotected.

She stood and found herself blocked by the solid plane of his body. He moved close, tracing the line of her throat with an achingly tender touch, while she held herself perfectly still. This man was unfathomable, a hardened warrior who suddenly looked at her as if she were the most precious treasure in the empire. No one had ever looked at her like that.

'Why now?' His fingertips hovered feather-light at the corner of her mouth. 'Why me?'

It was too hard to speak past the lump in her throat. Her survival instincts struggled to escape from the lure of him. 'A fair trade,' she forced out. 'You wanted this body and I wanted my freedom.'

His pupils darkened. 'You'll play the whore now?'

She pulled back her shoulders, drawing on the spirit of Madame Ling. 'In the end, seduction has little to do with the flesh.'

He took hold of her chin between his thumb and forefinger, his grip not quite forceful. 'Stop this.'

She steeled herself for his kiss, prepared to defend herself against the sensual invasion. He was close enough for it. Their joining had been rushed and fuelled by mindless hunger. Not nearly enough to satisfy either of them. Behind the shield of her callous words, her heart raced and every part of her came alive. Her senses reached out to seek the shape of him and the dark scent of his skin. If he drew her into his arms, she would succumb to him as she had done by the gorge.

When he didn't kiss her, the cold wash of loneliness swept over her once more. But with it came a sense of relief.

'I wish to return to my chambers now.'

Shaking free of his hold, she started past him. He waited until she was at the door before he spoke.

'It is still night time.'

She halted and turned. Irresistibly, her eyes lowered down his body. The hard outline of his arousal showed beneath the trousers.

Her throat went completely dry. 'I suppose we do have an agreement.'

'You know this is not a simple negotiation. It never was.'

The quiet edge in his voice sent a shiver through her. If it wasn't negotiation, then what was it? She didn't dare to think of it. Li Tao directed her to the bed, saying nothing as he lowered her on to the padding. Meanwhile his eyes spoke of possession. They never left her face until her back rested flat against the bed.

He left her and opened the door to call to someone outside. She lay docile, afraid what would happen if she allowed her desire to take over. After an agonising wait, Li Tao returned and set a basin on to the table. Steam rose over the edge as he lifted a damp cloth and wrung the water from it. She stared at his hands, captivated by the strength of his long fingers.

The sound of her own breathing filled her ears. He lowered one knee to the bed alongside her and parted her robe. The silk slipped away to leave her bare and vulnerable. Above them, the alcove of the bed arched like a cavern. The outline of his shoulders filled her vision.

He lowered the cloth and she recoiled in embarrassment, trying to sit up.

'Be still.'

With a hand on her shoulder, he eased her back on to the bed. Their coupling had occurred in the darkened study where she'd been able to hide. Now, his gaze roamed over her with excruciating patience. She flinched at the touch of the damp cloth at her shoulder and squeezed her eyes shut, mortified by the vulnerability of it as he bathed her in soothing strokes downwards over her stomach, following the curve of her hip. He lifted the cloth and dipped it again into the basin. The trickle of water punctured the silence and then he continued in the same slow circles until her body relaxed, growing accustomed to his attention. Cool air pricked at her skin following each pass of the cloth. Her breasts rose and fell in anticipation while her muscles warmed and loosened.

'You really must think me a beast,' he said.

She kept her eyes closed. His voice surrounded her, vibrating deep within.

'I never thought you were a gentleman.' She couldn't understand why her mind still insisted on sparring with him when her body wanted to lose itself to the sensations.

'You're right. I'm no gentleman.'

The cloth slicked its dampness over her legs. She squirmed, recalling the stain of blood on her thighs. Mortified, she tried to draw her knees closed, but his touch remained careful and utterly tender in a way that rendered her heart asunder.

When she dared to look at him, his head was bent in concentration.

'I was curious,' she admitted.

'Curious?'

'You asked me, why now? I wanted to know what it was. This power that could bring men and women to their knees. "The clouds and the rain", they call it, as if the joining of flesh could open the heavens.'

His smile touched his eyes more than his lips. 'I take it the heavens remain closed to you, Lady Ling?'

She had no answer for him. His embrace made her blood sing and her flesh ache, but he had climaxed inside her while she'd been left wanting. Even now, something inside her silently urged him to take her where his body had promised.

'I was to remain untouched in memory of the August Emperor.'

His hand stilled on her, the cloth resting at her knee. 'He is dead. You are not.'

For the last years, she had believed that peace was all she wanted, at the price of isolation. But when Li Tao was with her, she wanted something more. Something unnameable. But she wouldn't stay to search for it while war and death hung over him. She couldn't take that risk.

He set aside the washcloth and closed her robe, running his fingers along the silk. The brief caress was enough to make her want to arch towards his hand.

'You are a complicated woman, Lady Ling.'

Her skin missed his touch. She started to rise, but he stopped her.

'Stay,' he implored.

Because of their bargain? No, because of the way he was looking at her. Piercing her. Binding her to him, but only for one night.

His fingers gripped her knee lightly and her pulse quickened. He would take her again. She swallowed as he eased her legs apart. For a long breath, his gaze simply roamed over her, for once hiding nothing. His pupils grew wide and dark, taking the sight of her in. She saw passion there and hunger and pure admiration. Her nipples peaked against the sheen of silk. Soft abrasion.

He said nothing.

Li Tao bent and placed his mouth on to her sex. It startled her so much she jumped. Her body flooded with heat. Heat from him, from her. His tongue washed over her without giving her time to recover, licking a long path along her folds. She cried out in a breathless sob and he demanded more. He held her open with his fingers and tormented her until she was weeping brokenly, writhing with her nails hooked into his shoulders. Punishing him for making her feel this way. His hands rounded her hips, holding on as he angled her to the onslaught of his mouth. His tongue flicked faster and faster. She became nothing but pulse and radiant pleasure.

Her climax broke the surface and swept through her in wrenching waves. He held her through it, passing his tongue delicately over her sensitive tissue in a soothing pass before releasing her.

Then he stood and pulled the quilt over her shoulders. She would have called out his name, but she had no breath left. No strength left. The feeling of security that washed over her nearly brought tears to her eyes. But it was false and fleeting.

'When I return home, I will think of you,' she told him finally.

She turned from him and pulled the quilt around her shoulders. Her body still throbbed with his final gift. Li Tao remained close, though he no longer touched her. She listened to the broken rhythm of his breathing and kept her eyes squeezed shut, though she knew it would be a long time before she would be able to sleep.

Imperial Palace—ad 746
13 years earlier

Suyin trembled as she approached the imperial apartments. The silk robe they'd put her in brushed the floor as she walked and seemed to grow heavier with each footstep. The head eunuch walked in front of her down the long corridor. In the silence, she could hear the unsteady ebb of her breathing. A cloud of perfume hung around her. Orange blossoms, the Emperor's favourite scent.

She was sixteen, chosen into the court of women a year earlier. In that time, she had never been alone with the Emperor. After the selection ceremony, he hadn't paid her any notice at all. It wasn't uncommon for the chosen concubines to never know his favour. There were many poems of exquisite beauties left to languish untouched, their wasted youth a sacrifice to the whims of the Emperor. The Son of Heaven he might be, but he was only one man.

A man had only so many nights and while the Empress lived, she made sure those nights were with her. Now that the Empress was dead, the harem spent every hour pondering who would replace her in the Emperor's bed. That afternoon, the wooden tile with Suyin's name had been turned over. The first since the tragedy.

The other concubines cooed and sighed as Suyin was led away for the lengthy preparation. On their faces, she saw a mixture of curiosity, envy and fear. The Empress's poisoning had been followed by a string of indictments and executions. The Emperor was not known as a cruel man, but he enacted justice swiftly and unerringly.

The harem had been spared his vengeance even though the Empress had been last seen alive within the inner court of women. Suyin recalled that detail as she stood in the centre of the vast bedchamber and her palms began to sweat. When the Emperor emerged through a curtain, she jumped with alarm.

'Is the sight of me that frightening?'

She bowed her head low, not knowing how to answer. When he came to stand directly before her, she stared obsessively at his shoes. The blue-embroidery pattern made her eyes swim. Her neck started to ache from being bent for so long.

He lifted her chin with his hand, turning her head this way and that for his scrutiny. 'You have a face that haunts men's dreams.' The corners of his eyes creased in thought.

The Emperor appeared older than she remembered. Sad and grey. She prayed he couldn't read those disparaging thoughts on her face. He was supposed to be perfect and god-like in everyone's eyes. Her hands hung heavy by her sides while he continued to look her over. The first time he had seen her, he had asked her to play a song for him. That had been much easier. She had something to do to occupy her hands and her thoughts.

When he ordered the attendants from the room, her stomach lurched. Her heart pounded so forcefully it nearly drowned out the Emperor's next words.

'Do not be frightened, little beauty.'

It would be a long time before the sight of him didn't make her tremble. The entire palace, the entire universe, revolved around the Emperor.

'Your Imperial Majesty should know…' her voice barely rose above a whisper '…this concubine has never been with a man.'

'The Emperor knows,' he replied and his tone held a hint of kindness that made her hopeful.

In Luoyang, she had been a performer in the Lotus Pavilion among the courtesans and prostitutes. She wasn't ashamed of her past other than the Emperor might expect her to be skilled in the bedroom arts.

He took down her hair, pulling the pins free with strong, methodical hands while he watched her with a pensive expression. She thought she saw a spark of longing, but none of the hunger she had come to recognise in a man's eyes.

She flinched when he touched her cheek. Thankfully, he didn't seem offended.

'Go to the bed.'

Her thoughts raced as she passed through the curtain into the inner apartment. She lay down with her shoulder blades pressed flat against the mattress, still fully clothed. Would he want to undress her? Did he expect her to undress herself?

She stared up at the dragon carving overhead and tried to follow its serpentine curve through the rain and the clouds. This is what the court of women longed for when they primped and preened, hoping to catch the eye of the Son of Heaven. The Emperor's favour meant status and privilege. If she gave birth to a son, she might be elevated to imperial consort, her family showered with gifts—if they could still be found.

She didn't dare dream of being named Empress. 'Empress' had proven to be a deadly title to hold.

By the time the candles in the chamber burned low, she was still on her back and waiting. She rolled on to her side and peered through the curtain. She couldn't hear the Emperor or see his silhouette through the sheer material. He might be offended if she ventured out to search for him, but she grew tired of staring at the dragon above. The bearded, gaping mouth mocked her with its grotesque smile.

She didn't know when she fell asleep, but the chamber was dark when she awoke. The layers of silk and gauze she wore itched against her skin. She could feel the warmth from the Emperor's body beside her. He had not laid a finger on her. The only time the Emperor touched her that night was when his hand inadvertently grazed her shoulder while he turned.

The next evening, her tile was once again turned over. And again on the next.

After several nights in the Emperor's bed, she stood before him and untied her sash. Keeping her eyes boldly on his, she peeled the silk from her shoulders and let it fall down her body. His pupils grew dark, but he said nothing. He did not move towards her.

She saw the longing. She knew how to read a man's face and the tension in his body. The Emperor was not so old or unpleasant to look at. He had been unexpectedly kind. At that moment, she earnestly wanted to please him.

If she could give him a son, her sins would be absolved.

He looked at her for a long time while she stood with the silk dress pooled at her feet.

'Ling Suyin.' He finally rose and took her gently by the shoulders. 'You are very beautiful.'

He kissed her forehead and she shivered, folding her arms over her breasts. Her nakedness before him embarrassed her. It was only admiration she saw in his eyes, the way one appreciates a painting or the sky at dusk. She knew then that the Emperor's yang essence had somehow been damaged. The Son of Heaven, flawed and imperfect.

From that moment, she held something of value. The Emperor had only fathered a daughter with the Empress. There was no heir to the throne. The knowledge could endanger his entire rule and he needed her to keep his secret. Her life depended on it.

That night, while the Emperor slept with his back turned, her tears soaked the pillow beneath her cheek. The Emperor would protect her. Her position as his favourite was secure, but she was still young. She had hoped that, with time, she might have been able to fall in love.

Chapter Ten

Li Tao sat opposite the bed in his chair, keeping still so as not to wake her. Some time in the night, Suyin had rolled on to her side. Her fingers were curled beneath her cheek like a child, and her body rose and fell with each breath. It had taken hours before she had settled into slumber. At the first creep of the morning light, she was already stirring.

Her eyelashes fluttered open and her gaze trained onto him. 'You didn't sleep.'

'I need very little.'

She remained bundled in bed. His bed. A sultry murmur sounded in her throat and he grew hard. She didn't need coy remarks or artful glances to entice him. If she only knew how many times he'd kept himself from going to her throughout the night.

'I have decided not to fulfil our bargain,' he stated.

A dangerous glint lit in her eyes, followed by the ripple of tension down her spine. She snapped fully alert, with the watchfulness of a sleek cat preparing to pounce.

Her tone cut keenly. 'Even thieves and murderers honour their agreements.'

'I'm not a thief.'

'You have no use for me.' She held the sheet over her breasts as she glared at him.

'I disagree.'

'I already told you, I know nothing about Gao or your political entanglements.'

He laughed. Pure laughter this time. Had she forgotten how she'd writhed against his tongue?

She blushed, pink and perfect. She hadn't forgotten. Everything was changed, but the untouched consort couldn't know how much until now. Her robe fell from her shoulders, leaving them bare except for the midnight cascade of her hair against the pale skin. He let out a slow, steady breath. No, he was certainly not ready to let her go.

'Where will you go? To that forsaken house by the river?'

'Yes.' She dragged the sheet higher in defiance.

He stood and approached. 'You would wait helplessly until Gao's army marches through?'

She was too shrewd not to have considered all the risks. She knew Gao wanted her dead, but refused to tell him why.

'You begged for protection in your message to Emperor Shen. I have another proposal for you.'

'Hardly a proposal when I'm still at your mercy,' she remarked.

'Stay until the next full moon and I swear you'll have my full protection.'

'Your protection is worthless, Governor. In a month your head will no longer be attached to your shoulders.'

Was that sadness that flickered in her eyes? Her mouth turned downwards and, for a scant moment, a stab of regret bore into him.

'In a month, I'll deliver you into the Emperor's protection.' He lowered himself on to the bed and she didn't shrink away. A small victory. 'And I won't need to constantly guard myself against your elegant scheming.'

'And until then, I remain here for your pleasure?' she asked.

'The pleasure would be mutual.'

She flushed as he inched closer. Her armour of seductive detachment was gone, but he wondered who it had protected. He grew heavy, hard. He would have his mouth roaming over that soft skin soon. Her hand shot forwards to brace against his chest. The imperiousness of the gesture only inflamed him more.

With a smile, he lifted her hand to his lips. 'You were right all along. One night was not enough.' He planted a kiss against her palm. 'For either of us.'

Indecision hovered in her eyes, but she didn't pull away. She wanted this passion between them as much as he did, though she remained cautious as ever. He knew what it was like to be constantly on guard. He stroked her wrist lightly and her breath caught.

'My answer is no,' she whispered, unable to give the words any force. 'I won't stay.'

'Until the next full moon.' He lowered his mouth to press it softly against hers. 'Let me convince you.'

They hadn't kissed since he'd brought her back inside. He kissed her now. Suyin's grip loosened on the sheet between them as she responded, her lips warm and searching. The small surrender took away the last of his restraint and he pulled the sheet aside. She didn't require more urging than that to fit herself to him, soft curves to hard muscle. Her arms wrapped around him to grip his shoulders. His arousal lifted fiercely against her and her thighs parted instinctively at the pressure. But her mind refused to surrender.

'Why?' she demanded.

'I need to know what this is between us.'

He caressed her neck and stroked a reverent hand between her breasts down to the valley of her stomach.

'Desire.' She spoke the word dismissively, but her breath hitched. 'Yin and yang.'

'You know there's more.'

'I see.' Her cat's eyes glittered wickedly. 'You've discovered me untouched, so now you revel in being the only man to possess me.'

She shouldn't say things like that to him. Blood raged through his body, surging between his legs. 'No one can ever possess you.'

He had never allowed himself to desire anything with so much abandon. Certainly not any dream as sweet as this. His fingers dipped into the cleft of her legs. Her mouth parted in a silent moan as he drew small circles over her dampening flesh. Suyin could confound him, drive him to madness with her denials and half-truths, but the passion that glazed her eyes was real. Her hips lifted restlessly against his hand. He wanted her to let go. With him.

His arousal grew painfully, eager to sink into her heat. But there was more. At the moment, he didn't know what this feeling was that had taken hold of him. He only knew that he needed her to stay for as long as he could keep her. A month would have to be enough. A month set limits.

Watching her carefully, he pressed his fingers intimately to her. *'Tao.'*

With a shudder, her head fell back, neck exposed. He nipped at the pale skin of her throat and enjoyed the endless arch of her body into him. The blanket fell in a tangle about her legs and her toes curled tight into it. So beautiful.

Their first coupling had been rushed. He had been mad with waiting, lost the moment he buried himself inside her. This morning, he would hold back and take her to the heights of heaven. Then she could no longer question what held them together.

He stroked the smooth pearl of her sex, opening her. Her legs unlocked with abandon. Slowly, carefully he slid the length of his finger into her. She was tight, so tight around him.

'Stay,' he urged in a heated whisper. The same entreaty he'd given the night before. The only plea he'd ever uttered.

She shook her head, unthinking, lost in pure, mindless pleasure. She reached for him and cupped her hand over his swollen sex.

His patience was gone. He needed her now.

Through misted eyes, she watched him shed his clothes and slant his body over her to position himself. He could feel the tension building in her limbs as she anticipated his entry, bracing against the pain.

He kissed her throat as he angled his hips downwards and then forwards. Her flesh parted slowly and surrounded him, smooth heat tightening all around. She made a small sound in her throat and he slowed to stroke his hand through her hair.

She pressed her lips against the curve of his neck then. 'Don't stop.'

He gathered her to him and sank deeper. Her knees lifted to accept him. He paused, adjusted his hips and filled her completely.

* * *

There was still pain, but a welcome sort. It sensitised her, made the pleasure sharper. Her legs wrapped around his thighs and she dug her fingers into the bundle of muscle in his lower back. She closed her eyes to concentrate on the feel of him filling her. The pillow books spoke of coupling in vague, poetic phrases. It was none of that. This was wet flesh and heated skin, sweat and salt, vulgar and beautiful.

The muscles of his neck strained upwards. 'Suyin,' he groaned.

She loved that she could render such a powerful man helpless with her body. Loved that he did the same to her as hard as she fought against the surrender. He was no longer careful as his climax approached. He pushed harder, deeper into her, his thrusts taking on a restrained violence as if he needed to give her as much of him as she could take.

He took on an almost desperate rhythm, digging his fingers into her hips. She was rising again, chasing after him. At the height of it, the man above her disappeared. All that was left were the sensations he pulled from deep within her, the heady, spiced scent of him and the laboured pant of his breath in her ear.

Her inner muscles convulsed around him, squeezing him until he let out an anguished cry. He was releasing into her. She joined him and they crashed together in completion. This would never end. Still she held him tight. Still he thrust into her. They drifted into sleep that way, with his body embedded inside her and their arms entwined. Li Tao's skin glistened in the lantern light and she couldn't resist running her hand down his back to assure herself that his magnificent body belonged to her in that moment.

The clouds and the rain and the heavens opening. All that and so much more.

Suyin slept in satiated exhaustion, turning often in the strange bed. The awareness that Li Tao was close permeated her slumbered thoughts. Once, he reached out to pull her close. She dozed off tucked against his shoulder, but they didn't fit together as well as one would hope. They shifted apart in a haze of movement. When she finally opened her eyes, he was gone.

A hint of sandalwood and soap lingered on the pillow, combined with the unique scent of Li Tao's skin. She stretched her fingers over the rumpled space among the blankets where he had been. His absence was nearly palpable.

Her lover. She had thought she would grow old and silver-haired without experiencing what that meant. But the morning's passion and her unbridled response to him only left her with more questions. She couldn't be fooled by kindness. And the rapture between a man and a woman was natural. There was nothing special about these feelings. Nothing.

The scrape and shuffle of movement in the house meant it was past the quiet stir of the morning. Everyone would be up and completing their chores. Li Tao would be long gone to some unnamed duty that needed his attention.

She couldn't stay here, hiding away until he returned. Sitting up, she scanned the bed chamber, the contents pristine and unadorned. They belied his enigmatic nature. He should have at least woken her. It took some time to search out her clothes among the tangled sheets and even longer to arrange all the different layers into some semblance of presentability. Her hair was beyond repair. She smoothed down the length with her palms and tied it back. Let the servants whisper. They were all certain that their master had brought her there as his mistress anyway.

She pushed the door open and stepped into the corridor. Though it was unlikely he was still there, she paused at the entrance to Li Tao's study to listen for some sign of movement. The thought of seeing him again kept her on a keen edge of anticipation. What had she promised with her body? What had he? Her awareness reached out with tiny threads to search for him, only to be left to languish.

Beyond the front parlour, Auntie stood with her head bowed at the altar. The raised table held an urn of smouldering incense and took up a tidy compartment near the kitchen. Offerings of tea, rice and fruit had been arranged before a single thin plaque. For the first time, Suyin noticed the name carved into the wood. *Lei Hunhua—*

Spring Flower. A woman's name with no accompanying plaque bearing other names, a father, grandfather or great-grandfather to head the ancestral line.

Auntie bowed reverently before turning around. The deep lines around her mouth creased into a smile.

'Lady Ling, Master has spared Ru Shan and sent him away.' Auntie came forwards to take her arm, crowding close in confidence. 'Auntie sent special thanks to Master Li's ancestors for this mercy.'

Suyin breathed easier. 'Thank the heavens.'

She had known Li Tao wouldn't kill Ru Shan. Her instincts told her he was more than a senseless butcher, yet she was more confused than ever. Last night by the gorge, Li Tao had dragged her into his embrace with an almost fearful protectiveness. Then he'd waited until morning to seduce her with irresistible skill. The memories were both sensual and devastating.

Why did he want more time now? He didn't strike her as a man who was prey to his own indulgences. He didn't strike her as a man who was prey to anything.

'Do you know where Governor Li has gone?' she asked.

Auntie shook her head. No one ever seemed to ask where he went.

'You haven't eaten,' Auntie scolded gently. 'Let us go to your room. Auntie will bring you something.'

Suyin smoothed her hands over her robe and tucked her hair back nervously. The old woman said nothing about the scandalous way she had emerged from Li Tao's wing of the house so late in the day. She wondered if Li Tao had ever kept any mistresses. And there it was. The sting of jealousy.

She and Auntie made their way back to her apartments, while the other servants darted like fish at the edges of her vision, moving silently to their duties, but the atmosphere had changed around them. Soldiers were now stationed inside the mansion in addition to the patrols outside.

Suyin glanced back at the armed guards by the entrance to the garden. 'Auntie, what happened yesterday…I'm sorry for the pain I caused everyone.'

Auntie hushed her. 'Master Li, he worries too much.' Her voice dropped so low, Suyin had to strain to catch the words. 'Always watching his back. All this time.'

Suyin slowed her pace as they started up the stairs. 'You called him something yesterday.'

Tao-Tao. It had been so unexpected. A sentimental nickname someone would call a child.

Auntie chuckled and patted her hand. 'Would the lady believe he was such a skinny boy? His ribs used to stick out from him like the spokes of a wheel.'

'So Auntie knew the Governor from back in Luoyang.'

'Luoyang, yes. Dirty city. Smelly. He would run through the streets with his sleeves frayed and holes at his knees and Auntie would mend them up. Now see what he has become?'

There was pride there and, surprisingly, unbridled affection. She could hardly picture Li Tao as a lanky urchin wandering through the gutters. So he had risen from low birth. It wasn't unheard of in these times when the empire valued talent almost as much as it valued noble blood.

'Then you really are family?'

'No, no. Tao lived with his mother in the house next to Auntie. Such sadness.'

The more she learned about Li Tao, the more the mystery deepened. It was all in fragments, the streets of Luoyang, the daggers on display in his study. The hint of tragedy chased her away from prying any further. She had no business seeking out such personal details of Li Tao's life.

In the seclusion of her apartments, Auntie combed out her hair and helped her dress while deliberately avoiding any more talk of the previous day's confrontation. The silence tormented Suyin, leaving her vulnerable to thoughts of Li Tao and his unseemly proposal. For the first time in a long while, she wished for guidance from someone knowledgeable like Madame Ling. She had nothing to follow but her own instincts, which were suddenly murky and fragmented, and she certainly couldn't confide in Auntie.

Courtesans didn't enter into arrangements purely for pleasure. They vied for security, comfort and wealth. Li Tao had asked for a month. The scant number of days between one full moon and the next. Hardly the request of a man enchanted.

Li Tao was going to war. He wanted a brief, tidy affair and she—she didn't know what she wanted any more.

Auntie had a tray of food brought to her and Suyin saw with a wisp of tenderness that Cook had put a plate of steamed dumplings on it, another of her favourites. She finished the meal so as not to hurt Cook's feelings, and then carried her *qin* out to the garden for some distraction. Time was passing with painful slowness that day and it would be easier to detect anyone returning to the mansion when she was outside.

She seated herself in the pavilion and lifted the instrument from its case, pausing to run her fingers along the lacquered base. This was the first gift Li Tao had given her. It was one of the few belongings she'd have, when she left.

'Are you well, Lady Ling?'

She glanced up to see Jun standing before her with a canvas sack cradled in one arm.

'Yes, quite well.'

'You were sitting there a long time.'

Her fingertips rested against the strings, but she hadn't played a single note or noticed his approach. The youth continued to watch her with an inquisitive look.

'I knew Master Li would never harm the lady,' he said, surprising her with his directness. The last time Jun had seen her was after Li Tao had dragged her away.

'Thank you for your concern, young Jun.'

'Master Li has not gone far, in case the lady is wondering.'

'Pardon?'

'He did not ride beyond the bamboo forest today. Everyone thinks that Jun has one arm so everything must take him twice as long. I have time to explore the surrounding forest most days.'

For once, she found herself unsettled by the boy. He was staring at her with an intensity that transformed his usually gentle features into an uncustomary scowl, but a moment later it was gone.

'What sort of things do you see?' she asked.

'There are trails that lead up the mountainside. There is a lake where we catch fish for dinner.'

'How wonderful.'

Jun blushed and she wondered how old he must be. Perhaps only a bit older than she had been when she entered the Emperor's court. Jun simply longed for company, she reasoned. He was the youngest one in the household, with no one else to speak to and understandably awkward around women.

'Lady Ling.'

She waited so long for the next part that she had to urge him to continue. 'Yes?'

Lowering the sack, he shifted the weight of it against his hip. 'Master Li trusts very few people.'

'I suppose he has his reasons.'

'You affect him like nothing else. It is…unexpected.'

Strange conversation. Jun looked so anxious that she struggled to think of something to add.

'Everyone that we meet in our lives changes us,' she said. Had Li Tao changed in their short time together? Had she?

Jun nodded into the gap of silence. 'Take care, Lady Ling.'

'I will, Jun.'

The youth hefted the sack on to his lanky shoulders and turned to go. The off-centred nature of the conversation lingered once he disappeared into the kitchen. His words had a muddled sense of warning that she couldn't escape. She tried to chase it away with the first strum of her fingers over the strings.

Chapter Eleven

A sliver of peach silk fluttered just beyond the stone lions as Li Tao approached the mansion. A hint of movement and nothing more, but enough to awaken his pulse. He pulled the horse to a halt at the end of the dirt road, right before the walkway to the house, and dismounted. The rest of his escort continued to the stables. By then, Suyin had emerged, her hand perched tentatively against the statue's paw. The guard patrol tensed as she stepped past them, but they stood back after meeting his eyes for confirmation. The show of will was unmistakable. Suyin tested the boundaries at every opportunity.

She came down the steps, but stopped wide to stare uncertainly at his steed. Her dress smoothed over her elegant figure in the warm colours of a sunrise. The sight of her was always a new start, breaking the monotony of dirt roads, forest green and colourless sky.

'Lady Ling,' he greeted.

She cast her eyes downwards. 'Governor Li.'

The formal address hid a secret intimacy. That, and the way she had obviously been waiting for him, made his body tighten with anticipation.

On a whim, Li Tao beckoned her forwards. 'Don't be afraid.'

He held on to the reins with one hand and reached the other out to her. She hesitated before stepping towards him, staring warily at the horse the entire time. The animal let out a snort as she neared.

'He doesn't like me,' she complained.

'Come, I'll show you how. You can't be carried around in a palanquin all the time.'

Their eyes met and there could be no mistake about the thought that passed between them. She'd clung to him as their bodies joined. They had found release in each other's arms, skin to skin. The rest of this was merely distraction.

Her fingers remained stiff in his grasp as he lifted them towards the horse's neck. Suddenly the animal tossed his head in a violent motion. She gave a little shriek and fell back against him. He laughed as he held her and she curved into the contours of his body as if she belonged there.

'Black demon,' she cursed.

He didn't know if she was referring to him or the horse. 'He can sense your fear. If you remain calm, he'll remain calm.'

She looked up in awe. 'We didn't have horses in the village where I came from.'

'I was fifteen before I ever rode a horse or lifted a sword.'

Or learned to read and write. Lao Sou, lord of the assassins, had insisted he would need those skills if he were ever to be anything more than a gutter rat. He hadn't been born to the life of the warrior class, but he had adapted, much as Suyin had. They'd become what they needed to.

He pressed her fingers against the horse's neck again; this time the animal accepted the touch, his muscles straining beneath the sleek coat. Unaided, she stroked her fingers over the horse once more. Li Tao had thought of those hands often during the day, as well as her perfect mouth and the way she had been curled up asleep in his bed when he'd left.

The stable boy came to take the reins and they were finally alone together.

'Auntie didn't know if you would return today,' she said.

'Did you consider my proposal?'

Her lips curved slightly. 'You don't waste any words.'

'I don't have the time.'

'Only a month.'

She pulled away from him, her eyes growing sharp with challenge. This was the Lady Ling he'd come to know, always planning. It would be crude to remind her of how her nails had dug into his back as she shuddered beneath him. She was at once the innocent and the seductress, and both held him captive.

One month would hardly be enough, but even these moments were an extravagance he could barely afford.

'Walk with me.' She turned towards the path leading into the bamboo groves without waiting for his reply. 'I hear there is a lake nearby.'

Obligingly, he waved his men back. The area surrounding the compound was secure enough for them to take this short distance in private. Her arm brushed against his and she shifted away awkwardly, aware of every touch. The careless banter that always rolled effortlessly from her lips no longer served her.

'Auntie told me you spared Ru Shan's life,' she said after a pause.

'I didn't do it for you.'

'Still, I thank you.'

'Do not speak of him again,' he said stiffly.

They continued the rest of the way in silence. If Ru Shan ever came near her again, Li Tao wouldn't be so merciful. The need to stake his claim to her overpowered him, but he forced it back, remembering the dangers he faced.

Suyin hadn't given herself to Ru Shan or any other man, but that didn't mean she belonged to him. Not when he had no hope of holding on to her.

Li Tao walked beside her like a predator through the forest, no wasted movement, with a silence that unnerved her. This is how he chose to convince her to stay? She searched his stony profile for any sign of the passionate lover of that morning. They could spend a hundred years together and she still wouldn't be able to read him.

A boulder set beside the path marked the turn to the lake. A rough trail had been cut through the bamboo to the water, and she paused at the end of it to take in her first sight of the lake. Speckled light rippled along the surface as the sun dipped low in the sky.

Soon it would be evening. Li Tao always seemed more comfortable in the night.

Her gaze rounded the shore and found a patch of grass. She went to it and he followed her there, seating himself beside her. She smoothed her skirt over her knees and looked out over the water. The silence had continued for too long.

'So your answer is no, then,' he said tonelessly.

Her throat grew tight. 'What would you do if I refused to stay?'

'I would send you home tomorrow.'

'So simple for you,' she muttered.

'You should have at least that choice left to you.'

Did he do that deliberately? He would push her away until she was ready to condemn him and then twist her thoughts around. She picked up a stone and threw it towards the water. It skipped twice before sinking and Li Tao's eyebrows lifted in surprise.

She had no one left by her side. If she went now, she'd be alone and defenseless. Gao would come for her with a knife. Or, worse, with a proposition.

'We never did mention terms,' she said.

'The terms were very clear, though we were not speaking at the time. Pleasure for pleasure.'

'I hardly believe that's all you want.'

He ran his fingertips along her arm, stroking gently. 'The attraction of a man and a woman shouldn't be so difficult to understand.'

A shudder pulsed down her spine and she closed her hand over his to still it. She hated this power he had over her, yet she yearned for it. But she couldn't mistake it for compassion.

'You will have more freedom here than you would back in the imperial palace,' he said. 'And I believe you did not find my bed…' he paused to search for the word '…disagreeable.'

Her face grew hot under his gaze. 'There are armies marching against you,' she pointed out. 'I would be a fool to stay.'

'Let them come. You'll be safe long before anything happens.'

'You'd surrender me to Emperor Shen.'

He broke away and stared across the lake, his profile cutting a sharp outline against the forest green around them. A ribbon of sunlight danced over his face, reflected from the water.

'Shen is the only one who can keep you safe.'

His words left her cold.

'So you feel that war is inevitable,' she said.

When he didn't answer, she knew she had been right to try to escape. Li Tao would present a formidable defence, but how could he withstand the strength of two armies against his one? He met her eyes and she found it hard to breathe beneath his penetrating gaze. She wished she knew what it was he was looking for.

'You have not given an answer.'

'There really isn't a bit of poetry in you, is there?' she scolded.

He tensed beside her as he waited. His patience tore at her soul. If he was preparing himself for a life-or-death battle, why did he bother with something as meaningless as a brief affair? Why did his body call out to her in desire?

'Pleasure for pleasure, then.' A sense of dread weighed her down as she spoke the words, but beneath the fear laid a grain of hope.

She needed time to learn what Gao wanted from her. She needed protection.

Li Tao had given her power in this choice as his equal. For the first time, she was walking into danger's path willingly instead of hiding as she should. She had until the next full moon to sway Li Tao's course. In a month, she might be able to gain enough of his trust to convince him that there was another way besides war and death.

Li Tao said little to her as they returned to the mansion, but a quiet purpose had taken hold of him that was both frightening and exhilarating. He left her to Auntie, but his hand had lingered possessively on the small of her back for a long time before he retreated to his study. That night she dined alone with Auntie in quiet attendance after waiting for Li Tao to join her. He always took his meals alone and apparently didn't plan to change.

Suyin began to wonder what sort of arrangement she had agreed to. And with what sort of man?

As a wayward emptiness grew within her, she began to fear that she had agreed for more than merely pleasure or an opportunity to influence Li Tao. She feared she had agreed out of loneliness, a loneliness that all the nights before the next full moon could not appease.

If she had truly been an accomplished courtesan, she would know exactly how to conduct this affair. She would beguile and seduce and become whatever he wanted her to be. But she would not be his concubine.

Back in her chamber, she lit all the lanterns and stayed awake, stabbing an embroidery needle through a square of silk. When she finally inspected her work, her flock of cranes was crooked beyond repair.

The door opened with a slight creak of hinges. She gasped as the needle jabbed into her fingertip. Li Tao came to stand before her, his shadow falling over the embroidery. His nearness alone made her heart beat faster. Would it have been this way with any man who was her first lover?

'It is late,' she said.

'There was much to tend to.' Cocking his head, he peered down at the crippled birds with only mild interest. 'You are nearly finished.'

She fixed the needle into the cloth and set the frame aside. 'Sit and rest. You look tired.'

Such simple, meaningless conversation. The sort a master of the house would have with his mistress. She would call for tea and he would tell her about his daily routine. But they weren't those people.

Li Tao didn't move to seat himself. He remained over her with that inscrutable expression that always made her grasp for something to throw him off balance. She dropped her gaze from his face to stare at the line of his neck and the tap of his pulse. The urge to press her mouth against the tanned skin assailed her. Despite the neglect of that evening, she wanted him shamelessly.

'You are bleeding,' he said.

A spot of blood pooled on her finger. With a sureness that sent a flutter to her stomach, he took hold of her hand and raised it to his lips.

She snatched her hand away. *'Scoundrel.'*

His bottom lip curved just so and she shouldn't have been so charmed by it. Their gazes locked and the distance between them dissolved.

He touched her first, his hand to her neck to guide her to him. Always so direct. His lips descended warm on to hers. His kiss took her back to the morning when the heat of their bodies had mingled beneath the blankets. Had it only been just that day?

He lifted her to her feet, hands on her waist to anchor her hips against him. Finally, she wrapped her arms around him, breathing in his warmth and the distinct scent of his skin. She'd been waiting for this moment since opening her eyes to the empty spot beside her.

She learned about him in little pieces that she pulled from the haze of desire. Li Tao had no patience for preliminaries. Her clothes were pulled away and cast aside so that nothing shielded her from his eyes. And then he looked at her, long and slow with an intensity that made her tremble.

There were other little things she learned. Li Tao liked to keep the lanterns burning. He didn't care for moving to the bed and left their clothes discarded on the floor of the sitting room. Despite the hurried rush of their first coupling, Li Tao could be endlessly patient. His calloused hands slid over her, touching, soothing. And his mouth… He found places she never knew could cause such an ache within her: the base of her spine, the soft curve of her neck. His teeth scraped over her skin as if it wasn't enough just to touch and kiss and taste.

She knew things too. Nothing from pillow books or her vast, yet shallow education in Luoyang. Things that her heart told her to do. Li Tao shuddered above her as she ran her hands over each chiselled curve and plane. She had never been given such freedom, such power. His was a warrior's body, hardened through combat, nothing wasted.

Her hand slid down between his thighs to tease over his manhood, pressing her advantage on purpose. His eyes shut and his head arched back as she stroked. She watched his face, his expression tight, almost pained. His breath drained from him when her grip tightened ever so slightly. She wanted to know it all.

She was already wet before he slid his fingers over the pearl of her sex. Already straining for release when he rolled his tongue gently over her. His breath fanned hot against her flesh.

He dipped his finger into her and she grabbed on to the wooden frame of the *chaise* and bit back a scream. Li Tao liked to watch her lose herself, writhing and sobbing under his mouth. She glanced down to catch his gaze lift from the cradle of her thighs. With his eyes fixed on to hers, he urged her on with his mouth and the hard slide of his fingers until she climaxed, pulsing endlessly around him.

It was only then that he lifted her in his arms to carry her into the bedchamber. He laid her on to the bed and joined her. Her hips lifted towards him. There was a slight soreness that wasn't there before as he entered her. Her body was not yet accustomed to his impassioned love-making.

The nights. This is where they belonged. He thrust and thrust deeper. Slowly to prolong the pleasure. The muscles of his back tightened beneath her fingertips. His skin became slick with sweat. In the quiet pockets of the day, they didn't make any sense. The night could be what they made of it. If this was all he wanted, it was enough. It was everything.

She was climaxing again. She wrapped her legs around his hips and closed her eyes to let the lightning wash over her. He strained upwards, lifting himself higher on to his arms until he went rigid. His hips rocked into her of their own accord, thrusting deep one final time.

When she opened her eyes he was staring. That taunting curve of his lower lip had returned, smug this time. She lifted just her neck to press her mouth to his. It was a brief kiss in the aftermath of spent passion. She did it to capture that bare trace of a smile.

His muscles loosened and she released him, falling back languidly to watch him as he rose. One month. Long days, and nights that were too short.

'Will you stay?' she asked as he stood.

He was naked strength beside the bed. So magnificent. 'Do you wish me to?'

The wave of loneliness came back, but she answered with a languid smile, turning on to her side to see him better. That was all the answer Li Tao needed. As he turned to put out the lanterns, she saw the bare expanse of his back for the first time.

A bold design had been inked on to his skin just over his left shoulder blade. She detected the curved body of a dragon. Sleek bands of muscle glided beneath it as he moved. A mark of thieves and assassins. She had seen such marks in the dens of Luoyang and had been warned about the men who bore them.

He faced her. The look between them acknowledged what she had seen. What he had wanted her to see. He paused over the orb lantern, waiting. When she said nothing, he extinguished the flame inside.

Chapter Twelve

Shibao, Tibet—ad 745
14 years earlier

Li Tao plunged his sword into the Tibetan soldier's chest and pulled it out with the next motion. Even surrounded by death, his hands did not shake. Out of the corner of his eye, he caught the moment the August Emperor was thrown from his horse.

His focus narrowed in on the dragon insignia of the Emperor's breastplate. This was his time. Grand General Shen and his sons had taken to separate quarters of the battlefield.

The Emperor fought on foot with the confusion of the battle around him. With sword in hand, he struck at an enemy soldier, then scanned the field around him. Li Tao's task was clear: the Emperor had to die, struck down in battle by all appearances, a casualty of the war he waged.

Li Tao gripped his sword in one hand and reached for his knife with the other. He was close. Within paces of striking distance. The Emperor's gaze fixed on to him in recognition. He would deliver his death blow face to face. A warrior, a leader of men who fought alongside his men deserved more than a knife in the back.

All that was left to do was deliver the blow. At that moment, the Emperor's eyes widened. He called a warning as his focus fixed on a point just beyond Li Tao's shoulder. The Emperor lunged forwards as Li Tao turned to address the new threat.

The Emperor cut down the first attacker, but the second got through. Tibetan steel plunged into him and he doubled over with the impact.

Before he could think, Li Tao buried his blade in the enemy soldier's throat. His hands were not his own.

The Emperor fell, clutching his wound, and Li Tao whirled to face the next attack. All he remembered from that point on was the dull, tight exhaustion of his shoulders from swinging his sword as the Son of Heaven lay bleeding into the earth behind him. All other thought had been swallowed into the cold pit of shame in his stomach.

759 ad—Present day

Lady Ling glided along the bookshelves, trailing a careless finger over the spines. Every move was meant for him and he knew it. He thought of their nights and those endless hours, the sweet clench of her flesh around him, the perfume of her hair on his pillow. He set down his ink brush to savour the memories. Their nights proved that her sorcery over him was in no danger of fading.

'Sun Tzu, Tai Gung... War and flowery metaphors for war.' She cast out the exalted names with an air of dismissiveness as she slid the books out and back into the shelves. Suyin had a way of moving about a space as if she owned it and owned him as well. The insinuation alone excited him, even if it was an act.

'You know the military texts,' he noted.

'I was favoured concubine to the warrior Emperor,' she replied, slanting a glance at him over her shoulder.

'In name only.'

He thought he caught the satisfied curve of her lips as she turned back to his books. The extent of his possessiveness surprised him. Li Ming was in his grave and had gone there without ever enjoying the gifts of his infamous mistress.

'There is an interesting story about General Sun Tzu.' Still not finding anything she liked, she moved on. 'General Sun was challenged by the King of Wu to make an army out of his harem of concubines.'

Her voice flowed over him like soothing fingers. He found himself relaxing into her presence. His armies were in a holding pattern after all until he received more reports about Gao.

'He divided them into two companies, appointing the two favourite concubines as the commanders, but when he tried to instruct them, the girls merely giggled. He warned them that if the soldiers did not understand their assignments, it was the fault of the leaders.'

'The poor general. I know from experience even one imperial concubine can be a challenge.'

'Scoundrel.' She didn't even face him to fling the accusation.

'Go on,' he said, entertained.

Apparently she deemed the rest of the books uninteresting as well. She turned to him to finish her tale.

'When the harem continued to be uncooperative, Sun Tzu promptly executed the two favourites in front of the others. The king protested in anger, but the general replied, "When a general receives his orders, it is his duty to carry them out to perfection, even if the king protests."'

'And of course, the remaining women executed their tasks like trained soldiers,' he finished. 'I would not have been so exacting in my punishment.'

'Because they were defenceless women?'

'Because war is war and a general should know the difference.'

He looked up expectantly as she reached the end of the bookshelf. At the edge of the sealed cabinet, she seemed to lose interest and wandered back to where he was seated.

'Your tea is getting cold.' She lifted the teapot, her sleeve pulled back gracefully, balancing a finger over the lid to steady it. 'Do you know that there is an art to doing this? In Luoyang, rich noblemen would pay to sit and have tea poured for them.'

His fingers brushed momentarily against hers as he took the cup from her. The touch should have been insignificant after all they'd done together, but the sensuality of it was undeniable.

'Sit with me.'

Rather than indulging his request, she slipped behind him and placed her hands over his shoulders, kneading her thumbs against the tight bands of muscle. He turned his head to one side, then the other, the sinew giving with a slight crack. Following the line of his shoulder blades, she worked his back in slow circles until the muscles begrudgingly relaxed.

He let his head fall back until he could see her. The vulnerability of the position sank in—neck exposed while she stood over him. He swallowed past the knot in his throat, forcing himself to remain still while she cradled his face in her hands.

'You said a woman gave you this.' Gingerly, she ran her thumb along the scar slashing across his cheek.

His gaze flickered up to her. 'The woman I was supposed to marry.'

'Now, Governor,' she purred. Her hands lowered once more to perch on his shoulders. 'This story has become even more fascinating. Was she pretty?'

'Everyone in the empire knows this by now.' He straightened and her hands slipped from him. 'Shen and I have never been of the same mind. The August Emperor thought marriage to his daughter would repair the rift between us. I believed for a moment that the past could truly be forgotten. That I could raise sons, have a legacy.'

She reached for him again after a pause. Tentatively, she worked her fingers at the base of his neck.

'Honour was everything to Shen Ai Li,' he went on absently.

Suyin's hands paused. 'Ai Li?'

'She wouldn't have anything to do with me. Our marriage would have been a disaster.'

His betrothed had escaped from him and he'd hunted her to the very edge of the empire, defying several imperial sanctions in the process. But she hadn't been one of the corrupt ministers he was famous for tracking down. Ai Li was a wilful, rebellious girl who saw him for what he was. A rogue who was loyal to no one.

'The wedding was one final chance to reconcile with Shen.'

'Surely there are other ways to make peace with Emperor Shen.'

Suyin ran her fingers through his hair, her nails soothing against his scalp. He let his eyes fall closed and willed himself to relax.

'Shen never trusted me,' he said. 'Even before he was Emperor.'

'He needs allies like you. Especially while men like Gao continue to draw air.'

His breathing slowed as she stroked his neck, her fingertips cool against his skin. Was this merely the clever tongue of an accomplished courtesan? Or did she truly believe it?

'The princess accused me of being responsible for the death of her brother, Shen's fourth son. Another reason for the rift between us.'

'Were you?' she asked.

'Was I...?'

'Were you responsible for his son's death?'

The tension returned, coiling tight and refusing to let go. Suyin halted her skilful ministrations. He took hold of her hands and she grew still behind him.

'You do know how to charm a man out of his deepest secrets, Lady Ling.'

He turned to watch her reaction. She stood looking down upon him, her hand resting on him.

She refused to be redirected. 'Did you do it?'

He'd been called to answer this question before. 'There's no benefit to having the Emperor's fourth son killed. If I truly wanted to attack Shen, I would have targeted the elder ones who hold more significant power.'

'Benefit?' She dug her nails into his shoulders in agitation.

'No, I didn't do it,' he growled. 'And Shen knows I didn't.'

'Then how can Gao use this against you?'

'Because Shen still has his doubts.' The corner of his mouth lifted in a grim smile. 'Wouldn't you, with my reputation?'

His grip tightened on her wrists and her pulse jumped. He had been the August Emperor's enforcer and he was brutally efficient at it.

She wet her lips. 'It seems neither of us can escape such notoriety.'

'I tried to send you away, for your sake and for mine, but I couldn't.'

He directed her to the chair beside him. They were face to face now, on even ground. He held on to her, extending her arm across the corner of the desk to clasp her hand. She stiffened in his grasp, but didn't pull away.

'Perhaps I was tired of being cautious.' His gaze travelled her face: the elegant cheekbones, her sensual mouth, and always, always those eyes that would not let him go.

'It occurred to me that if you were sent here to gain my trust, then you've been remarkably successful.'

Her expression remained controlled, belied by only a minute tightening of her mouth. 'I told you no one sent me.'

Her eyes lit up whenever she was challenged. Whatever the mood, whatever her expression, she was exquisite, so beautiful he had to force his gaze away. He could see why the August Emperor would choose her for his deception. A man could easily become obsessed with her and forsake all others.

'I told myself that you might very well cut my throat in my sleep.'

She flinched at his words, but he held her fast.

'If you did, I would deserve it,' he continued. 'I'd consider it a testimony to your talents. You have me convinced in every way. And if I'm wrong, I can't say that I regret our nights together. This life might be worth it.'

He was being deliberately cruel. When they lay together, he surrendered himself to her for a mindless, staggering moment with every joining, and he accepted it. But he didn't like what she did to him when she looked at him in the glare of daylight, with that unbearable sadness in her eyes. She weakened him when he couldn't risk any weakness.

She didn't recoil as he expected. She leaned towards him, gripping his hand fervently in both of hers. 'Tao, it doesn't have to end in bloodshed. Shen isn't your enemy. You wouldn't send me to him if he was.'

'Shen and I have a respect for one another, despite our differences,' he said slowly.

'Then negotiate a peace with him. Is it so hard to recognise his authority? He wants what you want, for the empire to endure.'

'We've moved beyond that point, Lady Ling. The armies are moving closer to the river by the day.'

'So go directly to the Emperor. You must do it before his soldiers reach your borders. Don't let this be decided by imperial subordinates and that demon Gao.' Her pretty eyes held on to him, shining with a new fierceness. 'Shen will listen to you.'

'What makes you so certain?' he asked with dark amusement.

She let out a calming breath. 'He owes you a debt. Emperor Shen promised you his daughter. He'll feel the need to make amends. You know I'm right.'

He had to admire Suyin's perceptiveness, but her plan was madness. The days of strategy and planning were stealing away his strength. In the night, he lost himself to her softness and warmth whenever he could. Sleep was a distant memory.

'Governor Li?'

So she had reverted back to his formal title after her impassioned plea.

He folded his hands calmly in front of him, fingers knitted together. 'I wish that what you propose was possible. But Emperor Shen is not strong enough to hold the empire together. We must all fend for ourselves and protect the borders for as long as we're able. This has all been happening for a long time.'

She stared at the dragon signet on his finger. 'But you served the August Emperor without fail. You and Shen both. Loyalty must mean something to you.'

'Loyalty means nothing to me, though it is very touching how passionately you've defended me.'

His patronising tone angered her and he could sense her desperation building, a distant echo of his own fears.

'You won't consider another alternative. Not even to save yourself,' she said, every word steeped in bitterness.

'If the Emperor and Gao don't come for me, someone else will some day.'

Her gaze darted to the cabinet against the wall before quickly shifting back. He knew that she had seen the collection of daggers. He had suspected when she avoided it in her explorations.

'Those are a constant reminder of my failure,' he explained. 'Another reason you can't stay with me.'

'What failure?'

'To kill Li Ming.'

She jerked to her feet. The corner of the desk jarred against her hip as she staggered backwards.

'You are standing very far away, Lady Ling,' he said mildly.

'But you were part of his inner circle. You have had plenty of opportunity to kill the Emperor,' she said.

'If I had wanted to take his life, I could have. I'm a traitor to all sides.'

He pushed his chair back and stood, approaching slowly. He stopped just short of touching her. 'You see? All my secrets at your feet.'

She had to tilt her head up to meet his eyes. 'The mark on your back—'

'The mark of the *An Ying* clan.'

The Shadows. He made no effort to hide the symbol inked on to his skin when they lay together. She never asked about it, but he knew she had a vague idea of what it meant, how it branded him for life. Every year, Lao Sou sent him a gift to remind him of his betrayal. The old man would never forget, would never let him rest.

'I've never heard of it,' she said.

'You wouldn't have.'

His voice lowered until the tone was nearly intimate. 'I want you to know everything, so you will stop with this talk of duty and loyalty and the glory of the empire.'

'Do you—?' Her bottom lip trembled as she started to form the question. 'Do you still belong to them?'

'No, but no one can leave such an organization. Not without repercussions.'

Her breath came shallowly as she peered at him, eyes wide with fear and doubt. Yet still, she stayed. Her hands were clasped before her. He'd say her stance was demure, if he didn't know her so well. He wanted to take her in his arms and assure her there was nothing to be afraid of at the moment. Not from him.

There would always be unspoken secrets between them. It was something they silently accepted, but he wanted her to know so she could come to him without any illusions.

He lifted his fingers to stroke her cheek, but let his hand drop before touching her. 'Now you understand why there is no need to try to save me, Lady Ling. Death will come one way or another. This will never end.'

Chapter Thirteen

The faint glow of daybreak seeped through the windows as Suyin rolled on to her side beneath the quilt. Li Tao's back was turned to her. The edge of the blanket had fallen, baring the coiled dragon on his shoulder blade. Last night, she had awoken to the familiar shift of his weight beside her. He'd managed only to undress before collapsing on to the bed, asleep before he laid his head upon the pillow.

The last days had been torture. Li Tao had disappeared for a week and, hour after hour, she'd been left to imagine the worst. He would be carried home with a dagger in his heart or he would never be found. She would never see him again.

The month was nearly spent and she hadn't been able to convince Li Tao to negotiate. He had no reason to listen to her counsel, the advice of a woman he was using for his pleasure. Was that all she was? A last glimpse of beauty and warmth?

That was why he had asked only for a month. He was prepared to lay down everything in the impending confrontation. Li Tao was heading to his death and all she could do was watch the moon grow rounder with each passing night.

She curled close, careful not to wake him. The dragon rippled with the rise and fall of his breathing. Many paintings showed the pearl in the dragon's grasp, but here the dragon chased the orb, stretching out curved talons to capture its power. The markings and their hidden meaning frightened her.

Li Tao killed, not only in war or to defeat his enemies, but simply because he had been ordered, or paid. He had done so without regret, but hadn't she done worse?

With a low murmur, he shifted on to his back and his hand came to rest against her pillow. She traced the vertical line of his palm with her fingertip, unable to hold back any longer. Once he rose, it could be days before he returned. Some mornings she would awaken to find him already gone. The emptiness would linger within her for the entire day. This call of yin to yang went beyond any reason. But he was here now, restful and still enough for her to touch.

'What are you doing?' His eyes remained closed and his voice sounded far away, drugged with sleep.

'Watching you.' She stroked over the pad of his thumb. 'Do you know I can read palms?'

'Can you?' His breathing deepened as if he was drifting once again. He must have been particularly drained that morning to remain in bed for so long. 'What does mine show?'

'A strong life line and your head line curves downward. Your head will always rule your heart.'

'Hmm.'

His hand twitched reflexively as she drew an aimless pattern over it. His fingers were broad and long, the skin rough. He opened his eyes to gaze at her through heavy lids, the glint of his pupils tiger-like. They lay face to face. So close.

If he would only stay. If they could only remain like this, co-cooned together like two silkworms. Secure.

'Now I know all your secrets.' She followed the outline of his arm, trailing over the sleek muscle of his shoulder. 'All your weaknesses.'

'I have no weaknesses.'

'None?'

He squirmed as she explored his ribcage with a feather touch. Then she dug her fingers playfully into his side to make him jump. He jerked awake and surged over her, pinning her beneath his weight. Deep laughter filled her ears and she lifted her fingertips to the curve of his mouth.

He so rarely smiled.

Their bodies moulded together and she became keenly aware of the dangerous beauty of him: smooth, hard and strong. A perfectly tempered weapon. For a brief moment, she saw the longing in his eyes before they clouded with desire. The unexpected tenderness pierced deep into her heart.

Madame Ling had always warned her that these emotions were fabricated. She must never allow herself to believe the illusion. Never allow herself to fall in love. If she had lost her chastity in the pleasure den in Luoyang or in the Emperor's court, then her courtesan sisters could have taught her how to shield herself.

Li Tao hardened with arousal. They had slept unclothed with this promise between them. A moan caught in her throat as he settled his nakedness against her thighs, seeking her warmth. His skin flushed hot against her. She curved her arms around his neck and her hips lifted towards him without thought. He pushed into her in one clean motion. A soft sigh of acquiescence escaped from her lips as her body accepted him. The arc of sensation plunged her once again into dark waters, into the unknown.

His black eyes fixed on to her face as he thrust into her. His gaze became distant as arousal and need took over. This was the only way the barriers between them were ever removed. Only in the joining of their bodies, nowhere else.

She willed herself to be unmoved. This was nothing but flesh upon flesh. A man taking his own pleasure. But Li Tao continued in a steady rhythm and her body opened up to him, pulling her unwilling heart on a thread with it. Each penetration implored a new surrender from her that she knew she shouldn't give.

But her sex flooded and her heartbeat quickened despite her defences. Tao was still watching her, urging her to join him as the desire coursed between them, him into her and back again. Her breasts swelled, pressing against the hard plane of his chest. She forced herself to hold still, anchoring her hips down towards the bed.

His jaw clenched as he fought to force back the tide. Tension vibrated within his muscles as he held himself over her. It wasn't long before his eyes clamped shut and he sank his head against her shoulder, his thrusts growing more forceful. She wanted to cling to him, her fingers digging into his hips to urge him on. Instead, she curled them into the feather mattress as his ragged breath fanned against her collarbone.

He shuddered, every muscle locked as his passion overflowed and his seed spilled into her. Then, in a final exhalation, he grew still. For several long moments, he allowed himself to lie there, cheek rested against the swell of her breast; his skin was damp with perspiration. That space of idleness had to be an indulgence for him. Dawn was past and morning was upon them.

Without a word, he raised himself from her and left the bed to tug on his trousers. She kept her eyes fixed on the alcove above, listening to the faint sounds of his movements.

He returned to her and when he spoke his voice held a faint trace of humour. 'Perhaps I can please you tonight.'

His lips brushed against her forehead and she had to shut her eyes against him. She gathered the quilt around her, pulling the edge of it to her chin. His words reminded her too sharply of what they had between them. This was a physical liaison with an ending already foreseen. Why did her spirit insist on reaching out to him?

In the far corner of the room, she could hear the splash of wash water, the careful opening of the dresser door. He readied himself each morning without servants. Li Tao was a secretive, distant man even to those closest to him. This would never change.

She waited for a long time after the closing of the door before rising. She waited even longer, ensuring that he was gone from the mansion, before calling Auntie to her to prepare for the day.

His duties took him to the administrative offices in Rongzhou that day. It was the closest walled city to the bamboo sea and the provincial governor had summoned him there for a meeting. Yet when he arrived, it wasn't the bureaucrat that greeted him. Rather it was the bureaucrat's retainer.

The man droned on and Li Tao's thoughts drifted to Suyin. She'd been uncustomarily quiet when he'd left her. Perhaps she'd stopped playing the enchanting courtesan for him and this was her true self. It was impossible to discern and he didn't want to wonder about it. He wanted to enjoy her conversation and her beauty and the willing infatuation that came with being with a woman like Suyin.

But he did wonder.

This worthless functionary was still speaking his obsequious drivel.

'Why didn't the governor come to me himself?' Li Tao interrupted.

That slight show of ire was enough to make the man pale. He rambled off an apology about his master's inability to make the appointment.

Li Tao glared at the retainer impatiently. Men like this were suited only for carrying out simple orders. The provincial govenor was Li Tao's administrative counterpart and the man lived in fear of offending his superiors in Changan.

'If Governor Chou needs to speak to me, he can come to me himself.'

'But the provincial governor needs your assurance that there will be no conflict with the Emperor's armies when they arrive.'

What would Shen do? The imperial forces were already scattered wide. Shen didn't have the reach to oversee the southern district.

'Tell Chou I'll do what's necessary, as always.'

Li Tao made a motion to leave the meeting room, but the retainer rushed to block his path.

'Please! Governor Li must sign this.'

He stared down at the scroll as the retainer unfurled it. A declaration of undying and absolute loyalty to the Emperor, written in more lines than necessary. The servant flinched when Li Tao looked up at him. The hands holding the ends of the scroll visibly shook.

'Now, why would we need such a decree when we've already sworn to serve the empire?' he asked evenly.

This time, the man stood aside. In moments, Li Tao had his bodyguards gathered about him and he was back in the saddle, heading for the city gates.

A waste of time. Chou hadn't come to meet him because he didn't need to. All he needed was a piece of paper. The coward didn't even need his seal on that worthless declaration of loyalty. Chou could make a claim that he had attempted to defy the rogue warlord, in the name of the Emperor. He'd hide behind this flimsy show of alliance with Changan.

These bureaucratic games weren't worth his effort. Yet as they left the gates, he thought of Suyin's advice. Negotiate with Shen. It was too much of a gamble when Gao already had him defeated in the imperial court. Li Tao couldn't leave the district now with two armies bearing down on them, especially not to fight in the sophisticated battlefield of Changan where he was outmatched.

Li Tao directed his men east. He had planned to inspect the fortifications at the junction of the Tuojing and the Long River that day. His armies would need to hold the arteries that fed the southern province. Without those supply lines, neither Gao, nor Shen, could take him.

Once he was done, he'd have to ride late into the night to return to the bamboo forest. To Suyin. It certainly wasn't efficient or practical, but he'd told her he would. She had been in his bed when he left. She was bare beneath the covers with just enough smooth skin showing for the image to provoke him long into the day.

She'd let him leave without a charming look or clever word. That was how they would usually part, with her sultry teasing. It was expected and she obligingly did it to amuse him. The craft of the courtesan was in making a man feel like the lord of the earth, after all.

It was what he had wanted, wasn't it? Diversion. Something to think of besides civil unrest and warfare in the night. It was counter-productive to overthink. The bureaucrats could cower behind their scrolls and offices. All that mattered was that he and his armies knew what to do when it was time to act. Suyin would be long gone by then.

She had been waiting in the sitting room for hours by the time the chamber doors opened that night.

'I wonder,' she began, making a point of being the first to speak. 'I wonder if you imagine that I simply remain here motionless and vacant until the moment you return.'

Her back remained to him as she sat on the padded *chaise*. From behind her, she heard the creak of the door as it closed, followed by the measured pace of his footsteps.

'I do not think that at all,' Li Tao replied calmly.

Either he misread or completely ignored her acid tone. He was still bold enough to rest a hand on her shoulder, his thumb caressing the edge of her neck. A shiver ran down her spine despite her dark mood.

'Sometimes I imagine the way you look when I leave, asleep in my bed.' His voice resonated deep within her.

This was not working. She shifted away from his strong fingers, which had managed to seek out the most sensitive spots on her neck.

'Do you know it is past second hour?'

She turned in her chair to challenge him and was stricken by the sunken shadows beneath his eyes and the exhaustion that weighed down his shoulders.

'I thought for certain you would be asleep by now,' he said. 'Come, let's go to bed.'

At his whim and mercy. She wouldn't have it. 'There are things I wanted to discuss with you.'

'Suyin, we're both tired. We can talk in the morning.' He took hold of a strand of hair that had fallen loose and ran it through his fingers, his knuckles gently brushing her cheek.

His placating tone, the careless affection, and his assumption of command all combined to confuse her emotions. She was touched. She was enraged.

'Fine. Morning then.' She stood and cast him a pointed look before circling and heading for the door.

'*Suyin.*'

The tiredness and resignation in his tone was unmistakable, but she pushed through the corridor past his study and into the main house. With each step, she was well aware that no one followed.

The snap of the cold air in the courtyard shocked her and she pulled her shawl tight around her shoulders, even though the material was too thin to provide any warmth. She hurried along the stone pathway through the gardens. Through the side archway, she spied the lantern light from the night patrol as they walked the perimeter. Moonlight bathed the scene in a silver glow.

The moon that was growing rounder each night.

No lanterns had been lit at the rear of the house where her guest apartments were located and she was forced to slow. The last thing she wanted to do was wake Auntie or any of the others over a quarrel. With her hand on the rail, she felt her way up the stairs and navigated to her room.

The doors opened to a black void and the desolation of it encompassed her. It had been weeks since she'd occupied the guest apartments. She'd taken to sleeping in Li Tao's chambers when he was gone. Suyin hesitated at the threshold. Li Tao's bedchamber was at least heated and his presence beside her an undeniable comfort. But it was only temporary and she couldn't control her emotions when she was with him.

She shuffled into the darkness, her hands out in front of her like the sensing whiskers of a cat. Deliberately she left the door open, needing the glimmer of light it provided. After many slow steps, inch by inch, her fingers brushed against the polished wood of the sitting area. From there, she remembered enough to stumble towards the bedchamber.

The day had been agonisingly long, but at least Auntie and Jun and Cook had distracted her. Night-time was always the worst. After the evening meal, which Li Tao never shared with her, she had nothing to do but wait.

Her toe connected with a table and a vase struck against her arm before toppling to the floor. She only had a second to grope for it before it crashed and shattered. The violence of the sound made her pulse jump. For some unknown reason, that small calamity nearly set her to tears. She choked back the helplessness and felt her way to the bed, using her hands along the wall to find the alcove. Without bothering to remove her dress, she crawled inside, grateful that the covers hadn't been stripped now that she no longer slept there.

The space beneath the quilt was chilled and she curled up with the edges wrapped around her, willing her body to warm. Part of her knew this was irrational. She didn't need to exile herself like this. But in a way, she was still a prisoner in this mansion. Every night she waited, yet had no power to make any demands on Li Tao. Removing herself from him was the only privilege their arrangement afforded her.

The glow of a lantern illuminated the room just as a pocket of warmth gathered around her. She turned, surprised that she hadn't heard Li Tao enter.

'Suyin.' He spoke her name coiled within a long sigh.

She pulled the quilt tighter, as if she could burrow and disappear within the folds.

'There's a broken vase,' she warned begrudgingly as he approached.

The shards clinked against the floor as he kicked them aside. She rolled over to watch him as he placed the lantern on to the table. It cast the room in a muted, yellow glow.

He sat down at the edge of the bed near her feet and leaned back against the wall, exhaustion evident in every muscle. 'Come back to my chamber,' he implored.

'No.'

One of her hairpins dug into her scalp as she turned her head. She tugged it impatiently from her hair and threw it to the floor. She pulled another one and another and tossed them aside, realising then that she still had her slippers on as well. Li Tao surveyed the chaos that littered the ground, speechless.

He closed his eyes and passed a hand over his forehead, pinching at the bridge of his nose. 'Please come back, *Lady Ling*.'

Oh, Heaven and Earth, no one enraged her like this man.

'Why should I?' she demanded. 'Perhaps you should wait for me for once.'

'I do. Every hour of the day.'

Her chest grew tight and a stinging sensation crept into the corners of her eyes. She sank an inch lower beneath the blanket. Whenever Li Tao conceded anything, it was with such carelessness that he maintained the higher ground while she was left vulnerable. Even reclined against her bed, Li Tao's posture held a quiet, confident strength that filled her awareness. It made her mourn those empty hours without him.

'You're returning later and later every day. Sometimes not at all.'

'There is much to do. The northern roads have to be fortified and the grain stores—' He caught himself with a shake of his head.

'I want to know where you go. What you do.'

'It isn't important.'

'It is to me.'

She sounded possessive and she knew it. Like a mistress, like a wife. But she was neither. She was a temporary arrangement, a courtesan meant to stroke his ego and distract him from his troubles. Apparently she was a failure at that since she had set out to trouble him that night.

'Is this what you wanted to discuss with me?' he asked.

If she really wanted to know about his activities, she knew how to find out. She could massage the tension from his shoulders. Draw a hot bath for him. Pour tea and warmed wine and distract him with conversation, but she didn't merely want information.

She raised herself, propping herself up with one arm to be able to see his expression. 'This vigil is wearing you down,' she said.

'I'll be fine.' His denial was immediate, as expected.

'The month is nearly gone. What will happen when the armies arrive?'

'Either Gao and I will come to an understanding or there will be war between us.'

Perhaps the great Li Tao thought himself invincible, that he could take on both the imperial army under Emperor Shen's command and Gao's forces combined. He could be disillusioned enough to take on the demon armies of hell for all she knew.

'What about us?' Her words caught in her throat, but she forced them past. There was no way for her to ask this question and not leave herself exposed.

'You'll be under Emperor Shen's protection by then.'

She made an impatient sound and wiggled the slipper loose from her foot in order to kick it off the bed. 'The Emperor has no need for a consort. He already has a tigress of a wife. Who wants to be under another Empress's claws?'

'I wouldn't hand you over to be another man's—'

The steely sharpness of his tone startled her. What had he meant to say? Concubine? Lover? She froze just as she started to work off the second slipper. Li Tao took hold of her ankle to help her. The intimate touch sent a shudder through her. A rush of warmth travelled from his hand upwards until her face heated and she could barely breathe. This was what it meant to burn for someone.

'Gao wants you dead,' he said. 'You need the protection of someone like Shen.'

'Or you.'

'Yes.' Li Tao's hand remained on her, gripping her foot within his strong fingers. 'That was part of our bargain. I'll keep you safe as long as I can.'

'Our *bargain*,' she echoed.

'Which you are obviously no longer happy with.'

She could hear the strain in his voice as he fought to control his agitation. She didn't want that control. She needed to see what emotions he hid underneath, but he would never let go. Emotion was weak. It was without purpose.

'I don't have your way with words, Lady Ling, so tell me plainly what you want.'

He continued to touch her, belying his dark mood. He massaged the arch of her foot as he spoke, sending another web of sensation to tease her senses. Physicians taught that there were hundreds of pressure points in the foot, centres of pleasure and energy. Li Tao seemed to find each one.

'I want more.' She hated the note of desperation she heard there. It was hard to think when he was watching her so intently, yet caressing her with such tenderness, even while he was clearly unhappy with her tantrum. 'I want something more than the waiting and these few hours together.'

'There is nothing more.'

Her eyes narrowed and she shook her ankle free of his grasp.

He leaned back against the wall, resigned. 'I can see the Emperor's protection is no longer a suitable option for you.'

'Shen may be forced to order your execution. Do you think I want to be under his control?'

He frowned, but the wound she inflicted didn't give her as much satisfaction as she'd hoped. He took some time considering his next words and a small hope grew inside her.

'If you won't go to Shen, I can assign soldiers to protect you,' he began.

War. Still thinking of territory and battles. The disaster could be diverted, she had to believe that, but she couldn't make him see any differently, no matter what she did.

'I'll send you far enough away that the strife never comes to you. I can't afford to spare a single man, but I'll do it for you. You can spend the rest of your life with whatever wealth you need. Would that make you happy?'

She had never known the answer to that question. Suyin lay back down and dragged the cover up to her chin. 'All I want is to sleep right now. That would make me happy.' She squeezed her eyes shut.

Li Tao didn't move right away and she had to force herself to remain still, eyes closed, wondering with each heartbeat what he would do next. When he finally stood, she bit down on her lower lip to keep from sobbing. If he had moved into the bed and put his arms around her, she would have succumbed in a heartbeat. She would have forgotten this argument and buried her face against his chest. But she couldn't ignore the threat any longer.

He took a long time to leave, moving about the room. She heard the sounds of something heavy being dragged near the bed and couldn't resist peeking. Li Tao bent over a brazier, lighting the coals to warm the room for her. It must have been the influence of heartless women like Madame Ling that allowed her to keep from calling to him.

He straightened once the coals were smouldering and took hold of the lantern with one hand. 'Was it what happened this morning that has you upset?'

They weren't even battling on the same ground. He didn't understand her at all.

She rolled over and presented her back squarely to him, hip jutting in a sharp point in the air. The warmth of his kindness faded like morning fog in the sun. Every one of Li Tao's solutions ended with her being sent away. There could be no future for them, not in his mind. But that was what she wanted above all else, wasn't it? She needed to protect herself first.

She was indeed a heartless woman. But he was a witless man.

Chapter Fourteen

Li Tao took a moment to smooth out the folds of his tunic and straighten his sleeves with two sharp tugs before pulling his chamber door open. The unexpected presence of someone in the hallway elevated him to heightened awareness. He reached for the sleeve sword a moment before recognising Suyin's silhouette in the dim corridor.

'I had to rise especially early to catch you,' she said, oblivious of any danger. 'You usually leave before dawn.'

She wore a simple, unadorned blue-grey robe, and her hair had been pulled up into a loose knot. Her mouth remained soft and unpainted. She stood before him with a fresh openness that made her seem almost youthful. He wanted to draw her back into his chamber.

'I have given some thought into what you should give me—as my gift,' she added brightly.

'Your gift?' There had been no talk of anything of the sort.

'I want you to give me a day,' she continued. 'Today, actually.'

He folded his arms over his chest, in no mood to be charmed. 'They'll say I've been bewitched like the August Emperor, that I've forgotten all duty in my unnatural obsession with you.'

Her frown was immediate. 'What do you care about rumours?'

'Suyin.' He pinched at the spot between his eyes, willing the perpetual ache that had settled there to go away. 'Do you understand what is happening around us?'

'Of course I do. You'll be no match for Gao if you drive yourself to exhaustion.'

Thoughts of tactics and fortifications slipped from his mind as she pressed close to his side. The scent of jasmine and morning dew settled over him. If not for that baffling quarrel, he would have woken to her. They would have woken up to each other, but now he had to go.

'We should see each other in the daylight,' she coaxed. 'Not only in darkness like thieves.'

'Interesting way to say it.'

She curved her arm around his and urged him towards the courtyard, the look in her eyes unguarded and eager. He allowed himself to be led to the pavilion in the centre of the garden. The household lay in the last dregs of sleep before sunrise. He settled on to the bench and glanced up at her. Her skin shone with a pale brightness in the early morning. The crisp air brought a tinge of pink to her cheeks.

'I'll have tea prepared. Wait here.'

He watched her float to the kitchen, enjoying the infectious energy in her step. Her clear voice chimed from within and he imagined Cook's gruff reply. No one could resist Ling Suyin when she wanted her way.

She returned to sit across from him, folding her hands before her contentedly. For the moment, they sat regarding one another in the daylight, as she'd requested.

The excitement threatened to burst from her. 'I don't wish to be indoors at all today. We should see the bamboo forest, as much of it as possible.'

'I can't stay long,' he told her.

She went on regardless. 'Auntie tells me there are temples on the cliffs. And black-and-white *xióng māo* in the shade of the mountainside, feeding on the bamboo shoots.'

'They're very reclusive.'

'Like you.'

Her eyes sparkled as she teased him. Why this pleasantness now, when she couldn't stand the sight of him the night before? It would have made him wary, but he was too exhausted to be wary. At least of Suyin.

Cook brought the tray out to them himself, setting a plate of steamed buns on to the table. The old man arranged the cups and poured the tea, then nodded to them before shuffling back to his beloved kitchen.

She sipped at her tea while he watched, transfixed. There was always an effortless grace about her, especially in the most mundane of tasks.

'Auntie tells me this emerald tea is from Zhejiang. Good for increasing your energy and clearing your head.'

He lifted the cup and drank, barely tasting the steaming liquid. His head was anything but clear that morning. Suyin glanced at him over the rim of her cup and his chest clenched, a needle of pleasure piercing through.

'Every time I look at you, I discover something new to catch my attention,' he said.

No doubt she was accustomed to being scrutinised, so he was surprised when she blushed with pleasure. Her hands fluttered nervously as she pushed the dish of steamed buns closer to him.

'Please, eat.'

He picked at the bread, taking deliberate bites and chewing. She ate across from him in silence, her movements small and bird-like.

'You never share any meals with anyone,' she said. 'It's quite disturbing. I even once considered that I had made a bargain with a demon lover, like at the costume opera.'

The corner of his mouth lifted. 'You have an imagination.'

'But you are a man after all and not a demon.'

'We can share an occasional meal together, if you wish.'

He was content to sit back and let her fill the conversation with inane chatter. It gave him a momentary reprieve from thoughts of fortifications and the positioning of the troops along the Long River.

'You're thinking of what you would usually be doing right now,' she ventured. 'Riding out and seeing to your domain.'

'Yes.'

Her pleasant smile never wavered. 'You'd rather be doing that. This idleness is torturing you.'

He didn't answer. 'What did you want to discuss last night?' he deflected.

'Later, later. We have all day, do we not?'

Her form of persuasion was gently insistent. It disturbed him how much he wanted to indulge her. It lightened his spirit to see her smiling. Happiness was one emotion Suyin couldn't fabricate effectively, no matter how practised she was.

'Let us go before the sun is high.' She came to take his arm again as they stood, as if he'd escape if she didn't hold on to him. Her eyes were bright with excitement as she looked up, her impulsive energy almost child-like.

Reports indicated Gao had sent an envoy of five thousand men. Shen at least an equal number, perhaps greater. A bit more than one would expect for a peaceful diplomatic visit. They were only two weeks' march away.

He found himself nodding, conceding to her. All Suyin wanted was a day and they had few left between them.

The footpath cut deep into the bamboo grove, the air surrounding them damp and cool in the shade. Li Tao remained characteristically taciturn beside her. Every stone tormented her feet through the thin soles of her slippers, but she didn't want to complain. The path began to climb upwards and she couldn't remember the last time she'd walked for so long without stopping.

'Are we going far?' she asked mildly.

Li Tao looked back to where she had stopped. 'Do you need to rest?'

'A little while.'

Despite the coolness of the forest, she dabbed the perspiration from her forehead with her sleeve. The bamboo stalks climbed upwards until they disappeared to a point in the sky. Sunlight only pierced the forest in tiny pockets. The endless green was making her dizzy.

He came back to her side. 'I can carry you.'

She cast him a slanted look. 'You're leading me this way to torment me.'

The slight smile he gave was barely an answer, but he slowed his pace when they resumed walking. She took his arm again and this time his fingers curled around hers. Her chest shouldn't swell with happiness like it did, having him walk beside her as they spoke of nothing. In these moments, she almost glimpsed what it would be to sink comfortably into a life together. To be old and grey like Auntie and strolling through the garden on Li Tao's arm. To hear the laughter of grandchildren.

Whose dream had she borrowed? It couldn't have been her own.

They emerged on to a plateau overlooking the valley and the breath rushed out of her. The bamboo forest shimmered below, stretching outwards to touch the edge of the sky in the distance. The wind stirred the fronds in gentle waves. The slight rustle even sounded like water.

'A person almost could forget their sorrows here,' she murmured.

Li Tao came to stand beside her and, for the moment, they were the only people on earth beneath the sun and the clouds. She wished desperately for him to put his arms around her, but he kept his hands clasped behind him as he looked meditatively over the emerald sea. He was always so controlled. Only in the bedchamber did his restraint begin to crumble. His eyes would grow dark when he moved within her, falling closed only when the pleasure took them both. Her skin flushed so hot that she feared he could sense it through the space between them.

'What is that?' She pointed across the valley. A man-made structure interrupted the natural contour of the mountainside, partially hidden by the forest green.

'Observant,' he said with a note of admiration. 'There are watchtowers all along the cliffs. Guard houses, stockades.'

A numbness crept into her fingers. He revealed the information without reservation, without care. As if she were too insignificant to be a threat, or he no longer needed to hide his intentions. It certainly couldn't be that he trusted her. He presented a striking profile, his gaze fixed impassively on the distant cliffs. She searched the line of the ridge for the fortifications he spoke of.

'How many men do you command?' The words scratched against her throat.

He looked directly at her until she squirmed beneath his scrutiny. 'Old Gao has likely convinced the Emperor that I've raised an army of hundreds of thousands to oppose him.'

'But you have been building an army.'

When he didn't answer, she pushed on. 'You can't win like this.'

'I'm not so easy to kill, Lady Ling.'

'This is what Gao wants. On his terms.'

'Enough. This is not your battle.'

In other words, this was not her place. Li Tao wouldn't listen. He was a man of action, not words, and considered himself accountable to no one. In that way, he and Gao were very much alike. Her stomach sank with despair.

The more Li Tao built up his defences and withdrew from imperial scrutiny, the more his actions would incriminate him. All her knowledge meant nothing. Li Tao would never let her in.

'If you're so bent on war, why did you ask me to stay?' she asked in desperation.

'I wanted the nights.' His voice strained to near the breaking point. 'I wanted those hours with you.'

It was a generous admission from him—for Li Tao to admit he *wanted* anything—but she found no consolation there.

'A diversion,' she said bitterly. 'But now it's done.'

He caught her shoulders as she tried to go. 'It was a mistake to keep you here.'

A mistake. The pain bit deep before she could shield herself against it. She knew it was true, which made the pain worse. Someone had manipulated Li Tao to retrieve her. They were being compelled by unseen forces.

She twisted out of his grasp and moved back to the ridge to stare out over the bamboo sea, trying to recapture the sense of peace she'd had moments earlier.

'This is all we can have, Suyin.'

His words were a hollow echo of what he'd told her last night. *There could be no more.* She wasn't ready to accept it.

'It's always like this. First the August Emperor, and now you. Men only desire my company when the threat of death hangs over them.'

Li Tao came close enough for her to sense the heat from his body, so warm in contrast to the coolness of the forest. His arm closed around her waist, the other one about her shoulders to hold her against his chest, fitting her back. With a sigh, she sank against him and let his presence envelop her. He never embraced her in daylight, she realised.

'I see your face in front of me every moment of the day. I think of your skin, your voice, the way you taste.' His lips brushed against her hair. He held her even tighter. 'But this was always meant to end. It has to.'

She squeezed her eyes shut at the last part. She'd known his lover's words wouldn't be allowed to stand untouched. There was always bitterness to follow. He was convinced that they could not be, and Li Tao never backed down from his convictions.

He turned her in his arms so they could finally face each other. Without another word, he took her mouth with a kiss that only filled her with more longing, more doubt. His fingers curved over her hip possessively. She clutched at his robe and dragged him closer, as if he could be any closer. When they broke apart, he still wouldn't let go.

'You say these words. You insist on these things, but then you—' She struggled for words. 'There has to be a way.'

He rested his forehead against hers. The way he held her could be so deceptively tender. She still couldn't catch her breath and she didn't want to. She knew now, more than ever, that she couldn't lose him.

He kissed her again; this time his touch was rough and impatient. 'These men are more experienced than I at the art of war. At every step, I sense I'm making the wrong move, falling deeper into someone's plans.'

This was how she had felt in the palace, always fighting against the hold of powerful men and feeling that there was nothing she could do to be free of them. She'd felt that way with Gao and his minions. In a way, even Emperor Li Ming had imprisoned her to his will.

'You don't want to be a part of this,' he said.

'But I'm already a part of this.'

'No.' A single word. It rang as a final declaration. He ran a possessive hand along her spine. 'This was not part of our arrangement. I can't have you here.'

His black eyes claimed her completely even as he denied her. She cradled his face in her hands, running her fingers over the rigid line of his jaw, waiting for him to turn away, but he didn't. Though Li Tao would never admit it, she still had some hold over this indomitable man. For once, she didn't want to use this power for her own gain. She only wanted to find some way to help him. It wasn't enough for her to merely survive, to simply *exist* any longer.

Again she caught the phantom of a dream. The two of them, many years later, walking together. Li Tao was still tall and majestic beside her. His shoulders only bowed slightly with time, his hair grey. He had spoken once, and only briefly, of family, of a future. A legacy. She wished with all her heart those were things she could tempt him with.

'Perhaps the solution is beyond what you and I can accomplish alone,' she ventured.

He frowned at her, not comprehending. She was only starting to form the idea herself.

'What if you went directly to Shen? He doesn't want civil war. Humble yourself before him.' She knew nothing about battles and armies, but she knew men like Li Ming and Emperor Shen held themselves to a higher moral standard. 'Appear before Shen without your army, one man to another. Lay your sword at his feet and tell him that everything you do is for the sake of the empire.'

'Like a dog baring his throat for slaughter,' he scoffed.

'A grand gesture,' she argued.

'It's suicide.'

He let go of her abruptly, distancing himself from her as well as her counsel. His stark silhouette against the bamboo spoke of isolation and solitude. This was why Gao targeted him, the same reason the crafty governor had been able to use her while she was in the palace.

Li Tao was alone. He had no allies.

She wished she knew what he was thinking, but he had closed himself off. When he turned to tell her that they needed to go back, she had no argument. Suyin walked silently beside him down the trail. Around them, the forest chirped and clacked with life. Li Tao didn't look at her. He only barely slowed his stride to accommodate her smaller steps. She searched for something to say that wouldn't reveal her desolation.

He probably thought her mad to suggest he make himself vulnerable to his enemies, or perhaps he was finally convinced she was there to lure him to his death. She had no place preaching honour and sacrifice when she'd done unspeakable things for her own protection in the past. Experience had taught her what she needed to do to survive. That was all she had ever known, but she wanted more now. Even if it wasn't possible, she wanted.

Suyin didn't bother him for the rest of the day. To his surprise, she excused herself when they reached the manor. Li Tao returned to his study to wait for more reports. The battle lines were forming, the supply lines were ready. He called for his messengers and issued commands, but it was nothing more than moving pieces aimlessly on the board from one position to another.

War was coming upon him, fast and winding like a viper, but he wasn't afraid of death. He had bartered away his life long ago when the first knife had been thrust into his hands. As he watched Suyin disappear into the recesses of the house, he wondered what else he had given up.

Suyin continued to haunt him. She was so close. He could go to her at any moment, if he so desired. He stayed shut away on purpose, trying to work while he dreamed of her mouth exploring his skin. His hands fit around her waist so easily. He would lift her on to him. Watch her face as she sank on to him. Over him. It had only been one night without her in his bed. One long, empty night.

It was night once again when he finally extinguished the lanterns to return to his empty chamber. The bedroom door opened only moments after he had shut it. When Suyin stepped into the room, he was flooded with a feeling that bordered on gratitude.

By then, his hunger raged inside him and she looked so magnificent that he wanted to take her, hard against the floorboards as they'd done the first time. Holding back nothing. But she stood with hands clasped, her eyes full of questions.

He led her to the bed and let her hair down, running his fingers through the black silk. With reverent hands, he slid her dress from her shoulders, kissing each spot of smooth skin as it was revealed. Outwardly, he remained gentle. Inwardly, he wanted to devour her.

'You truly can lure a man to his ruin.' He let her hands roam over his shoulders. 'Seduce him into forgetfulness.'

'But that wasn't me,' she protested. 'It was all lies.'

'No, it wasn't.'

So many poems and paintings centred on Ling Suyin. None of them captured her essence. She could seduce men to madness without ever wielding her body. He brushed his lips over her eyelids, her cheek, and finally found her mouth. For a long, drawn sigh they did nothing but kiss. Her lips parted for him beautifully, allowing him to taste her, to take his fill. The questions were still there, unspoken. She'd withdrawn from him since their morning together. He could sense it in her hesitation now.

She wanted to know if this was the last time.

He had no answer. He stroked the graceful arch of her neck and trailed downwards to run his fingertip over the swell of her nipple. Her flesh peaked beneath his touch. Rewarding him with her response. He lowered her on to the bed, his arousal straining against his trousers.

'I'll go with you,' she offered.

He couldn't understand her meaning. The blood pulsed hot within him.

'To Emperor Shen,' she continued. 'We'll go together.'

'You'll stand by a traitor?' he asked harshly. 'That's senseless.'

She shook her head in vehement denial. Her arms curved around his shoulders to hold on to him and her soft breasts pressed against his chest. She was offering to put herself at risk. For him. He couldn't understand why, didn't want to think of what it meant. Not yet. He reached for the ties at his waist.

'This is my burden. There's nothing for you to do.'

Her lips found his throat and she tightened her arms around him. 'Please, Tao.'

She needed to stop speaking, to stop thinking of what came next. He could make her forget. A few strokes of his fingers against the tender cleft of her sex and she was ready for him. He slid himself into her, welcoming the arch of her body and the sweet sigh of surrender and acceptance he'd come to know so well.

Suyin closed her eyes at his penetration. When she tried to speak he kissed her hard, moving into her until all she could do was moan. He shut his eyes to listen to her impassioned cries and concentrated on the sweet, wet clasp of her body until he was consumed within it.

Chapter Fifteen

Suyin woke with a start, cursing at the empty spot beside her in the bed. She dressed in a rush and flew from the chambers to an unusual amount of activity at the front of the house. Her shoulders sank with relief when she saw that Li Tao hadn't left. He stood beside the stables, overseeing his men as they loaded packs on to their horses.

'Where are you going?' She moved to stand beside him, ignoring the chill of the morning air.

'You and I are going to see Emperor Shen.'

Her mouth fell open, unable to find words. She blinked at him as questions filled her mind. He inspected her from head to toe and her skin warmed beneath the thin robe she'd pulled on hastily.

'You'll need to change your clothing.'

Frowning, she folded her arms over her chest. He gave her nothing but a half-smile in grim enjoyment at her confusion. Too many questions hovered on her tongue. When had he decided? What had made him change his mind?

'I'll never understand you,' she said.

He guided her towards the house, keeping her close to his side. His warmth was more than welcome in the cool morning.

'It occurred to me, Lady Ling, that you have a history of surviving the worst of circumstances. I'd be wise to follow your lead.'

He was trying to make light of the situation, which only made her more nervous. 'I know Emperor Shen will listen to you. He must. He needs you.'

'I should let you speak then, as confident as you are of this plan.'

'Tell him everything you've done is for the sake of the empire. Don't be so stubborn. Admit your mistakes...' Her voice trailed off as she realised he was mocking her. 'Can't you pretend to be humble?'

He shook his head. Everything about him was so direct and uncompromising. No wonder Gao could spin his traps so easily. Imperial politics required a delicate balance of persuasion and intimidation. She didn't know that this was the right thing to do, but it had to be better than staying here to wait for death to march upon them.

They halted at the front hall. Finally alone, he turned to face her, cradling her cheek against his palm. She wanted to close her eyes and savour the caress.

'You know the danger of declaring your allegiance to me,' he said.

'I do.'

'I will not blindly surrender to Shen.'

Her heart plummeted at his warning. 'I know that as well.'

It was a great concession for him to consider negotiating with the Emperor, but Li Tao would stand behind his principles to the death. It was in his blood and nothing could change that about him. To approach the Emperor was a great risk, but for the first time in a long while, she dared to hope. Li Tao wasn't resigned to civil war and execution as she had feared. He was considering another way.

His face showed neither hope nor relief as he watched her. If anything, the tension had become more clearly etched in the lines around his eyes.

'See what power you have over me,' he said.

She tried not to be wounded by the bite of cynicism. 'The Emperor is an honourable man. Shen will be moved by your gesture of compromise.'

'I can still fulfil our bargain and relinquish you to Shen, as we agreed.' His jaw tightened even as he suggested it. 'You can stay clear of this conflict and go free.'

Li Tao was in an unpredictable position and his domain was the heart of danger. She would be reckless to stay, she couldn't ignore that. Survival was a matter she knew more than a little about. She'd always managed to choose the right side whenever the current changed within the imperial palace.

But what life did she have alone, running and hiding? She didn't have Changan any more or the mansion by the river that the late emperor had built for her. Li Tao, as calculated as he was, was willing to take a chance. She could be his equal beside him. She could try. Wasn't that what she was asking for, what she hadn't known how to ask for, just several nights ago?

And delicate politics was also a matter she knew more than a little about.

'Tao, let us be honest.' She took his arm. 'Our original agreement was an illusion. It means nothing any more.'

Li Tao was stepping into the unknown and doing it willingly, but he didn't like it.

It was like the first time he had taken a knife in his hands. He hadn't even known how to grip the weapon. It was like his first battle. It was worse. He was no longer a man with only his own life to lose.

If his negotiation with Shen failed, then it meant war for him and for the empire. Imperial and regional armies fighting and killing one another. The neighbouring kingdoms and the barbarian invaders of the west could simply wait for the empire to burn down its own house. Li Tao had come to realise that he didn't want that either.

Suyin was seated before him in the saddle. She was becoming more accustomed to the ride, no longer digging her nails into his arm. The best swordsmen of the first battalion rode at the flank and rear guard. They were safe within the borders of the province, but he couldn't guarantee anything beyond the barricades.

He'd been content to take orders under the rule of Emperor Li, but those were different times. The Emperor had given him command of the district and Li Tao had known nothing about how to govern, how to lead men, how to gain respect. He had studied warlords like Shen and Gao, but he'd always known that he couldn't mimic them. The August Emperor had needed a different sort of force. Li Ming had known about the balance of power and how it was so easily toppled.

They cleared the shade of the forest and Suyin tilted her face up to the sun to soak in the light.

'You look like you've been released from prison.' His arm tightened around her.

She leaned back against his shoulder and glanced at him through her lashes. 'I've seen nothing but the same rooms for days and days.'

It had been nearly a month since he'd first found her. 'You were content to stay by your river and wither away.'

'No longer. When we return, you should show me every corner of this province.'

Her tone was too bright, lacking in its usual fluid harmony. He'd come to expect more subtlety from Suyin. He moved his focus to the road ahead.

'Be assured of your success and you cannot fail,' she said quietly.

So they had become adept enough at reading each other's moods. She pressed close and he touched his chin to the top of her head in silent acknowledgement.

This venture was not at all assured. He would meet Shen face to face, without soldiers and courtiers, if Shen would even allow it. Suyin was asking him to rely on the Emperor's sense of honour and sentiment. He'd criticised Shen for those very same traits. Honour and sentiment were unpredictable.

Their first stop was an instalment of soldiers positioned at the crossroads. A guard station had been built to provide rudimentary shelter for the men. The structure stood out as an ominous reminder that the roads winding through the province were no longer open to all.

After a short rest, they rode on.

* * *

By night-time, they reached an encampment outfitted by a thousand soldiers. A span of tents swept through the clearing and the men milled about around the crackling bonfires. This was the Rising Guard, the specially trained warriors of Li Tao's first battalion.

Suyin scanned the barracks. 'They're waiting for battle, aren't they?'

'I need them centralised so they can move quickly.'

'There are so many…'

'This is not even a fourth of my army.'

She twisted around to face him. 'Gao has accused you of raising an army to challenge Changan.'

'Half of which is true.'

He dismounted, then settled his hands around her waist to lift her from the saddle. He could see her questions taking shape, but he shook his head once, sharply. Suyin clamped her mouth shut.

'Good decision,' he murmured close to her ear before ordering the men to ready a tent for the night

She aimed a piercing look at him. 'Later,' she promised.

This was not the time to question his authority, but he was certain she would interrogate him until dawn when she had the chance. He left her with his head guardsman and went to inspect the camp. He trusted her opinion on matters of the court. For now, she would have to trust him when it came to commanding an army.

When he finally retired to his tent, Suyin was seated on the cot that constituted a bed in the field. A lantern flickered beside it.

'Your bodyguards wouldn't allow me outside.'

She held herself with slender shoulders pulled back regally. Her hands were folded over one knee. Elegant to her very fingertips, even in these less than luxurious surroundings.

He refrained from going to her. 'Women are a rare sight in camp.'

'Would I really have anything to fear amongst your disciplined soldiers?'

'No.' He was certain of that. 'But why torment them needlessly?'

The way every glimpse of her tormented him. Each time they parted, the reunion was always like this. A small bit of diplomacy exchanged to renegotiate the terms between them. He was in complete control. She was a glorious and mysterious woman. He was not in complete control. His heart took a running leap, falling just a drop faster. Rising just a bit more.

'Your army must be tens of thousands. Large enough to challenge the Emperor,' she said.

'That would be rash. An attack against imperial forces would only incite the other warlords.'

'That wasn't what I was asking.' There was more sadness than accusation in her tone.

He went and seated himself beside her. 'Only the strong survive amongst the *jiedushi*. Gao has been looking to the south for years, gradually poisoning the court with rumours. I knew I had to strengthen my hold. If I wasn't a threat, then I would have been destroyed long ago.'

Her knee brushed against his leg as she turned to him. He still couldn't absorb the incongruity of having this enchanted creature here with him, among the dusty barracks.

'Don't you see? Gao pushed you to this,' she insisted. 'You played into the rumours.'

'There was nothing that could be done for that. Gao's family is of noble birth, intermarried with the imperial line in past generations. He's always shunned those of the lower class who were elevated in rank.'

'You're wrong.' She shook her head for emphasis. 'Perhaps some of the other warlords feel that way, but not Gao. The reason is never personal for him. He's very much like you, in that respect.'

His eyes found hers. 'You seem to know much about Gao.'

A look of pain crossed her face and she started to make her escape, but he caught her gently. As gently as she would allow.

'Do you think I would turn you away because of a past association?' His arms closed around her. 'I know you were somehow associated with Gao. It's not unexpected, the way alliances are made and broken within the court.'

But now she was by his side. His.

Suyin finally ceased struggling and he lowered her on to the mattress of rugs and furs, laying himself alongside her. The discussion about Gao had stolen away her poise.

She lay stiff in his arms. 'I escaped from Gao's grasp long ago. He hoped to use me when I became the Emperor's favourite. But I freed myself. I found a protector more powerful than Gao. I escaped.'

And now, years later, Gao wanted her dead. Anger flowed hot through his veins. Suyin was wrong. His reasons could be very personal.

'Gao won't ever come near you again,' he vowed.

'He uses others to achieve his goals. He never acts himself.' Her voice sounded drained, listless. She blinked up, focusing on nothing in particular. 'It's madness to go to Shen, but it's madness not to. I'm not certain this was the right path.'

'I don't know either,' he said after a pause.

The men who served him were loyal, steadfast and followed orders impeccably. Suyin was the only person who ever questioned him without fear. She had made him realise that there was no way to win if he stayed in the south, barricaded in a defensive position. He'd defeat Gao's first wave, only to be attacked by imperial forces as well as the other warlords who would swoop in like vultures for their share of the kill.

Gao was too powerful. Li Tao needed to do something unexpected to challenge him.

Suyin turned in his hold to nestle against his shoulder, and he pushed the thoughts of war to the corners of his mind. He fought these battles in his head all day and in his dreams. These moments of peace were his only luxury.

'Tao, what made you change your mind?'

'Isn't it clear?' His hand trailed a soothing path along her spine.

'No,' she whispered mournfully. 'No, it's never clear with you.'

He didn't know what else she demanded. He shifted and took her face in his hands, kissing her with his lips pressed earnestly to hers.

She broke away. 'You'll never say the words.'

His muscles wound tight, as if he was readying himself for impending battle. He didn't have an answer for her.

He kissed her again with a growing urgency, tasting her as she opened herself to him. He'd make love to her if he could. They could lose themselves in each other. The roughness of the bed would fade quickly.

But the warmth didn't quicken into passion as it always did between them. Gradually Suyin sank against him, too exhausted to stay awake. He was weary as well. The day had been full of changes. Instead of removing her clothes, he brushed back her hair and pressed his lips to her forehead. Her breathing had grown heavy and he imagined she was already asleep.

Chapter Sixteen

The city of Chengdu stood on the bank of the Jin River, which divided the southern province from the central empire. A sturdy wall of grey brick and mortar enclosed the provincial capital. Within the gates, the streets were paved and rows of buildings lined either side of the crowded avenues.

It had been a long time since Suyin had been around so much activity. The babble of the crowd left her dizzy and disoriented. The military installations had increased as they travelled closer, yet the citizens of Chengdu wandered through the markets buying and bartering as usual.

Li Tao handed the reins to one of the bodyguards and they continued through the streets on foot. 'Wang told me you barely ate last night.'

Wang, the head guardsman, had been tasked with taking vigilant care of her

'All I wanted to do was sleep,' Suyin said.

'I forget that you're not accustomed to such travel.'

'I am not helpless.'

The reply came out more abruptly than she intended. She wasn't helpless, but she was weary. Suyin wasn't used to riding on horseback the entire day. She wasn't used to riding at all. At night, they slept at roadside inns or in tents that were hastily erected at sundown. The gruelling routine drained the last of her strength. The continued uncertainty drained the last of her patience.

Li Tao directed the party towards the busiest thoroughfare to search for a tavern. He ignored her protests and insisted on a proper meal before heading to the river crossing. Soon they would be in imperial territory, outside his jurisdiction.

'I didn't expect to be so tired,' she said, her tone conciliatory.

'You'll feel better after eating.'

She took his arm and he surprised her by resting his hand against the small of her back, urging her closer just so. Such a subtle suggestion of possession, of intimacy. He was being uncommonly attentive. She forgot the thick of the crowd and the armed men on every side of them. For this moment, she floated content.

The simple affection in his touch hinted at something she hadn't felt before in all of their heated nights. Perhaps there could be peace. There could be happiness like this, side by side.

His bodyguards surrounded them, taking positions at the front and back. Her uncertainty returned. Li Tao had become more withdrawn as they neared the capital, so much so that the mere touch of his hand brought forth all of her hidden longing. He had never mentioned anything as ephemeral as happiness. Li Tao only spoke to her of survival.

They needed to be free of Gao before there could be any peace. She had bested the old warlord once before, but that was another era, another emperor. And her victory had only been temporary.

A set of red and green banners hanging from the second floor marked the restaurant almost as clearly as the spiced scents floating from the open windows. Li Tao guided her inside.

'Governor, welcome!'

The proprietor recognised Li Tao right away. He ushered them to the upper floor, spouting a list of the kitchen's specialties as they climbed the stairs. On the ground floor, a group talking loudly in the corner hushed as they passed by. A thread of tension spun from guardsman to guardsman.

'Rumours about Ru Shan,' Li Tao explained when she looked to him.

She didn't expect to hear that name again. 'But you released him.'

From behind them she heard Wang and the others conferring. The word 'traitor' emerged from the murmuring.

Li Tao guided her upwards. 'It's nothing. A minor concern.'

But his gaze turned inwards. Ru Shan's release was another decision she had coerced upon him, against Li Tao's judgement. Was he regretting his show of mercy?

A private banquet room awaited them at the top of the staircase. Servants appeared with trays of wine and tea, eager to serve before the party was even settled. Li Tao seated her beside him and Wang stayed close. The threat of danger was always present. Suyin was never allowed to forget that.

She waited until the servers left before speaking. 'Will we continue with only your guards?'

Li Tao smiled ruefully. 'You advocated a grand gesture, Lady Ling.'

'Perhaps a few more men would be appropriate.'

'Marching a sizeable army against Changan would look like an open challenge, would it not? We'll join a small escort at the crossing.'

She nodded, but a sick feeling curdled her stomach. The forces of Shen and Gao were closing in on them like the two claws of a black scorpion. These men led armies in the thousands and tens of thousands while she knew nothing about warfare. Yet she had directed Li Tao into the path of danger.

'I've sent messengers ahead to notify Shen of our intentions,' he said.

'I imagine that the illustrious *Emperor* Shen would respect an appeal for peace.'

'*Emperor* Shen,' Li Tao corrected himself with some distaste.

Suyin had to remind him of such nuances. Any offence would be scrutinised and worked over by the court until it resembled high treason. If anything, she believed that Li Tao held a begrudging respect for Shen. If she could only guide him when he stood before the Emperor, but Li Tao wouldn't be schooled and controlled. Not the way she'd allowed herself to be controlled when she had lived in the palace.

An arrangement of cold plates was brought before them. The proprietor himself took the dishes from the serving trays to place them on to the table.

'Please enjoy,' he urged.

Suyin lifted a set of wooden chopsticks from the bamboo container. It had been fifteen years since she'd been in a public place, sitting out in the open. She was stunned by the novelty of it: the diners in their drab grey-and-brown clothing, the scrape of the dishes, the worn edges of the tables. Every detail took on an uncustomary significance.

Li Tao was looking down at her curiously. A smile formed on her lips.

'You wouldn't understand,' she said.

But perhaps he did understand. Li Tao had lived his own sheltered existence for so long. Something inside him had reached out to her, long before they could speak so freely. She still hadn't found the right words to penetrate the armour around him.

She started to comment about the ordinary becoming remarkable, but a sharp, frantic knocking came from outside.

'Governor!'

The conversation in the banquet room halted. Li Tao continued drinking his tea, but he edged closer to her. His shoulders raised slightly, muscles tensed. Two of the guardsmen moved to the door and opened it. Li Tao glanced briefly at the new arrival before beckoning him forwards with a curl of his fingers.

The messenger bowed as he entered. His clothes were covered with dust. 'Governor Li,' he greeted. The man appeared haggard, as if he'd ridden a great distance. He looked uncertainly at her.

Li Tao confirmed with a short nod. His men were so attuned to Li Tao that his commands were expressed with the most efficient of gestures, no effort wasted.

'We've captured a group of men attempting to slip past the western barricade,' the messenger reported.

'And?'

He looked uncertain. 'They'll speak only to you.'

Apprehension filled the room. She couldn't comprehend the

unspoken signals between them, but there was obviously danger—danger and something more insidious.

She touched her hand to Li Tao's arm. 'Who are these men?'

'I don't know, but there's more.' His expression grew cold, unreadable.

The messenger bowed again, almost an apology. He took a letter from the fold of his tunic and placed it on to the table. Li Tao read it in the stark silence of the room.

'Why was this not given to me sooner?'

More silence. Finally the messenger, whom Suyin surmised had to be one of Li Tao's trusted men, spoke in a lowered tone.

'It was taken and suppressed by Governor Chou.'

A muscle ticked along Li Tao's jaw. He regarded her for a long time before he finally spoke. 'Lady Ling, it seems we must put a stop to our journey.'

A feeling of dread stopped her breath. 'We have to go to the Emperor before it's too late.'

Li Tao had a way of turning away from her when he absolutely would not answer. The gesture was final, the decision was made. He did it now.

'Tao, you must reconsider.'

She could talk until her mouth ran dry and it wouldn't move him, but she had to try. She wanted to stand and order the men from the room. She would demand to see that letter and insist that Li Tao listen to reason. This was their one chance, the one time he'd given her his trust, at least enough to take her counsel.

But he didn't give her another opportunity. He took hold of her arm, not cruelly, but without any warmth. They stood and he pulled her close as he led her back through the streets. The guards parted the crowd before them and they moved past the shops at a determined pace. Li Tao's grip on her was no longer reassuring.

The horses were ready and waiting for them by the city gate. Wang and half of the guards separated from the others. Hope dwindled inside her. The men knew. They already knew and she didn't.

'What's happening, Tao?'

The patient, indulgent lover of the morning was gone. He was now the warlord who expected his orders obeyed. 'You will be returned to the bamboo sea.'

'Whatever this is, your men can handle it,' she insisted. 'You must go to the Emperor.'

He was already shaking his head before she finished. 'It's not safe for you here…with me.'

She wanted to shout at him that nowhere was safe. They had discussed how important this was. This was Li Tao's last chance to fight the accusations of treason. War would follow if he didn't appeal to Shen. Death would follow.

'Tell me,' she implored, trying to command him the way he commanded his men. With will alone.

A look of pain crossed his face, or was it anger? She would never be able to read Li Tao. He always warded her away, building the barriers higher and stronger.

'There are soldiers,' he told her. 'A regiment heading for the provincial border in advance of the approaching armies.'

'Imperial soldiers?'

Li Tao didn't respond. He led her to where Wang waited astride a horse and lifted her up behind the head bodyguard.

'Please, think carefully about what you're about to do.' She grabbed on to Li Tao's wrist when he tried to let go of her. 'Gao Shiming wants this. He wants to prevent you from meeting Shen.'

His eyes met hers one final time. The emptiness behind his gaze chilled her. All her charm and grace and persuasiveness meant nothing. They were strangers again.

'There's a man in this city I need to see to,' he said.

The statement was not quite directed at her. There was no more time for questions. Wang directed the horse towards the gate just as Li Tao's soldiers assembled behind him, disciplined and ready. The last thing she saw was Li Tao stalking toward the city centre with sword drawn.

Li Tao rode down the dirt path with his personal guards beside him. It had only taken a day to secure the provincial capital. His men had surrounded the administrative offices and wrested control with hardly a fight. The fight would come later. Another day to have the prisoners brought to him so he could learn exactly why they'd come. More days and more hours to organise his troops.

Once the capital was under his control, he headed back to the bamboo forest. They switched horses frequently at relay stations to travel as fast as possible. The days and hours were in short supply; every minute carried countless demands.

The mansion emerged through the forest. He should have sent a messenger. Wang could have been trusted to carry out his orders, but Li Tao came in person anyway. There was no doubt in his mind about why.

Suyin emerged before the entrance like a goddess in blue silk. She paused at the top of the steps with the stone guardians framing either side of her. Again he sensed the echo of that first hunger of his youth, but stronger this time. Suyin had grown into her power and beauty. It hurt to look at her. The ache of wanting.

A woman like that could convince a man of anything. He'd allowed her to convince him that there was one last chance for peace. He'd wanted to believe so much that he'd been weak with it. She'd wanted to believe as well.

He chose his words carefully as he approached. Nothing soft and flattering came to mind. There was only hard truth.

'There will be no meeting with Shen,' he said.

She paled, then took a steadying breath. 'Come inside.'

Auntie and the servants were gathered in the front parlour. She went to Auntie first and squeezed her wrinkled hand. 'See, he's alive.'

The old woman nodded. At Suyin's quiet instruction, Auntie took the others back into the recesses of the mansion.

Suyin turned to him once they were alone. 'We all were frightened for you when you didn't return.' She was feeling her way around him, hesitant.

'There was an important matter I needed to see to.'

'You must be tired. Cook has supper prepared.'

He shook his head in a flash of anger. They just did not have the time any more. Not for simple pleasantries. Not for indecision. Not for this game of power and desire they always played.

'Come with me,' he said with a roughness that only revealed his anger, but none of the rest. None of the bitter disappointment. None of the faint hope that was now gone.

She took his hand and the cool touch of her skin soothed him beyond comprehension, but he denied the comfort she offered. He needed to remain alert, honed. He tightened his grip as he led her down the corridor to his study. They were barely inside before he shoved the door closed and dragged her into his arms.

Her breath caught as his mouth found the delicate skin of her throat. She shuddered, arching her neck to give him more. His arms tightened desperately around her. He wasn't being gentle, but Suyin knew he wasn't a gentle man.

Li Tao anchored his hips against her. He wanted to lift her in his arms and take her there, against the wall. He would lock her away and lie with her until neither of them could stand.

Suyin wrapped her arms around his neck. 'Tell me everything.'

Her voice cut through the grip of desire. The tension drained way and he let himself just hold her. Soft curves and jasmine perfume surrounded him. Suyin always managed to penetrate deep to the soft, vulnerable organs hidden inside. It was too tempting to keep her near him. Tempting and dangerous.

'It was Gao. One of his regiments has slipped in close while the provincial governor withheld the reports. The messengers I sent to Shen were also stopped.'

He'd always ignored Chou as a harmless, gutless bureaucrat, but his counterpart wasn't as worthless as he'd thought.

'I stripped Chou of any authority so he can no longer be a nuisance.'

She stiffened against him. 'You've wrested control of the entire province.'

Suyin's tone was full of regret. Li Tao had none. He'd spent over a year building an army for this moment. All lesser obstacles had to be removed to prepare for the greater threat.

'My soldiers protect this district and keep it safe from invaders. This province was always under my control.'

He could see how she rebelled against his claim of authority. What would she suggest now? More peaceful discussion? It was much too late for that.

'Was the governor allied with Gao?' she asked.

'He was simply not allied with me. He wanted to make that clear to anyone who would question it.'

His hold tightened around her waist. The silk of her robe slid wondrously beneath his hands. She smelled so good. War was all but upon him, but he insisted on taking just this moment.

Li Tao didn't have a moment to waste on anything but the defence of the province, but he was still right to come back. He'd needed to see her and to hear her voice. And he'd needed something else.

He lifted his head to catch her gaze. 'Tell me why Gao wants you dead.'

She paused, breath held back. Still hiding. 'I don't know.'

'Suyin.' His tone carried a hint of warning.

'I've been trying to figure out why since I came here. I truly don't know.'

'The men we captured were messengers. Gao wants a meeting.'

'A meeting?' A hundred thoughts flickered across her face. 'He must want to negotiate a deal with you directly.'

'That will never happen.'

Li Tao couldn't attack Gao's troops directly. That would be the last evidence the old warlord needed of Li's defiance. Yet Gao had made a move to circle around the imperial forces in order to arrive early. Li Tao had miscalculated. Gao wanted something else besides bringing him down.

'I need to know everything about Gao, starting with why he sent men after you. Gao wanted you dead and someone else wanted you alive.'

'I have no loyalty to Gao. You believe that, don't you?'

She blinked up at him, her eyes wide and vulnerable. Involuntarily, his hand tightened around her waist. He'd already risked too much for her. He might be foolish enough to risk even more, but he wanted to know what he was facing. He wouldn't be ambushed in a blind alley.

'Tell me everything,' he demanded softly.

He guided her to a chair and relinquished his hold on her to face her. She smoothed her robe over her knees. Elegant, graceful, biding her time. He waited.

She managed a small, mournful smile. 'So now you're my interrogator?'

When he refused to be charmed, her shoulders sank. 'Gao was the one who discovered me in Luoyang.' She exhaled slowly, with some effort. 'He brought me before the August Emperor.'

'You were under Gao's control from the beginning.'

She flinched. Her lips parted to deny it, but she couldn't. 'It would be easy to think that all of this was part of a larger plan, an intricate plot. I was only fifteen. I knew nothing about emperors or palaces. Gao came with a party one night to the pavilion. I didn't know who he was, but Madame Ling fawned over him. He came back the next evening alone to watch me from the other side of the curtain.

'My hands trembled so badly, I could barely play. I sensed he was a man of influence. That night he paid to be able to look at me with the curtain pulled back.'

His knuckles clenched. 'Only to look?'

She nodded quickly before continuing. 'The next night Gao came back with a note for five hundred *taels* of silver and ushered me into a litter headed to the imperial palace. Madame was happy to comply. Her fame in the pleasure district would be immortal.'

'Gao thought your beauty would easily capture Li Ming's heart.'

She stared down at her hands. 'Gao always thought he owned me, but even with all of the warlord's manipulations, the Emperor never called me to his bedchamber. I became worthless to him.'

Li Tao struggled to remain dispassionate as he listened to the explanation. Suyin had done what was necessary to survive. He'd done the same.

'What did Gao tell you to do?' he asked.

A hand fluttered nervously to her throat. She swallowed. 'I didn't want to be noticed. I tried to disappear. I was only one pretty face among hundreds. You've heard the stories, haven't you? Of concubines being pushed into wells, strangled by eunuchs, slaughtered by jealous emperors.'

For every ten poems speaking of the virtues and graces of the Emperor's concubines, there was one tale of sorrow.

'You still haven't told me anything that would cause Gao to come after you,' he said, his voice hard, his heart harder. He had to remember how clever she was. Suyin had risked her life by agreeing to go with him before Shen, yet she still kept her secrets.

'Please, come sit, Tao.'

She gestured to the place beside her, but he didn't comply. He moved around to sit down in the chair opposite her, where they could remain eye to eye. After a pause, she withdrew and sat with her hands curled together in her lap, acknowledging the small defeat.

'Beautiful women are so very expendable to men of power,' she remarked lifelessly.

The accusation wounded him when he should have been impervious, but he revealed nothing. He merely stared at her, willing her to continue.

'I could describe schemes against the throne, against other warlords, against you.' Suyin pierced him with a glance. 'Sometimes it was as simple as a small remark to the Emperor or finding a bit of information that Gao wanted. I would later discover that someone had been exiled from court, or even executed. Did I cause these things to happen? I don't know.'

'Tell me everything.'

She looked up, surprised at how he mirrored her words. 'I murdered the Empress,' she said quietly.

'What?'

'I killed her. And her child.' Suyin wrapped her arms tight in front of her to keep from shaking. Her eyes filled with tears. 'Not because she threatened me or because I held any ill will towards her. I did it because I was alone and I was weak.'

Chapter Seventeen

Imperial Palace—ad 743
16 years earlier

It was a misconception that castration rendered the palace eunuchs effeminate and passive. Yao, the Empress's eunuch, held the knife to Suyin's throat with more viciousness than any man.

'Do you understand, whore?' The high pitch of his speech chilled her spine.

She gave the tiniest of nods, biting her lip to hold back a sob of fear. Two months in Changan and she already knew the palace of dreams for what it was: a gilded nest of snakes. And now she didn't have Madame Ling to protect her. The den mother's motives had been callously self-serving, but Madame had needed her and had kept her safe in the pleasure district of Luoyang.

Yao had stolen into her room in the dead of night to threaten her. The eunuchs were given access to the women's court as if the only danger a man could pose was between his legs.

He hissed his orders in a harsh whisper as she scrambled up from her sleeping pallet. She passed a hand over her throat as she dressed in the dark, the press of the knife looming oppressively over her.

'Take this.' At the door he placed a cup into her hands. Then he waved the knife in front of her face and pointed across the quarter.

Yao had made himself clear. She would bring the brew of herbs to the Empress. Suyin could not protest that this was not her duty. She was a chosen concubine by title and not a servant, but once the women had learned a woman of the evening had wiled her way into the Emperor's court, it became a harem pastime to heap a mountain of trivial abuses on her, the punishment of a thousand cuts.

The lanterns were lit in the Empress's palace at the south end of the women's quarters. Suyin hurried through chamber after chamber with the eunuch at her heels.

The Empress lay reclined inside her private apartment, her face nearly as pale as her sheer nightdress. She glanced up and frowned. The palace touted the Empress as a great beauty, but whenever Suyin looked upon her, her face was always twisted into a sneer of displeasure.

'Empress, to your health.' She held the cup with outstretched arms and bowed her head low.

The Empress winced in discomfort. Her hand rubbed absently over the rounded swell of her stomach. The unborn child she carried was said to cause her turmoil quite often in the late hours of the night. The fortune tellers crooned that this meant she carried a restless baby boy who would be eager to challenge the world.

The Empress rubbed a hand over her throat and squeezed her eyes shut to fight off a wave of sickness. 'She doesn't have the sense of the lowliest of attendants,' she said in disgust.

'You must drink before the Empress,' the eunuch snapped.

A chill raced down her spine. The Empress glared at her impatiently. Yao nudged her in warning. The knife was out of sight, but she knew it was there, waiting for her.

The Empress's eunuch was highly regarded in the palace. If she tried to expose Yao, she would be the one they hanged. With stiff arms, she closed her eyes and lifted the cup to her mouth. The bitter brew slipped past her lips and she forced it down her throat.

The Empress held out her hand. 'Be gone from here.'

She stared at the Empress's belly as she handed the cup over. As soon as the Empress bent to drink, she couldn't hold back.

'Empress,' she choked out in alarm.

Even though the jealous Empress had been the worst of her antagonists, she had to try to warn her, as one woman to another.

But Yao grabbed her before she could speak. 'The Empress is tired. Leave her.' He made sure she could feel the tip of the knife through his sleeve before he shoved her towards the door.

Suyin ran. The poison swam black though her veins. She knelt in the damp moss of the garden and forced a finger down her throat until she coughed and retched into the dirt. Her heart raced with fear. Had the poison already crept too far into her? She had only taken a small swallow of it.

She had to go to someone about what she knew. As she dragged herself to her feet, she realised with a growing emptiness that there was no one. Yao had singled out the one girl who had no friends, no allies. He held enough influence in the palace to ensure her silence.

With a sick heart, she crawled back to her pallet and curled into a tight ball. Within the hour, sharp, needlepoint stabs racked her stomach. She was dying, dying alone and lost in the hidden compartments of the palace. Her ghost would never be able to find its way home.

Wicked nightmares descended on her. Yao chased after her with his knife. If the poison didn't kill her, he would. But death didn't take her, as she deserved. She emerged from her sickness to find the women's court in chaos.

The Empress's body had been found that morning on the floor of the Temple of Spirits. She had dragged herself there in the night, as if seeking protection in her last moments. The eunuch Yao was discovered hanging from the rafters of his bedchamber with a rope pulled tight around his neck.

Li Tao sat across from her. His hands were curved over his knees as he stared, unmoving. The dragon ring gleamed upon his second finger. He had been charged to destroy the emperor's enemies and show no mercy. That was how he had gained favour.

His gaze was calculating now, starved of passion. Without any of the warmth she had come to know. She had earned a measure of trust on the journey to the capital, but it was spent now. She had lost him. Somehow, that made it easier to speak.

'Gao gave the order to the chief eunuch. He wanted the Empress dead and I did nothing to stop it.'

'Suyin—'

A deep line creased his brow. Her vision was too blurred with tears to tell if it was concern or anger. Or horror. She recoiled when Li Tao reached for her. Her pulse raced and her stomach twisted into vicious knots, sickened by all that she had seen. The memories refused to be denied. At times, the images would fade, but the debt always remained. Stones upon a scale. She had to be done with this.

'I was Gao's puppet,' she confessed. 'I had no one to go to in the palace. At times he wanted me dead, and then he would seem to protect me. I could never predict what would happen next.'

Li Tao closed his arms around her, pulling her to her feet. He insisted on dragging her against him. Impossible man.

'So many people were implicated in the Empress's death, but never me.' She forced herself to face him. 'Never the Emperor's precious consort.'

The warmth of his body wrapped around her, but she didn't deserve the comfort. He attempted to stroke her hair while she struggled in his hold like a trapped fox. Still he held on, his arms a steel cage around her until she tired.

His voice was low and close. 'I'm not going to hurt you.'

She squeezed her eyes shut and sank against him. 'When you first came to the river, I thought you knew. I thought you had come to fulfil your vow to the August Emperor. You were charged with hunting down all the conspirators.'

He stiffened against her. His chest rose and fell against her cheek and she held her breath as the knowledge filled him. There had been such disorder in the palace over those days. The only one who had seen her enter the Empress's quarters in the middle of the night had been the chief eunuch. Suyin never knew whether he'd taken his own life or Gao had him killed. She was certain Gao would have her killed as well, but he'd let her live to use her.

'You were forced,' Li Tao said finally. 'And Emperor Li is dead. That era is gone.'

'But you were always so loyal.'

'I'm anything but loyal.'

There was such a fearful beauty in his harsh features. His gaze held fire and unspoken determination. He was a puzzle she would never resolve. She had exposed her most guarded secret, but he gave nothing in return.

'Why are you still fighting so hard to maintain balance?' she asked.

'Because it is the only way the empire will survive.'

'You truly believe that?'

'Yes.'

His hands strayed down her back and she flushed beneath his touch, her body moulding to him. She considered urging him to leave this losing battle. The empire was vast and they could hide away and live out their lives as they pleased, as she'd once tried to do. But he would never agree. Li Tao believed in duty, if not honour.

She traced the edge of his tunic. The first time she'd dared to touch him after her confession. 'You and Emperor Shen are more alike than you know. Everything with you is black and white. You can't defeat Gao like that.'

He released her, but remained close. 'Gao wants a meeting between us. I already know he wants me to join with him against Shen. There would be no need for secrecy otherwise.'

'That was never Gao's way.' She exhaled, trying to dispel her memories of palace conspiracies and all the old fear in one breath. 'Gao would rather employ his network of spies and connections within the capital than risk open rebellion.'

His mouth twitched in what was almost a smile. 'Perhaps you can be useful against Gao after all.'

She knew more about Gao. Those plots seemed insignificant compared to the Empress's murder, but woven together they formed a pattern of treachery.

'I can go with you—'

'I don't want Gao anywhere near you,' he interrupted. 'There is nothing for me to discuss with him. I'll meet Shen and Gao's forces directly. Gao can voice his accusations out in the open.'

'We can still send a message to the Emperor.'

'It's too late.'

Once Li Tao had decided, he became immovable. Suyin wanted to believe he could face both of the approaching armies and prevail, but there were dark shadows beneath his eyes. Li Tao had been forced to the edge of a cliff. The conflict was wearing him down.

If they could have reached Emperor Shen sooner, he could have denied Gao's accusations. She would have used every skill in her, every bit of diplomacy she'd learned, to defend him. But Shen wouldn't come down to Chengdu himself. He would send some subordinate who would be easily manipulated by Gao.

'Everything will happen quickly now. I'll return to Chengdu tomorrow. The border fortifications are in place. Gao will know when I don't go to him that the negotiations are over.' He spoke plainly. No emotion to obscure what was inevitable. Then he paused. 'I shouldn't have even come here.'

'Why did you?' She pressed her palm against his chest and watched it rise and fall.

'You know.'

She didn't know anything. All she had was hope and only a thin thread remained. She listened to the beat of Li Tao's heart against her, not quite in rhythm with hers. She wished she did know something valuable, something that could actually hurt Gao and put the power in her hands for once. But she searched through her past and found nothing.

Gao could bring about an empress's death and go unpunished. The warlord had enough power and influence to bend the court to his will. She was nothing but an emperor's ruse, created to allow a dying man to rule a little longer. Only Li Tao had the strength to challenge Gao openly. For that, Gao would destroy him.

She lifted her fingertips to his face, running them gingerly along his sharp cheekbones, the thin scar. He didn't look away as she pulled him towards her. She brushed her lips over his. At first he didn't respond, but finally his hands curved around her and he closed his eyes, letting her lead.

He was always so direct and demanding. In contrast, she savoured the contours of his mouth, their breath joining delicately. They didn't have time any more, but they could create the illusion. They could explore one another and stretch out the hours of the night as far as they would allow.

And while he kissed her, she willed herself not to waste any time questioning him, issuing demands that neither of them could fulfil. She knew that Li Tao had already made his decision. What she didn't know, was what that decision was.

Li Tao returned to the study in the still hours that night. He navigated the corridors without need for light. His eyes were still trained to gauge the shadows and dim edges of space after all these years.

At the desk, he lit an oil candle and set it down beside the ink stone. The pool of light fell over the papers as he worked with quiet efficiency, grinding the ink, opening the empty pamphlet to begin his missive. The characters flowed out in tight columns from the tip of his brush, as unembellished as the orders they contained.

He never knew why Lao Sou had taken the time to teach him these things when all he was meant for was one kill on a faraway battlefield. Not all members of the *An Ying* clan were so carefully tutored.

He considered Suyin's proposal. He could denounce Gao, but it would be his word against the senior warlord. The truth mattered little when Gao had the support of the noble families and lesser generals.

The whisper-soft fall of slippered feet interrupted his thoughts. Suyin's silver voice curled around him. 'You never rest.'

'There's much to do.'

She came into the halo of light and he feasted with his eyes. It had been too many days without the sight of her. Unbound hair against cream-smooth skin. A slip of blue silk moulded to her curves like water. He was already hard. His body didn't know or care that he couldn't keep her with him.

'I've never slept much,' he recalled. 'In Luoyang, I could wander the ward all night and not be tired. I would sleep in the hour or so before dawn and then the ring of the market gong would wake me.'

'Luoyang.' She said the name with all the sensuality and decadence the eastern capital deserved. 'To think that we might have crossed paths a long time ago.'

'I would have only seen you as a silhouette in a window.'

There had been gongs to signal everything in the city. Gates open at dawn, gates closed at sundown. The sprawl of the city devoured the weak. It had destroyed his mother, a disgraced woman abandoned in the crowded wards. But Suyin had survived.

She stood beside the desk. 'I waited every night while you were away. When I closed my eyes, I hoped only that you would be there when I opened them.'

'You don't have to wait for me any longer.'

Suyin smiled, not detecting the true intent of his words. These insignificant snatches of conversation always seemed to make her happy. She leaned against the edge of the table, revealing a glimpse of ivory skin where the robe parted. He wanted to reach out and pull her on to his lap, let his hands roam beneath the silk that barely covered her.

He rested his fingers gently over her wrist. 'Do something for me.'

For a second, her breath caught. 'Anything.'

There were so many things he wanted from her. Everything between heaven and earth, in this life and the next.

'I am sending Auntie and the others away. You must go with them.'

Her wistful smile faded. 'No.'

'It's not safe here.'

'I thought I was safe when I left the palace, but my enemies found me.'

He pressed against the space between his eyes. The ache there had become a constant throb. 'There is nothing more important to me than knowing you're far away from danger.'

This had to be done. He needed the freedom to think and plan and act. He couldn't worry about the people under his protection. He couldn't keep thinking of Suyin and what she meant to him. To face the approaching enemy, he needed to stand alone. With nothing to lose.

'Auntie will not go unless you do,' he said.

'Bastard.'

He knew he had her. 'You're clever and resourceful. You'll always know what to do.'

He started going through the logistics: the route they would take, the cache of gold and silver he would send with them.

'I can be of use to you in Chengdu,' she argued.

'I believe it.' He looked up and watched the firelight dance over her face. 'But that's not what you are to me.'

Her fingers tightened over the edge of the desk. Her eyes glistened, but she held back the tears with a fierceness that shook him. He had never desired her more.

'First you demanded one night, then a month,' she accused. 'Stay when you tell me to stay, go when you say to go.'

'I always had the better part of the deal.'

He was going to win this battle. He'd planned his attack with careful precision, but Suyin switched tactics.

'You think I don't know what you're doing.' The softest of threats lurked beneath her silken tone. She ran her finger along the part of the robe, offering him a scant hint of skin, the tantalizing rise of her breast just beyond sight.

'You're trying to tell yourself what we had was nothing. That you were only seeking diversion.'

'I wouldn't lie to myself like that. Or to you.'

What they had was everything, but even perfect moments were meant to pass. His heart threatened to punch a hole through his chest. He sat back, his hands rounding over the arms of the chair while she stood over him. He could reach for Suyin and tear that scrap of silk from her. He could bury his face into the valley of her breasts and take his fill, but it would destroy them both if he held on to her.

'There was only one thing I was ever certain of with you,' she went on sadly. Her hand slipped beneath the edge of the robe, where he wanted desperately to go. 'You want this body. If I were truly wicked, I could make you keep me with you. I could seduce and beg and you'd say yes.'

Desire roughened his voice. 'It was always more. I didn't want it to be, but you were always more than that.'

His shaft grew thick as he watched the silhouette of her fingers circling, making him ache with each slow pass over her nipple. He wanted to close his mouth around her like that, run his tongue against the hard little peak and suckle her breasts through the maddening barrier of cloth until she demanded his hands on her, inside her.

She removed her hand. Her scent swirled around him, the faint hint of jasmine and the feminine musk of her skin.

'I don't want to go.'

'You must.'

She was breathing hard, cheeks flushed, her eyes dark and illuminated with passion. And beneath it all, she was angry. 'You told yourself one night would be enough. Then it was one month. What are you telling yourself now?'

She climbed over him, her thighs parting over his lap, an offering and a challenge. The blood pounded in his ears and his body grew painfully tight, straining towards her. His next breath would not come.

'That you are beautiful beyond words, Ling Suyin.'

'Promise me you'll come for us.'

The muscle along his jaw tightened. He said nothing. This was always meant to end. He had set boundaries to assure that, but Suyin challenged him. She defied him. He reached for her and cradled her cheek against his palm, but she twisted away. She didn't want his tenderness.

'Promise,' she pleaded.

'I'll try.'

His half-attempt at a vow rang hollow in the chamber. He had only spoken out of weakness—weakness for her and a distant longing that refused to let go. Suyin squeezed her eyes shut and nodded, forcing herself to accept.

He kissed her then with his hands buried in the endless river of her hair, too hungry to be gentle. She moaned against him and he drank in the sound. He invaded her mouth with his tongue, pushing inside her, kissing her until she went weak against him.

Her hips sank lower, grinding her soft weight against his arousal. Her arms circled his shoulders to cling to him. The seductress slipped away and he could see the fear in her eyes. For once, she did nothing to hide the vulnerability. She reached down to pull apart his robe and loosen the ties on his trousers.

'Wait—' He tried to stop her, but she wouldn't let him. Soon he was sliding against her damp flesh in a streak of unbearable pleasure.

His hands dug into her waist to hold her away while his body begged to sink into her.

'Is Ling Suyin your true name?' Suddenly he needed to know.

'They gave me this name.' A look of sadness crossed her face. 'I don't even remember what I was called before Luoyang. And you?'

'Tao. Just Tao.'

Her fingers circled his shaft. Gripping her hips, he slid into her in one smooth, deep stroke, and she let out a purring moan as he penetrated endlessly into the snug heat of her channel. Soft, sweet music. Her body resisted the thick invasion before yielding and stretching around him. Her back arched. A muted sound of surrender caught in her throat as she lowered herself fully, fitting her hips against his. Heaven.

He searched her face as she rode him, a pool of shadows with the candlelight behind her. Once again he was in Luoyang, looking up with yearning at the lighted windows, hearing the laughter. He never imagined that nameless urchin would one day hold the most beautiful creature in the world in his arms.

Before long, his climax was upon him, surging through him. He reached for her, her breast filling his palm as he came in ragged bursts, pouring his essence deep into her.

He remained inside, wanting more even as his strength wound down. The position became awkward once their passion was spent. Suyin sank her head against his shoulder and he stayed like that longer than he planned, listening to her breathing until it slowed.

Boundaries. He needed to remember, but he wanted to forget.

Chapter Eighteen

Li Tao carried her from the study back to his bedchamber. They made love again, then he held her until she drifted. Not long after her eyes closed, he rose from the bed. She stirred awake as well. There could be no rest for either of them.

The spot beside her was still warm and she could hear Li Tao moving about the room. With a murmur of protest, she entrenched herself beneath the blanket. She didn't want to open her eyes and find that it was morning. She wasn't ready.

'Is it light outside?' she asked.

'The moon is still out.'

She sighed with relief and rolled on to her stomach. The room was dim, lit by a single oil candle placed upon the bedside table. She searched for him through the halo of light. He wore loose fitting trousers and the flicker of light danced over his bare torso. Beautiful in form.

He came to sit beside her on the bed and placed something on to the table. It appeared to be a thin bamboo instrument atop a folded cloth.

'What is that?'

'A needle and ink.'

She started to rise, but he eased her back to the bed, his hand rubbing slow circles over the curve of her back.

'It's all right.'

She closed her eyes and savoured the sensual brush of his palm. 'What is my mysterious lover scheming?'

He propped one knee on to the bed and lowered his voice even though they were alone. 'Will you allow me to inscribe a mark on your skin?' His palm rose gently along her spine to rest over the plane of her left shoulder. 'Here.'

She held her breath before releasing it slowly. 'The same design that you have?'

'In essence. I'm not as skilled an artist.' His fingertip traced a curved pattern against her shoulder, sending a lazy shiver down her spine. 'The pain is not much. The needle only stings slightly.'

The pain of it was the least of her worries. Within hours, she'd be gone. Li Tao would ride out to the front line and the mansion would be locked down and abandoned. Could she allow him to brand her for ever with the mark of thieves and assassins?

She turned away and pressed her cheek against the mattress. 'You ask too much.'

'It's for your protection. I have one enemy more persistent than Shen or Gao.'

His hand grew still, resting possessively against the curve of her back. Li Tao was sending his most trusted bodyguards with her along with an armed escort, but she didn't want to be protected. She wanted to stay and hold on to what she had, despite the risk.

'You think your Old Man will come after me?'

'He'll try, once I'm gone.'

His answer made her insides go cold. 'Don't talk like that.'

He tensed beside her, but said nothing. His fingertips stroked her hair and the stillness between them overwhelmed her. This was the only sign of permanence he'd ever offered. She was glad that her face was turned away so he couldn't see the tear that escaped down her cheek

She wiped it away and twisted to face him. 'Yes,' she said. 'I'll wear your mark.'

He nodded and turned his attention to the items on the table. With a sense of ritual, he poured a few drops of water on to the flat stone dish and then lifted the ink stick. He ground the charcoal mixture in circular motions to yield a pool of glossy black liquid.

With careful fingers, he brushed her hair from the back of her neck, combing it to one side. She shivered as the strands tickled across her skin. He moved fully on to the bed and his thigh brushed against the outside of hers as he positioned himself.

His breath fanned warm over her as he planted a kiss against her shoulder. Then he reached for the thin bamboo quill. The end of it tapered to a point and she caught the gleam of several small needles at the end.

He smoothed his hand down the line of her spine. 'Lay flat.'

She obeyed, folding her arms beneath her head as a pillow. There was nothing to do but accept. He ran one hand over the area beneath her shoulder and then paused with fingers outstretched to pull the skin tight. She winced when the needles bit into her, but remained still, anchored by his hold.

He stopped the motion of the instrument. 'How are you?'

She gasped. 'You startled me.'

'Breathe through it. The sting will fade.'

Perhaps on tough hide like his. He moved the bamboo stick a fraction inwards and stabbed again and then again, repeating the motion. She pressed her cheek against her arm, her eyes squeezed shut. The sharp pricks continued until the pain coalesced into a burning sensation. She wavered between asking him to stop so she could catch her breath or remaining silent so it would be over quicker.

The needle stabbed up and down in a rapid staccato, boring the black ink beneath her skin. Her fingers dug into the soft flesh of her upper arms. She tried to concentrate on the scritch-scratch sound of the instrument to distract herself.

Li Tao wiped at her skin with the cloth and then continued. Little by little, the sharp sting of the needles began to blur. The pain never faded, but it receded to the edge of awareness as her body acclimated. The muscles of her back loosened and accepted the pain.

Soon the pain floated above her body, replaced by a warm halo that curled throughout her limbs. With a sigh, she let her head sink in the cradle of her arms. The sensations melded together: the searing prick of the needle, Li Tao's firm but careful hand on her.

His fingertips stroked lightly between her shoulder blades. 'Am I hurting you?'

'It's not so bad.'

As the burning receded, every other sense grew sharper. Her skin became suffused with warmth. Her breathing slowed to match the steady draw of his above her. She wanted to curl into his touch. Li Tao's hard thighs straddled either side of her while she lay naked beneath him. The feeling of being sheltered overwhelmed her and it was impossible to deny the sensuality of the experience.

She wished she could see his expression, but she didn't dare move while he drew the dragon into her. She closed her eyes and surrendered into the jumble of emotions that swirled through her, not at all surprised when her skin warmed and her sex grew damp with longing as the needles continued their relentless path over her. But it would only torment her if they made love again. She would always want one last time.

'I am in love with you,' she said when he was done. They didn't look at one another. 'You must know that already.'

He spoke after a heavy silence. 'No. I did not.'

There would be no poetry or words of great feeling. Li Tao was more complicated than words allowed. Her love for him was the same; she couldn't say when it had begun or when she had stopped pretending. When it had become more important to protect him, than to be protected by him.

She breathed in his scent and tried to capture the feel of being close to him. The design was complete and soon it would be time to go. The mark stung upon her shoulder blade, but she welcomed the pain. She hoped the memory of it, and of Li Tao's hands on her, would last long into the journey.

Only hours later, Suyin stood outside the mansion. The rest of the household was gathered there as well. The span of the bamboo forest engulfed them. A temporary shelter waving farewell with the breeze. All of their belongings had been stowed away in two wagons. Servants didn't own many possessions. Suyin realised she didn't have much of anything either. It was the same as it had been when Li Tao had first come for her by the river.

Li Tao helped Auntie on to the back of the main wagon, seating her beneath the awning rigged to provide shade. They would be packed in amongst the trunks and supplies. It appeared as if they were simply preparing for a trip to the market except for the armed escort assembled around them.

Suyin stood beside the caravan as the last of the goods were loaded, wanting to hold back the inevitable as long as possible. It seemed they all moved slower. Cook inspected the sacks of rice over and over before climbing on to the driver's seat and Jun took more time than usual using his good arm to hoist himself up beside Cook.

The mark still burned, her skin raw beneath the thin material of her robe. Every twinge reminded her of Li Tao's mindful touch and the tender pressure of his lips against her back. He had marked her as his, only to send her away. The ache of loss overwhelmed her and she had to look away. She wouldn't show any tears. Not when he could carry about unmoved, without a trace of emotion.

This was just his way, she told herself. An impassive face to the world that challenged him. But he erected the same wall against her, despite all their nights and mornings and moments.

Wang and the elite guards flanked the supply carts on horseback. An additional armed escort of twenty men would take them beyond the bamboo sea to the southernmost corner of the province. Li Tao was sending his most trusted bodyguards with her and leaving himself unprotected.

That was nonsense. Li Tao had an army of thousands at his command. He didn't need these swordsmen at his side. He didn't need her.

'Lady Ling.'

Li Tao crouched on the bed of the wagon, holding his hand out to her. So they were done. There was nothing left to wait for. She placed her hand into his and her heart sank as his fingers closed around hers. He pulled her upwards. The arm that circled her waist was unnecessary, but welcome. She leaned against him to savour a final moment of closeness. She hoped that she had said everything in the night, with words and without, because there was no time now. And she couldn't form any thoughts.

'Please be careful.'

His gaze fixed on to her as hard and unyielding as ever. But there was darkness there, a flicker of pain that was only a mere echo of what she felt inside. He didn't speak as he led her to sit beside Auntie. Then he only said her name once, low so only she could hear, as he brushed back her hair.

He turned and lowered himself from the wagon. His boots landed with a solid thud on to the packed dirt road. She followed his every movement as he walked to the front of the wagon.

'Take care of them,' he told Jun. The boy straightened an inch and nodded.

She knew at any moment the wagon would lurch forwards and the mansion would disappear in the distance. Her mind had woven that picture into her dreams throughout the night. She scrambled forwards to lean over the front of the wagon.

Surely she would have something to say to him. Something that could help. She had conversed with philosophers and diplomats and generals.

'Li Tao.'

She didn't have to call him. He was already watching her. He stood tall and starkly handsome and immovable. No matter how hard she searched, Li Tao never showed any sign of doubt or regret. His expression remain stern and fixed, so much like the late Emperor Li Ming, her once protector. A man who had irrevocably decided his fate and was living on borrowed time.

'There is nothing honourable about fighting to the death,' she beseeched him.

'You already know I'm not an honourable man.'

The wagon lurched forwards, the wheels groaning beneath the weight of them. A muffled sniff came from Auntie's side. Suyin looked back, as she always did.

Li Tao remained alone in the centre of the road with the curtain of bamboo behind him. She forced her gaze away before he became nothing but a dark shape in the distance. Her life had been a string of unwanted journeys, from the humble river bend to the imperial palace. She wanted to believe that this time she would be able to return home, that fate would allow her to come back to find it unchanged.

The ache inside her took over as the mansion disappeared from view. She stared down at her lap, her own hands feeling like they weren't a part of her anymore.

They were going to a remote village. Cook's family would take them in and they could disappear amongst the fields of rice and yams. Li Tao believed they would be safer there than walled inside one of the fortress cities under military control.

Now that the journey was underway, the silence became unbearable. Suyin needed some distraction. At least until they were far enough away that she knew Li Tao couldn't come after them. Until then, she harboured a desperate hope. She kept looking behind them, imagining the sound of hoofbeats in the distance.

Auntie gripped Suyin's hand tight and she laid her head against the old woman's shoulder. Auntie never spoke of any children. Certainly her protectiveness toward Li Tao was much like a mother's love.

'Sleep,' Auntie cooed. 'You look tired.'

Suyin had barely closed her eyes all night. She and Li Tao had been greedy for every last moment together.

'Maybe a week from here,' Cook said from the driver's seat. 'I'll make the Lady some special yam noodles when we get there.'

They were trying so valiantly to cheer her. She realised then that she wasn't alone this time. Li Tao had sent more than his bodyguards. He'd sent the only family he had while he stayed behind.

The day ebbed away in stretches of silence. Cook and Auntie begged her to tell stories about the imperial palace. She described the lake and the plum blossoms in the spring, the great halls that towered over gleaming stone courtyards, making it sound like a faraway place among the clouds. There were thousands of these stories in her head about emperors and concubines and crafty servants.

'Not these fables.' Jun's protest surprised her. 'Tell us one of your stories, Lady Ling. About something exciting that happened to you.'

He leaned over from the front of the wagon eagerly, gripping the wooden plank for balance.

'My life was very ordinary, young Jun. I walked about the palace and looked pretty. The Emperor's caged bird.'

'What of the insurrection? The palace was under siege for days.'

There was a gleam in Jun's eye she had never seen before. Auntie shushed him for prying.

'There is nothing exciting about rebellion.' Suyin met the youth's gaze. 'I was very frightened. The August Emperor was dead and armed men took the inner palace by force. I thought I would be killed.'

'For the secrets you kept.'

Jun didn't wait for her response. Satisfied, he turned around to take the reins from Cook.

Where had this morbid curiosity come from? Jun had changed since they'd left. He seemed to stand taller with a newfound brashness. She dismissed it as a boyhood fascination with danger, but a sense of wariness remained with her.

Two travellers approached them, requesting water midway through the next day. They didn't appear to be beggars, just worn and dusty from the journey. As soft-hearted as she was, Auntie couldn't refuse. She rummaged through their stores for wrapped dumplings and sat them down in the shade of the wagon.

The men stared at the retinue of armed soldiers as they ate. One of them had a beard that had grown scraggly around the edges. The younger one's face had a touch of gauntness, his skin pulled back over a pronounced forehead and sharp nose.

'Rioting has broken out in the south,' the bearded one said.

Suyin pulled Wang aside. A whisper would be too easy to detect so she spoke quietly and calmly. 'Do not trust these men,' she said, before retreating to the other side of the caravan.

Their manner was a touch too forward for peasants. If they were merchants, they carried nothing. When they finally departed, the bearded one raked his gaze over her with such lurid contemplation that Jun edged closer to her. She was touched by the fierce protectiveness that vibrated through the youth.

Was the rest of the empire becoming like this? The roads so unsafe that every stranger was cause for fear?

Wang and the bodyguards discussed the news of rebellion as they continued on the next leg of the journey. Their loyalty was first and foremost to Li Tao and they wanted to send a message to him. Once again, she heard Ru Shan's name.

Li Tao was fighting a rebellion from within while he also prepared to defend the territory against invaders. The mood grew sullen the further they ventured. The first, feeble attempts at conversation had fallen away to silence, punctured only by the grate of the wheels.

As the wagon rumbled on, Suyin considered how easy it would be for her to convince the party to turn around and return to the bamboo sea. Cook missed his kitchen and Jun fidgeted restlessly on the seat with no gardens to busy himself with. Auntie had stopped reassuring her that Li Tao would be fine. They all wanted to go home.

Once again, the earth element in her reached out to absorb everything around her, seeking an anchor. She yearned to stay and belong somewhere. A place where her life could take root and grow. But Li Tao had sent them away to safety for a purpose. He was counting on her to lead these people. He wouldn't let anything like sentiment muddle his judgement.

Evening came and they pulled the wagons aside. Suyin sank back as the men set up camp for the night in the wild grass beside the road. She closed her eyes against the weariness that sank deep into her bones.

'Lady, are you not well?'

Auntie knelt over her, holding out a cup of tea. Suyin glanced over to see Cook already tending to a cooking fire for the evening meal.

'I must have fallen asleep. I've been so tired lately.'

Ever since the failed trip to see the Emperor, she'd been exhausted, as if she had never recovered from the strain. She sat up, feeling selfish for complaining when she never lifted a finger. The entire household had chores that kept them busy from sunrise until sundown. She really was little more than a songbird.

'I am fine, Auntie.' She rolled her shoulders to shake off the feeling and sipped her tea.

'How long have you been feeling like this?'

'It must be because I haven't slept. Too much worrying.'

Auntie's voice dropped into a whisper. 'Do you ache? Here?' The woman touched a hand to her own breast.

Suyin's eyes widened and that was all the confirmation the old woman needed.

'My girl, you must be with child!'

Could it be? Suyin's hand trailed down to her stomach. 'So soon?'

Auntie cradled her face affectionately. Her hands felt like soft, worn leather. 'Monkey, it only takes once. All that old gossip of you being barren.' Auntie sniffed dismissively.

'Auntie!'

They were whispering to one another, sharing a woman's secret. Suddenly, Suyin was filled with a new sense of purpose. She was with *child*. She was with child. Such terrible power in that thought.

When the Emperor had chosen her for his charade, she had thought her life as a woman finished. No lovers, no husband, no children. Yet here she was, carrying Li Tao's child, a part of him growing inside her.

Her eyes stung with the threat of tears. The heavens were capable of kindness after all.

'I have to go to him,' she whispered.

'Lady, you can't.'

'But he doesn't know!'

'We have the child to think of now.'

Her spirit plummeted after soaring so high. Auntie was right. Li Tao had sent them away to keep them safe. He would insist on the same for his child. Yet the need to have him beside her devoured her heart, greater than any pain she'd ever known.

She sank her head into Auntie's lap. 'Oh, Auntie.'

'Think good thoughts for your little one.'

Auntie smelled like an herb cabinet, earthy and medicinal. She stroked Suyin's hair, telling her gently once again that everything would be all right. Some part of her, deep inside, yearned for this coddling. She closed her eyes and tried not to think of Li Tao riding into battle.

'What was Tao like, as a boy?'

Auntie told her about the textile ward, the hovels stacked together wall to wall. The seamstresses would rush to finish the sewing in the daylight because candles were expensive. Suyin was reminded of the thatched house by the river she had lived in when she was a child.

'What of his mother?'

Auntie sighed above her. 'His dear mother, the sorrow.'

'Li Tao's mother was lost when he was young.'

'Yes.'

'Did she take her own life?'

Auntie hushed her. 'The sorrow,' she murmured once again. Speaking of such sadness would conjure up the restless spirits that hovered between the living and the dead.

Li Tao remained such a mystery. On their first night, after he'd taken her on the floor of the study, she had escaped to the edge of the gorge in tears. Li Tao had rushed to her side. It was the only time she'd seen fear in his eyes. He'd pulled her into his arms to protect her. The cold-hearted warlord had always tried to protect her. He was trying to protect them all.

If they hadn't wasted so much time fighting one another, she might know him better. This man who had irrevocably become a part of her.

'One day Tao left and Auntie did not see him for years. Auntie knew he was alive and that he remembered, because he would send gifts. Money and rice. When Auntie saw him again, he was no longer a boy.'

Suyin started to drift, soothed by Auntie's touch and voice.

'He had grown tall, his shoulders wide,' Auntie continued. 'He said we were going to Chengdu. When Auntie asked him if he worked for the military governor, he told her that he was the *jiedushi*.'

Suyin remembered the stir within the court. Li Tao the war hero, the Emperor's relentless executioner, given the command of an entire military district. A great honour for one so young.

'So you see, Tao will know what to do,' Auntie murmured.

Auntie's voice was beginning to fade to the edges of her consciousness. Suyin was getting so sleepy, lying there in the wagon. Her thoughts drifted to her baby. She didn't want to send a letter, a feeble scattering of characters on paper in the hands of a messenger. She wanted to tell Li Tao herself. She wanted him to put his arms around her.

Heaven and earth, she didn't even know how he would react to the news. Li Tao had never spoken of the future.

'This turned out to be a happy day after all,' Auntie said.

'I'm very happy,' she echoed obediently. A child was supposed to be a joyous thing. She was supposed to be elated and suffused with warmth. In truth, she was confused. The future rippled like the surface of a pond, blurred and unknown before her.

Cook was calling them to dinner, but her body was so tired. She wanted to stay and rest. She would close her eyes and think of Li Tao. Suyin wrapped her arms around herself, feeling small beneath the open sky. At that moment, only she and Auntie knew that everything in the world had changed. It was a secret.

Once again, she had a secret, but one that was more momentous and devastating than any she'd ever kept.

Chapter Nineteen

Suyin couldn't open her eyes. She tried to, tried to force herself awake. How long had she been asleep and where was she? It was dark. A rushing noise filled her ears, like the rustling of cloth in the wind. Heat lashed at her.

'Lady Ling is in there!' Auntie's voice cut through the blackness. 'She's in the wagon.'

No, she wasn't. Her thoughts were coming one moment too slow. Coarse grass pricked against her cheek. Her fingers scraped against hard earth when she tried to move them. She wanted to say something, but her lips refused to move.

I'm over here!

But that was only her mind crying out. An arm hooked around her waist and hefted her up with a grunt. All around her, she could hear footsteps pounding and the clash of swords. Auntie was still screaming.

A shoulder jostled against her stomach as she was lifted up over someone's back. Her first thought was of her baby. Whoever held her started running and the sounds of the camp faded in the distance.

'Stop…please.' Her mouth formed thickly around the words. Her throat was so dry. She needed to tell them to be careful. Please, please be careful.

The shouting was starting to fade. She tried to call out to the swordsman Wang, to Cook. Even to Jun, but she was so weak. She tried to dig her nails into her abductor, but her fingers fell away, slack. She couldn't feel her hands. Her breathing slowed and she slipped away again, her mind going slippery and dark as if sinking into black water.

When her mind broke through the fog she heard strange voices. Her first thought was of Gao. He had broken through Li Tao's defences to capture her.

'Lady Ling, drink this.'

The familiar voice filled her with relief. 'Jun?'

Daylight filtered through her lashes and she could see Jun holding out a cup folded from a palm leaf.

'Please drink,' he urged. 'It's water.'

She remembered him in the wagon last night, much in the same position as he offered her a bowl of rice soup. It was her last memory before the fire. Her eyes narrowed.

'Jun,' she said again, her tone accusing.

He looked stricken as she struggled to sit up. She needed to force this cloud from her mind fast.

'So this is Li Tao's woman.'

They weren't alone. The unfamiliar voice and the underlying threat in it sent her pulse skittering. There were two men standing behind Jun.

'This must be *An Ying*,' she said evenly.

Jun's eyes widened at the mention of the secret name. The bearded man grabbed him by the shoulder, yanking him back before he could respond. Water flung from the cup and the droplets splashed over her.

'Your job is done, boy.'

She squinted listlessly at the shadowed figure, exaggerating the effect of the drug. She recognised the unruly beard and the thick eyebrows. It was the ragged stranger they had encountered on the road. His gaunt companion with the pointed, badger-like face stood behind him. At first she thought Gao had abducted her, but he didn't need to employ such guile. Old Gao would have killed her immediately.

'Ling *Guifei*,' the bearded man pronounced her title speculatively. His tone sent a shiver down her spine. 'Li Tao is a lucky man.'

'Don't touch her, Zheng.' Jun tried to force himself between them. 'Where are the others?'

'Dead,' Zheng declared.

Her heart stopped. For a second, she thought he was speaking about Auntie and the servants.

'The boy didn't tell us the swordsmen with you were the Shining Guard.' Zheng took hold of her chin, lifting her face to his. She had no choice but to let him. 'We sacrificed many of our men.'

Wang and the rest of Li Tao's guards had put up a fight. She prayed that Auntie and Cook had escaped. The brutal calculation in Zheng's eyes knotted her stomach, but she stayed silent, afraid to goad him. She had faced death before and survived. That knowledge and the need to see Li Tao again gave her strength.

Jun continued to lunge forwards, ignoring Zheng's greater size and strength. 'We are to bring her back unharmed. My orders come from Lao Sou.'

The Badger pulled Jun back. 'We have orders too,' he said calmly.

The mention of the Old Man made Zheng hesitate, but it was clear the two of them not only outranked, but could overpower, Jun. Zheng had no intention of taking orders from the boy.

He scrubbed a hand over his beard. 'All I want is a taste of what Ling *Guifei* gives Li Tao so freely. No harm at all.'

Choking back a cry, Suyin wrapped her arms around herself protectively. She wouldn't show any fear. She wouldn't show any emotion at all.

'Li Tao will find you and kill you,' she promised.

Zheng loomed over her and her bravado faded. She shrank back, turning her face aside. He leaned close enough that she could feel the swipe of his breath against her cheek.

'I will be waiting,' he said with a mock intimacy that made her blood go cold.

He hooked his fingers into her bodice and wrenched downwards. Her robe split at the seam, the rending of silk deafening. She bit down on her lip and willed the pain to take away her fear.

Jun struggled free, only to have Zheng swat him back. His meaty arm connected with the boy's jaw. She cringed at the sharp impact. All she could think of was Li Tao and their baby. A surge of protectiveness seized her and she squeezed her eyes shut. She would survive this. No matter what they did to her, she had to stay alive.

'Is that all you have, Ling *Guifei*? No fight left in you?'

Her eyes flew open. Zheng was breathing hard, aroused. This went beyond lust. He was savouring his power over her and, more importantly, his power over Li Tao. There was an old grudge there. She was certain of it.

A cry rose behind them. In a whiplash of motion, Jun snapped forwards, a knife gleaming in his good hand. Badger staggered backwards with blood seeping through his fingers.

'We have orders,' Jun snarled.

This could be her only chance. She shoved at Zheng and scrambled to her feet. The ground lurched unexpectedly and her vision blurred. Her skirt clung like a net about her ankles when she tried to run. A trace of whatever Jun had put into her food remained in her.

A hand grabbed her roughly, tugging on the silken robe. It was Zheng again. He forced her to the ground and threw himself on top of her. His knee wedged between her thighs. She tried to claw at him, but he pinned her arms against the jagged ground.

'Hold!' It was Badger that spoke. 'Back off, Zheng. You saw it.'

Zheng's grip tightened defiantly on her wrists. 'It means nothing.'

'She's been marked,' Badger insisted.

Zheng returned his attention to her, his gaze cold. 'The mark of a traitor means nothing.'

The tattoo. The assassins of *An Ying* spoke in language and codes of conduct that no one else could understand.

Jun came close. 'You have much to answer for if you touch her.'

He clenched his fists so tight that they shook, but there was nothing the youth could do against the two more experienced assassins. Zheng sniffed dismissively, but his wiry companion came up behind him. His long shadow fell over her eyes.

'Release her,' Badger said. 'She's untouchable and you know it.'

Suyin clutched the edges of her robe together the moment Zheng's grip loosened. He removed himself from her, but his eyes clamped on to her.

Jun moved to help her stand, but she refused his hand. Of the entire household, she'd been kindest to the boy. His attention had seemed so genuine that she'd left herself vulnerable. Apparently she wasn't immune to deception either.

Horses had been stowed in the brush along with travel packs. Suyin fought a wave of panic. The assassins were taking her far away. She prayed that the swordsman Wang and the rest of the bodyguards would organise a search party—if they had survived.

Jun stayed close, as if he could still fulfil his promise to Li Tao to take care of her. He held out a cloak. 'Put this on.'

'I won't accept anything from you.' She clutched the torn silk to her breast as the men prepared the horses.

'Lady Ling, please.'

His words held no hint of plaintiveness. Jun was hardly the awkward boy he had affected so flawlessly. The look of innocence was gone, replaced by a hardness that set her on guard.

'You were one of them all along,' she said. 'Ever since Auntie took you in.'

'Yes.'

'A frail helpless orphan.'

Jun smirked. 'What would the great Li Tao have to fear from a cripple?'

It was more than that. Lao Sou knew what Li Tao had been, the streets that he had prowled. The Old Man had held up a mirror to Li Tao and he had been unwittingly fooled by his own image.

She watched Badger and Zheng as they readied the horses. According to their account, they had sacrificed many others last night in order for Jun to be able to steal her away. The Old Man wanted Li Tao alive.

She needed to work out which one of these men was the most dangerous. The two larger men were brutes, used for ramming through fortress gates and scaling walls. They had nothing like the stealth of Li Tao or Jun. Li Tao had hidden within the Emperor's army for years. Jun was possibly even more skilled.

'Not many people can fool me,' she said coldly. 'That takes a special breed of treachery.'

Jun fell silent and she saw a trace of the same austere discipline that had been instilled in Li Tao. He stood rigid beside her, battling within himself. He was uncomfortable with her anger. Jun might be a trained assassin, but he'd been fed on Auntie's kindness. It gave her a small spark of hope.

He held out the cloak once again. 'Take this.'

Badger came up to them, ending the argument by grabbing the wool and jerking it over her shoulders roughly. 'Zheng needs no more encouragement.'

Despite her defiance, the cloak provided a semblance of comfort, some armour against these dangerous men. She stared at the spot where Zheng waited by the horses. The memory of him pinning her against the ground made her go cold. She longed for Li Tao so much it hurt, but he was far away, occupied with the approaching armies.

Had anyone been left alive? Inwardly, she wept for Auntie, for Cook, for the servants who had become like family. She prayed for their safety.

'Where are you taking me?' she asked.

Badger answered, direct and simple. 'The Old Man wants to meet you.'

He took a knife from his belt and slashed a line on to a nearby tree before directing her towards the horses.

Chapter Twenty

Luoyang—ad 739
20 years earlier

After his third job, Feng invited Tao to join his gang. When Tao refused, Feng sent a gutter rat after him, someone larger, more experienced, but not as desperate to draw his next breath. The first rat, then the second, turned up dead and Feng stopped cluttering the alleys with his urchins.

Tao never joined any of the other street gangs. He didn't want the shackles of such an association even for the protection it provided. He worked the dark corners and outskirts of the territories, carving out his own domain.

One night he found a grey man in a grey robe leaning in one of his corners.

'Old man,' he called out.

'Young boy.' The street lanterns revealed a twist of a smile on the old man's face.

He took no offence even though he was no longer a boy. Pride could be deadly in these streets.

'I am looking for the one they call Tao.'

'That is me.'

The old man's eyes gleamed with enjoyment. The oddness of

it made Tao slip his knife into his hand while he hung back in the shadows.

'Just Tao? Not Tao the Knife or Tao the Tiger?'

The grey man shook with laughter, utterly at ease in the back streets, which meant he was drunk or mad or dangerous.

'Who are you?' Tao demanded.

'You had it right from the start. They call me "Lao Sou".'

Old Man.

'I have never heard of you.'

'No one has.'

Tao stepped back and his gaze darted to the rooftops, to the far end of the alley. He saw nothing, heard nothing, but he knew the grey man was not here alone.

'I have a job for you, Tao the Silent.'

'Tonight?'

The Old Man chuckled. 'No, no. Not until you're ready. Put away your knife and walk with me.'

She knew the sound of water, even from a distance. The ebb and flow of it grew louder as they rode. They must be nearing the banks of the Jin. They veered into the thick of the forest, dismounting to continue on foot.

'You're not going to cover my eyes?' she asked.

Zheng snorted. '*An Ying* is everywhere. We can disappear like the blowing wind.'

'How poetic,' she remarked blandly.

He shoved her forwards. The forest gave way to a stone path, encroached and overgrown with roots. The broken tiles led to a sudden part in the trees to reveal the face of a once-grand temple. The cracked paint lent it a hint of antiquity, a venerable sheen.

Zheng clamped a hand on to her shoulder. She shook him free and stepped forwards of her own volition, searching among the pillars and alcoves. There had been sliver of movement among the shadows, she was certain of it. Jun's hand slipped to the knife in his belt.

'You've never seen Lao Sou, have you?' she asked.

'Few have,' Jun replied.

'Yet you serve him above the people who cared for you.'

'Don't let her bewitch you, boy,' Badger drawled from behind them.

She slid him a look over her shoulder and Badger flashed a crooked smile. *An Ying* was an odd collection of characters.

They stepped around the broken incense urn in the yard. A set of weathered steps led to the open doors. Zheng took hold of her again as they crossed the threshold. She peered through the dimly lit interior to the man seated where the altar once stood. The effect of it was akin to an emperor on his throne.

'Fine work, young Jun,' he said.

Li Tao had told her that Lao Sou preferred to wear drab clothing and disappear unnoticed in a crowd, but the man before her was dressed like a nobleman, his robe richly embroidered and of the finest silk. His face remained shadowed.

'The notorious Ling *Guifei* honours us with her presence.'

'Lao Sou,' she greeted. 'Your servant has his hand on me. I beseech you to have him remove it.'

'Zheng, show respect for our guest.'

His hand tightened momentarily, anger vibrating through his fingertips. Then, without a word, he let her go. And just like that rank was established. She met Lao Sou's gaze with a look that said, *We are equals, you and I.* Even though he held all the power.

He beckoned her with a wrinkled hand. 'Come closer.'

She stepped on to the raised platform, noting how he was alone in the chamber. No, not alone. Once again, she caught a ripple of movement in the niche of the altar. Lao Sou didn't want to appear as if he needed protection, but there was no way to tell how many guarded him.

'Closer, closer. I am not the demon Li Tao described.'

He remained seated, his head tilted as if gauging each step. His eyes remained unfocused and blank. Blind. Li Tao had not told her that. How did a blind man command the respect of this horde of murderers and spies?

'Li Tao never spoke of you as a demon.'

He raised a thick grey eyebrow. 'No? What did he say?'

'That you would come for him some day.'

He nodded, seemingly pleased, and a wave of powerlessness swept over her, weakening her resolve. It was as Li Tao had said. They were being manipulated, their fate not entirely their own.

'Come closer, my lady.'

Lao Sou pushed off against the arms of the chair and stood, reaching out to her sightlessly. She found herself obliging him, taking his arm as if he was an old grandfather rather than the killer she knew he was.

'My eyes are old and dim. I have never regretted it so much as now.' He chuckled softly as he gestured toward the adjoining chamber. 'I would have liked to look upon Ling *Guifei*'s renowned beauty.'

The old man led the way to a second chamber and they left Jun standing with Badger and Zheng in the centre of the room. The arm beneath hers was tough with wiry muscle and his step was agile and confident. He needed no assistance, she realised. Lao Sou was holding on to keep control of her.

A guard stood just inside the room. She saw no weapon, but she didn't doubt that he was armed. He remained silent with the dark-eyed lethalness of a predator. This was what she had expected from the clan.

The chamber was furnished lavishly in contrast to the spare altar room. The Old Man seated her himself, pulling out a chair at the table for her before seating himself. She watched as he placed two cups before them, gauging the distance with his fingers before pouring wine from the jug.

'Li Tao will not come for me,' she began.

'He will.'

'He is not a sentimental man. If I were of any value, he would never have let me go.'

Her heart ached, yet she continued to torment it. Maybe if she heard the truth enough times from her own lips she would finally accept it. Li Tao knew what was important and he chose his battles carefully. They had said their farewells. She should consider it a blessing that he wasn't the sort to rush in to save her. It would mean his death.

Lao Sou folded his hands before him. 'What you mistake for coldness is single-mindedness. He cares for you more than you know. I've been paying close attention.'

'With your spies?'

He reclined in his chair, more than pleased with himself.

As much as she wanted to see Li Tao again, she prayed the old man was mistaken. She was fighting for her life and the life of her child. Li Tao couldn't also fall into this madman's grasp. She needed to find a way to escape on her own.

'I know Li Tao better than you,' she challenged. 'You never thought he would betray you for the August Emperor.'

Her remark seemed to wound him. He frowned, but then shrugged and took a sip of his wine. 'Li Tao has marked you with our symbol. The dragon and the pearl.'

She touched a hand to her shoulder. The tattoo lay just beyond her reach. The memory of the needles made her skin tingle. She had never seen her design. She only knew it was a rough likeness of the symbol inked on to Li Tao's body.

'Do you know what the pearl represents?' Lao Sou asked.

'No.'

'It's a mystery. A powerful mystery. The dragon doesn't know what it is, but he chases it anyway.' He nodded with satisfaction. For a moment, it appeared as if his eyes actually focused on her. 'That mark means he will come for you.'

Li Tao knew the moment his scouts reported that the wagons were returning. He took a horse out to intercept them and the look of defeat in his soldiers' eyes told him what had happened. Auntie was speechless with grief. She tried to call out to him as he dug in his heels, riding hard in the direction they'd come from.

The horse's stride pounded out a rhythm against the dirt road. In his head, Li Tao retraced his mistakes. The clan had remained dormant for so long. The armed escort was only a cautionary measure. He should have known his former master would strike now, when he was vulnerable. Part of him must have known. He had given Suyin the mark of the clan as a last defence. It was a promise written in blood and now he had to deliver.

The swordsman Wang had not returned with the others. He and the other elite guards had stayed to scour the area, but they would never find Suyin. The *An Ying* clan would move quickly. Their minions would scatter like ghosts in the daylight.

Li Tao returned alone to the location where Suyin had been taken. The assassins had left behind their marks on the trees. Their secret language. Lao Sou wanted to be discovered, but only by Li Tao. So he followed them.

Like a dog baring his throat to slaughter.

The music came through the forest, lilting notes that drifted into a song meant only for him. He recognised Suyin's skilful touch on the strings. Li Tao dismounted and walked towards the sound. At last, Suyin had the grand gesture she'd asked for, except it wasn't before the Emperor as she'd intended.

Your woman is still alive, his former master was saying. Come to me if you wish to see her again in this life.

His armies awaited his command at the front line, but instead he'd come here. This was the price he paid for letting Suyin inside. If he ignored the Old Man now, she would be the one to pay.

The music guided him to an abandoned temple. The columns were painted red, though the colour had faded and the woodwork had warped and cracked. Li Tao stood at the open doors, alone as he had been in the streets of Luoyang when Lao Sou had first come to him. He had always been able to empty his head in those dank alleys. He would block out the emptiness in his belly and the chill in his fingers, and simply survive. This moment was not so simple.

He stepped beyond the threshold into the darkened interior. The shelves and altars were empty of the customary statues and relics that adorned such temples. Instead of offerings of rice and tea, there was only dust. The air was clogged with it.

Li Tao found Suyin immediately. She sat at a low table, a focal point of sound and colour, wearing the same blue silk she'd worn when challenging him beside the gorge. He should have known then he'd fall to her. Her fingertips were poised over the *qin*. The song halted and she looked up at him, her eyes growing wide with surprise.

The Old Man sat beside her in the temple alcove. His men were stationed around the chamber as if he were holding court. These cold-hearted killers would cut out Li Tao's heart on a single command from the Old Man, but they faded before him. There was only Suyin.

'Are you hurt?' he asked.

She shook her head. Her palms flattened over the strings, fingers splayed to still the last murmurs of sound. Her lips parted in shock.

'I thought—' She swallowed, fixing her gaze on to him and delving deep, deeper than he'd ever allowed anyone. 'You're here.'

She had doubted he would come. The pain of that doubt cut deep. He bled inside.

'Of course,' he said evenly.

'You shouldn't have come.' She met his eyes with an odd, pleading look, trying to speak without words. He couldn't understand.

'Li Tao.' The Old Man spoke his name like a grand proclamation. 'It's been fifteen long years.'

The attention of the entire chamber focused in on him as a single target at the centre. He sensed a mix of emotions: awe, anticipation and fear. So he still had a reputation.

One face among them was blatantly familiar. Jun. The one who had betrayed them. Li Tao marked him with a stare, but Jun refused to flinch.

Li Tao returned his attention to the old man at the front. 'You have something that belongs to me.'

Lao Sou's arm rested across the edge of the Suyin's table. The placement of it was like the casual drape of a lion's paw over its prey.

'I told Ling *Guifei* you would come for her across the span of the earth. Tell me, is she beautiful?'

'Yes, she is.' The sight of her would always take his breath away.

Lao Sou turned to Suyin next. 'Is he kneeling?'

She looked to him. 'No,' she replied softly.

'No,' Lao Sou echoed with a drip of venom.

The years had worn his old master to the bone. He seemed gaunt, grey, the lines in his face cut deeper. Apparently Lao Sou was blind now as well, but still far from harmless.

'When I found you, you were a stray wandering the gutters.' Only the flex of the Old Man's fingers against the corner of the table hinted at his anger. 'I gave you an assignment and you failed.'

'I made a choice.'

'You have no choice!'

Lao Sou's voice thundered through the chamber. Suyin jumped at his sudden outburst and the entire assembly hushed.

It was true that Li Tao had been nothing when he was taken from the streets. Lao Sou had trained him patiently. Some would say, as a father might a son. Then his master had sent him to the imperial army to die without a qualm.

'What do you wish of me now?' Li Tao asked calmly.

Lao Sou shook his head. 'Still insolent.'

'I am at your mercy.'

The Old Man snorted. He wanted something more. After fifteen years of waiting, he wasn't getting the confrontation he so eagerly wanted.

'Where are your armies?' Lao Sou asked.

'By the river.'

'What will your soldiers do if you're not there to lead them?'

'March on their own. An army can't live or die by its one general.'

Lao Sou shook with anger. 'Look at you. Bringing war upon this empire like you're the August Emperor.'

If this was revenge, it was a twisted beyond recognition. Suyin's hands were locked fearfully in front of her. Li Tao wanted this finished for her sake.

'What do you want, Old Man?' he demanded. 'An apology on my knees?'

'Emperor Shen and Gao's armies gather on the other bank. You have a chance to redeem your past failure.'

'By taking the life of another Emperor?'

'No, *boy*. You have been agonising for months over this problem and the solution is in front of you. Kill Gao Shiming.'

At that, the Old Man's hand shot out, quick as a cobra. Li Tao ducked aside as the dark blade embedded itself with a thud into a wooden pillar behind him.

Suyin sprang to her feet, but the guards restrained her. Li Tao dug his nails into his palm to keep from rushing forwards.

Lao Sou stood triumphantly. 'There. I will even give you the knife.'

'Is that is all you want?' he demanded.

The Old Man snorted. 'When I hear of your success, I will release her. And you *will* fulfil your duty this time.'

And that was all this was: duty. One death to make up for the one he'd failed to deliver years ago.

If murdering Gao would resolve his problems, Li Tao would have done it long ago. But Gao's death would only urge the forces behind him to rise up. The old warlord's army would be left in disarray—a serpent coiling and writhing without a head. It went against everything Li Tao had fought to maintain: balance, order, stability. Lao Sou was bleeding him of every last bit of will. The Old Man wanted it all back—everything he'd built in the last fifteen years.

Li Tao met Suyin's eyes. He wished he had held her longer the last time they were together. He wished that he had given her everything she'd ever asked for.

'It's good to see you.' He tried to put the world into his farewell, but he'd never had any talent with words. They fell heavy into the silence.

Suyin started to respond, but the guards took her away. She disappeared through the heavy curtain at the side of the room. Her cries became muted.

Li Tao ground his teeth together. He dragged one breath into his lungs, and then another. He couldn't go to her. He needed to focus. Lao Sou wouldn't harm her if he did what he was told. That was the entire purpose of this game. Control.

The only way he could guarantee Suyin's safety was to kill Gao. The elder warlord already planned to meet with him. Even with the guards surrounding Gao, he could do it. A single man with a blade.

The coldness seeped into his skin as he accepted the inevitable. This is what he had been trained to do. His body remembered.

This was the last he'd ever see of Suyin. She had been frightened and he could do nothing but watch as she was dragged away. There was at least one small comfort his last act would earn him: Gao would no longer threaten Suyin.

Li Tao faced his former master. 'If you hurt her—'

Lao Sou dismissed him with a snort. 'Go. And don't disappoint me again, Tao.'

Suyin swiveled against the henchmen who held her. Tears stung at the corners of her eyes and her knees threatened to collapse.

Li Tao had come for her. She could hardly believe it. He had always insisted on discipline and control. Even when they argued. He fought for it when they made love. Seeing him had filled her with hope, but all hope fell away when she saw the look in his eyes. They were flat and devoid of light. Dead.

The Old Man would now destroy him for this one weakness, the weakness she'd caused. He was still so close. She could *sense* him. If she called out to him, Li Tao would come rushing back to her and the assassins would put a knife in his heart. So she bit her tongue and remained quiet.

She needed so desperately to tell him about the child growing inside her. She was certain she was pregnant now. The soreness in her breasts and the constant exhaustion were accompanied by waves of sickness from the moment she awoke to late each afternoon. For days, she had fought to hide these signs. They would only give the Old Man more to hold over Li Tao.

The hands clamped around her relaxed as Lao Sou appeared through the curtain.

'He is gone.' He bristled as he strode into the antechamber. He nearly knocked over the chair before righting it and swatted away the attendant who tried to help him.

'Leave me,' he growled

His attendant slipped outside the door and Lao Sou dropped on to the chair. He made a noise in his throat—a half-grunt, half-snort like a little boy trying to get attention.

Men of power had few ears to spill their troubles to. This was something she understood as a courtesan, but she was in no mood to indulge him. He had sent Li Tao to die out of spite.

She remained standing with her back to the corner and her hands balled tight. The pain of having Li Tao close enough to touch only to lose him again cut deep.

'Do you even have a name?' she asked petulantly. 'You certainly were not always an old man.'

'I hardly remember it.'

'Quite sad.'

He twisted in his seat to face her. '*An Ying* has controlled the fate of emperors and generals. This empire has risen in its wake.'

'A lofty description for a den of thieves and murderers.'

'Thieves? Murderers?' He stood, shaking with anger. His sightless eyes searched the corner for her.

Li Tao spoke of the clan as a mysterious force with fingers winding into all corners of the empire. For all she knew, these were only myths to frighten people.

'Assassins hiding in the dark,' she accused.

'You know nothing about *An Ying.*'

'I know you sent Li Tao off to die for your petty revenge.'

Using the furniture as a guide, he attempted to advance on her. The effect was almost pitiable. She was tired of men of power controlling her fate. She had already lived a lifetime of conspiracy.

'If Tao had simply done what he was told years ago...' he ranted.

'What was the price for the August Emperor's head?'

'No price. I called the order on that bastard.'

'Emperor Li Ming was a good man.' Even after his death, she felt the need to defend her protector. Especially against this goat.

'Warmonger with the head of a baboon!' Lao Sou slapped his

palm against the table. 'He would have brought the empire into one battle after another until it fell into ruin. If he had fallen at Shibao, Emperor Shen would have taken the throne fifteen years earlier.'

She realised then that Lao Sou had once operated in the inner court. Perhaps before the reign of the August Emperor. He could be a minister or a general. It was the only way a secret clan could gain such influence.

Boldly, she took a step closer, loud enough that he knew exactly where she stood. She wasn't afraid. She was tired of being careful.

'Li Tao described you as a cold, calculating mastermind. I see a bitter old man, buckling under the weight of time. You're angry because Li Tao wouldn't grovel before you after all these years. Even if he did, you wouldn't have the satisfaction of seeing it.'

The room fell silent. Lao Sou stopped with a huff of breath. He pointed a wrinkled finger at her accusingly. 'I was always told that Ling *Guifei* was charming and sweet-tempered.'

'Whoever told you that?'

'Plant more flowers than thorns, they say.'

'Why should I be flowers and perfume when you deal in knives and poison?' she demanded.

He grunted and struck his hand against the table top. Then, to her surprise, he chuckled. He turned and found his seat, sitting back with his hands propped upon his knees. It seemed their altercation had drained the bile out of him.

'She-demon,' he remarked with an inexplicable amount of glee. 'No wonder Li Tao is so smitten with you.'

Chapter Twenty-One

Imperial Palace—ad 746
13 years earlier

'These men owe me a debt of blood.' The August Emperor pushed a scroll across the desk to Li Tao, then slid his dragon ring beside the edict. The ruby eye sparked red against the dark wood.

'Take the LongWu Guard.'

The Emperor's elite guard was recruited from amongst the aristocratic families of the empire and he, a commoner, a bastard of low birth, was to lead them on a mission of revenge.

Li Tao turned the ring over in his palm. 'As the Emperor commands.'

He slipped the ring on to his finger and lifted the scroll to search the characters. Men of title and rank. Some of them within the first order, closest to the Emperor. There were close to a hundred names.

'The Empress was carrying my son.' The Emperor's voice faltered, but his next words were spoken with steel-cut clarity. 'I intend to settle the debt in this lifetime.'

Li Tao nodded and rolled the edges of the scroll closed. There would be no stalking in the shadows this time. The Emperor had issued a public decree that these men were already dead. He simply needed to hunt them down and deal the final blow. The Emperor's hands would remain clean.

Perhaps Li Ming had known what he was all along: a killer. A man with a knife.

The message came to him in the middle of the night. Li Tao was stationed in the fortress tower at Chengdu, overlooking the Jin River, and he'd been far from asleep. It was less than a day since he'd left Suyin in the hands of his enemy.

The walls of the Chengdu made it suitable for a siege. Throughout the province, he had regiments in reserve. Key points along the bank were fortified. His army was ready. But now there was another urgent message. Another clandestine meeting, but not with Gao.

Li Tao crossed the river with a small escort. They used lanterns to light their way in the darkness. A tent had been raised on the far side of the shore and was guarded by only a handful of soldiers. The camp was marked by torches. Everything had the mark of such haste that Li Tao suspected an ambush at first. He dismissed the possibility as he assessed the banner that flew over the meeting area.

He was surprised, he had to admit. Very surprised.

The soldiers at the entrance bowed and pulled the canvas aside to admit him. A table had been set up inside. The young man seated behind it looked more worn than he, if that was possible.

'You are lucky my archers recognised the imperial insignia,' Li Tao said. 'You might have been shot on sight.'

'I don't believe that, given your reputation for discipline.'

He would have recognised Tai Yang from his voice and speech alone. The Emperor's middle son had the characteristic high cheekbones and serious, deep-set eyes of the Shen family. When Li Tao had first encountered Shen Tai Yang, he'd received a commission in the Emperor's LongWu Guard due to his name. It was an illustrious name to live up to.

Now he was a prince.

Tai Yang gestured for him to sit and poured a perfunctory cup of wine for each of them.

'You are a difficult man to defend, Governor Li.' The younger man drank his wine before setting the cup down with agitation.

That amused Li Tao, for reasons he didn't understand. 'I've heard a similar sentiment expressed recently.'

'How many summons did my father send you?'

'Three.'

'You're a bastard, Li.'

Tai Yang had picked up some fire in the year since Li Tao had last seen him. Shen's middle son was known for maintaining a calm head in the worst of conditions.

'Circumstances were not favourable for me in Changan, as the prince can understand.'

'Drink your wine,' Tai Yang muttered.

He complied. The small act of civility seemed to calm the younger Shen considerably.

Tai Yang smoothed a hand over the front of his robe to right himself. 'Have you spoken to Gao?'

'Tomorrow.'

Tai Yang let out a breath of relief. 'I nearly killed that horse to get here in time. I told my father that you would never ally your-self with that old wolf. We believe there must be some reason for your actions, as questionable as they seem.'

'Is that why you've been marching an army of thousands toward these borders?'

The prince tensed, then reached to pour more wine as a distrac-tion. 'If my father wanted to have you defeated, he would have sent one of my brothers.'

They faced off across the table, the threat wisping between them like fog, not yet solid and real. The Emperor's two elder sons were formidable warlords in their own right. Their regional armies held the northern part of the empire. It was the combined forces of the Shen family that allowed them to emerge as the dominant power after Emperor Li had died without a successor. Rival warlords

accused Shen of seizing the throne, while they crouched in their
fortresses, hoping to do the same.

'I came here to negotiate with you, Li Tao.'

'Despite my many offences?'

If Shen's son had arrived sooner, before Suyin had been captured, then there might have been some hope.

'The Emperor wants the same thing as you. Gao only wants disorder so he can feed off it. Swear loyalty to my father, Governor
Li. Others will follow your lead.'

'Not all.'

'We know this. We understand that Gao has been building up
his forces. The other warlords will declare their alliances openly.
Division is unavoidable now.'

The prince had served in the imperial army as had all of Shen's
sons, but Tai Yang usually much more conservative in his actions.
It was a surprise that he'd ridden into the centre of the brewing
battle so unprotected. It seemed now was the time for bold gestures. Nothing else would suffice.

'The Emperor is prepared to denounce Gao?' Li Tao asked.

Tai Yang shifted uncomfortably. 'If he has to.'

Gao was too powerful. Emperor Shen had to acknowledge his
influence to a point. It had held Shen back from acting sooner.

'What if charges could be brought against Gao?' Li Tao thought
of all Suyin had confessed. He didn't like using her like this, but
perhaps it was the only way to fight the old warlord.

'What sort of charges?'

'Murder. Treason.'

Tai Yang straightened with interest, but his frown deepened. 'We
need your loyalty first, Governor Li. Unconditionally,' he added.

That was the twist of the knife. Shen wanted him under his command.

'You only need my army.'

'We need you,' the prince insisted.

Tai Yang's proposal brought up new possibilities, but none that
could save him. In order to free Suyin, he had to kill Gao. By tomorrow night, he and Gao would be gone. The struggle for balance

and power would have to continue without them. His army would need strong leadership or it would fall to ruin.

The hour was late and the sense of inevitability was closing in on him. 'So Emperor Shen finally understands that peace is impossible. Between Gao and me, he's chosen me as the less dangerous enemy.'

'You were never our enemy. I never believed you had anything to do with my brother's death.'

'Your sister thought differently.'

The prince shook his head wearily. 'That was a mess.'

'Are you saying that to be diplomatic?'

'I'm saying that because it was a mess. We should be family by now.'

Li Tao thought back on the past year, on the failed betrothal and the missed opportunities as he and Emperor Shen had tried to preserve the balance of power in their own way.

'You cannot force an alliance where there is no affinity between the two parties,' Li Tao replied.

'My father should have listened to you. I should have as well, but no one wanted to believe that the empire would break apart.'

They remained silent for several beats, as if in mourning. Tai Yang regarded him thoughtfully. It occurred to Li Tao that someone had to have been his advocate within the capital. A quieter voice to counter Gao's strident one.

'Tell me what you have against Gao,' Tai Yang said finally.

'No matter now. You won't need it.'

Li Tao straightened and rose from his seat. He thought of Suyin and their failed attempt to go to the Emperor directly. She knew enough to expose Gao, but only if Shen was ready to denounce him. Gao had foreseen this possibility and tried to have her killed to remove the threat.

It was down to timing and missed opportunities. If they had succeeded in reaching Changan, or if Tai Yang had come before he'd sent Suyin away… It was useless to think that way. There was only one solution left to him.

'I regret not being able to speak with your father,' Li Tao said. 'But you are a worthy ambassador.'

'As Emperor, my father can't meet with you directly—'

'Until it's clear where I stand. I know.'

'Governor Li.'

He stopped out of respect. Tai Yang had taken a great burden on to his shoulders for someone so young.

'If you are seen negotiating with Gao, it will be difficult for anyone to defend you,' the young man warned.

Li Tao allowed a cold smile. 'I won't be negotiating with him.'

The prince's eyes widened with understanding. 'Governor Li, wait—'

'You'll have my answer tomorrow.'

He slipped from the tent and Tai Yang didn't call after him. Outward appearances were still important. The imperial army was here to secure his allegiance or take him down, whatever was necessary.

He returned to the fortress, to the temporary shelter of the stone walls. His first battalion was stationed there in the capital to await the approaching armies. The Rising Guard was rumoured to be undefeatable, the captains recruited from among the fiercest warriors of the old Dragon Guard. All legends and rumours. General Sun Tzu spoke the truth when he wrote that the greatest battle was won far from the battlefield. Lao Sou and Gao Shiming had outmanoeuvred him at every turn. And now Emperor Shen wanted his loyalty, in blood.

An intrusive memory filled his head. Suyin stretched over him, her feather weight anchoring him to the mattress while she whispered in his ear, *'Let the legends fight their own war.'*

What she had asked for was impossible. But her arms had circled him, her breasts supple against his chest. When he ran his hand down, he could feel the downward slope of her back and the curve of her hip all in one motion, and he closed his eyes to lose himself in the dream.

Suyin had wanted them to leave and disappear into the depths of the empire. But people like Ling *Guifei* and Governor Li Tao could not disappear. When he was tasked with the execution of the Empress's murderers, the conspirators had gone into hiding and he had found them all. Except for Gao. Except for Suyin.

His life was not his own. Perhaps it never had been, from the moment he had first plunged his knife into another man for silver.

The hilt of the sleeve sword pressed against his wrist. There was still one skill he excelled at. The Old Man was right. This was a clean end to things. One knife. Two deaths. Gao and then himself, soon after.

It wouldn't be the end of the conflict. Gao had his heirs to succeed him. The warlord's forces would regroup and reassess. Perhaps they would come after his domain for revenge, but Li Tao had no successors for them to hunt down.

The thought gave him his only moment of regret. He had no heirs. No legacy.

Enough. He was already making a mistake by thinking too much about his target. He had brought this moment upon himself; he had no choice but to face it.

Li Tao allowed himself to think of Ling Suyin one final time as the sun rose. He would not see her again, but Lao Sou would be true to his word and release her. Li Tao needed to bind that belief to his soul and hold it deep where it was hidden. Then he would banish all thought of her. Emotion would make his heart pound and his hand shake. If he hesitated for even one moment, he'd falter. All his sacrifice would be for nothing.

Chapter Twenty-Two

'You should get a walking stick, old man.'

Lao Sou grunted at her suggestion. He held onto her arm as they navigated the woods and gestured with his free hand. 'Go that way.'

Of all things, he wanted her to take a stroll with him outside the temple. As if she was a nursemaid instead of a prisoner. She had been counting the hours since Li Tao left. He would be heading toward the Jin River, toward his death if she couldn't get free.

'How much can you see?' she asked.

'Everything is murky. Shapes and shadows and only in the sunlight. Here, come here.'

He beckoned her close and then took hold of her face. She fought the urge to pull away from the leathery feel of his hands against her delicate skin, but there was something vulnerable in the way he peered at her so intently.

'I used to see everything. Faces were like books. I could read the tiny movements around their eyes and mouth and their faces would speak to me before they had said a word. Now I see nothing.' He let go of her. 'Everyone grows old.'

'So you can no longer read the intentions of those closest to you.'

He frowned. 'What do you mean by that?'

'Nothing at all.'

Lao Sou made a sound of annoyance. 'Your veiled hints of conspiracy bore me so. This old dog knows what you are trying to insinuate. Do you know why I brought you out here?'

She looked back on the two guards following behind them at a distance. Lao Sou grabbed her attention with a yank on her wrist.

'Li Tao cannot protect you. Come and work for me.'

'Old Man, in case you do not know, we are enemies.'

He waved away her declaration as if swatting away a gnat. 'I need your eyes, your ears.'

'When you surround yourself with liars and thieves, you have to watch your back all the time.'

'We're not thieves.' He sighed, exasperated. 'You have a talent for reading people and discovering their intentions. How else could you turn someone like the righteous Ru Shan?'

'How do you know of that?'

'Of course I know. I know everything about your beloved Li Tao.'

'Don't mock me, Old Man.'

It was a painful reminder that this was all a game. He took pride in manipulating the world around him, in controlling the lives of men.

'You're not saying anything, Ling *Guifei*. Not like you at all. Tell me, what expression are you wearing right now?'

'Disdain.'

'Indeed. Well, answer me.'

Insufferable man. She glared at him. 'Why would I serve you? You sent Li Tao to die.'

'He put himself in this situation,' he muttered. 'Besides, it is the only way. Gao Shiming must be destroyed. Honourable men like Emperor Shen need men like us to do the unspeakable.'

She wanted to shout that he wasn't doing anything but sitting back and pulling strings.

'I swear I will put a knife in your heart the first chance I get,' she vowed.

'No, you won't.'

It was strange how they spoke of revenge and death so civilly, their voices lowered in the midst of the morning stroll.

'You are not cold enough,' the Old Man scoffed. 'I could always see people's strengths and their weaknesses. I knew where to place them to make things happen.'

'You were wrong about Li Tao.'

'I was not wrong! *An Ying* has its share of killers. They have their uses. But the most critical tasks require sharp instincts and a strong will. Both make a person unpredictable.'

Life and death meant nothing to this man. His heart was deadened to it. The thought both chilled and saddened her. Would this have been Li Tao after a lifetime of ruthlessness? Was he already like this?

'Think of it, you stubborn old fool. How long is your beloved empire going to last if you keep killing its leaders?'

His hand tightened around her arm. 'You have a wicked tongue, but somehow, I like you, Ling *Guifei*. Do you know I saved your life? I learned about Gao and his amateur assassins. All it took was one message to Li Tao.'

'Why save me?'

He shrugged. 'You played the *qin* so beautifully. It seemed like a waste.'

'Crazy old man,' she muttered.

'Ungrateful she-demon.'

Lao Sou wasn't doing this out of hatred, but she couldn't work out what it was that tied him to Li Tao so obsessively. For whatever reason, the old man enjoyed it when Li Tao did his bidding, whether it was reacting to a mysterious warning or assassinating a warlord.

She knew he wasn't insane, despite her insults. He was shrewd and manipulative. But however formidable the clan leader had been in the past, she was beginning to see his weakness. He'd grown self-centred, vain and indulgent—on the outside.

Lao Sou was lonely. She understood that sentiment more than she would care to admit. He had built his organisation, kept too many secrets all his life, and now there was no one to share his glory. In time, she could gain his trust, but she didn't have time. She needed to find Li Tao and prevent him from sacrificing himself.

'If you discovered Gao's plot, then you must know why he wanted me dead,' she ventured.

'Why else do men act rashly? Jealousy, greed…'

He was rambling now. He didn't know about Gao's plans. She'd have to persuade him another way.

'Which of those explains why you sent Li Tao to his death?'

'Simple.' The old man snorted. 'I needed that bastard Gao removed and Li Tao is my finest weapon.'

'You're a sentimental fool.'

She witnessed his anger rising, the instant regaining of control, and, a second before that, a glimmer of contemplation. Lao Sou didn't care at all about Gao Shiming. This was a personal grudge over Li Tao's defiance. She pounced.

'You made a mistake, Old Man. You acted out of emotion.'

'She-demon,' he grumbled. He had run out of responses.

'Li Tao is more useful to you alive.'

'Not if he doesn't follow orders.' Suddenly, a slow grin spread across his face and Suyin doubted she'd won the battle at all.

'Can you control him, Lady Ling?' he asked.

This was precarious ground. 'No one can control Li Tao.'

Lao Sou shook his head. 'Nothing so sinister, my lady. I have a feeling you can persuade him where no one else could. Yin balances yang, does it not?'

This was what she had wanted, wasn't it? A chance for a compromise.

'What do you require from him? One thing only.'

Lao Sou stroked his beard, enjoying the moment. 'That requires some thought.'

After all their days and nights together, Li Tao still remained impenetrable. She wouldn't try to deceive him, not even to save him. And he would never allow anyone to speak on his behalf.

She was being asked to make a promise she couldn't keep, to a man she didn't trust. But Li Tao was going to die if she didn't do something. He would die without knowing he'd fathered a child. She was falling into a chasm, air rushing past her, almost certain death below.

'Take me to him.' It was a good thing the Old Man couldn't read her expression and couldn't see her doubt. 'Li Tao will listen to me.'

The meeting point was further along the Jin River, in a remote location between major cities. A tea house rose along the banks to serve weary travellers, but the owners had evacuated weeks earlier when the barricades formed.

Li Tao's army held the southern bank. He approached the tea house with only two of his bodyguards. Gao had done the same. He could see the horses tethered beside the bridge that spanned the water. The enemy was camped on the far side, out of sight.

Li Tao left his men by the bridge. He took the path slowly, using the time to empty his head of all doubt. The instinct was still in him. He didn't need to search deep to find it. The coldness was there, sleeping just beneath his skin. It had always been there.

With steady breaths, in, then out, he slowed his heartbeat. Gao would be able to smell any fear on him, but he'd show none. He only needed to get close enough to strike.

Soon all his debts would be paid. His debt to Lao Sou. His debt to Suyin. He would end as a lone assassin, the same as he had started.

The tea house was a magnificent one, rising several floors with an elaborate frame of wooden beams and columns. Li Tao entered with all senses on alert. His footsteps echoed in the wide open spaces of the tea house. The tables and chairs were all empty. No ambush awaited him.

Gao had seated himself beside the window with the best view of the river. His guards stood against the wall, one on either side of the table. Only two men. Li Tao could take two.

The ageing warlord waited with a tray of wine set before him, looking formal and cultured in a silk robe trimmed with brocade. The blade at his side was likely tarnished from disuse. The warlord had gotten heavier in his grey years, but Gao's advanced age gained no sympathy. His look was as shrewd as ever.

'Governor Li.' Gao's tone could be described as jovial. And smug. 'I'm pleased you've come.'

Li Tao's very presence would have to mean he was considering the deal. Gao was a politician who trusted that two warlords would never draw swords directly against one another. That would be unfathomable. Uncivilised. Barbaric.

With a steady heart, Li Tao approached the table head on. He hadn't yet drawn a path in his mind. His hands remained loose by his sides. For this sort of task, it was better not to plan too far in advance. Success or failure would be decided in a grain of time. A perfect moment.

No need to risk signalling his intention too soon.

Gao watched him with single-minded intensity, his eyes like dark glass. 'No greeting, Governor Li?'

A nod. 'Governor Gao.'

Li Tao stopped and planted his feet firmly against the floor boards. A coil of readiness wound within him, but outwardly he remained uncommitted, his shoulders relaxed. Utter stillness before the strike. Lao Sou trained assassins who could slip in and out of locked rooms. He recruited men and woman who killed with poison and made death look still and natural. Li Tao had never been one of those stealthy operators. He dealt death swift and clean.

Gao must have tasted something in the air. 'Won't you be seated?'

The old warlord's gaze veered out to the river. Li Tao knew without reason, knew it in his blood that it had to be then.

He lashed forwards like an arrow, brash and blind.

Li Tao narrowed in on a single point: Gao's throat. The killing instinct was there in his hands and in his blood. Gao's smooth exterior faded. He opened his mouth to utter something, whether it was a question or a cry for help, Li Tao didn't know.

He no longer thought of the man as his enemy. Gao no longer existed.

Chapter Twenty-Three

Suyin rode behind Jun in the saddle, clinging to youth's waist so tightly that her arms ached. The forest rushed by on either side of her in a flood of browns and greens. This time, the blind fear came not from the horse or from the speed of the ride. Her fear came from the inevitable drip of time.

She held her breath in a useless attempt to hold back the minutes. Her heart beat out each second, one after another. She urged Jun to go faster, but she didn't know whether he heard her. The rush of the wind swallowed her shout and swept it away.

Li Tao was somewhere close, ready to plunge a dagger into Gao's heart. A cold sweat broke out over her brow and an odd sensation caught in her throat. She fought down the wave of nausea. Whether it was from the motion or from pregnancy, she couldn't tell.

She had to stop Li Tao. She had to.

A red bridge appeared ahead, with the tea house beside it. The ornate building stood over the river in a deceptively tranquil welcome. *An Ying* knew of the meeting place between the two warlords. Their spies seemed to know everything.

Jun dismounted just outside the tree line and helped her down from the saddle. Her legs wobbled as her feet hit the earth. She tried to centre herself, inside and out. Success. She'd only think of success, and not failure.

The boy steadied her with one arm awkwardly around her shoulders. Jun wasn't merely a boy any more. He didn't appear so young and vulnerable when she looked at him now.

'Be careful, Lady Ling,' he said, before pulling himself back on to the horse.

'You're going?'

The corner of his mouth lifted in a rueful smile. 'You forget how I betrayed Governor Li.'

'I didn't forget.'

'Neither will he.' He nodded toward the tea house in the distance. 'Go quickly, Lady Ling. They're already inside.'

She turned to the river and spied the horses beside the bridge. Beside them, Li Tao's guards stood in a silent watch. They faced away, their attention focused on the opposite bank, in the direction of the approaching armies.

When she looked back, Jun had disappeared. She heard nothing, not even the stamp of hooves to signal his retreat. The woods were silent and shadowed as she searched the dark patches between the light. Was the clan hiding in there, watching and waiting to report on Li Tao's failure or success?

She hurried to the tea house and slipped in through the side entrance. The echo of voices floated through the deserted structure. She heard two, both resonating down to her very bones. One was Li Tao's, deep and familiar, curling around her and tugging her forwards.

He was alive. She quickened her step.

The second voice was one she hadn't heard in years. One she'd hoped to never hear again.

Suyin came to a halt in the main room. Li Tao's back was to her. He was stalking forwards with deliberate purpose and she caught sight of a long-forgotten face over his shoulder. Gao Shiming. The man who wanted her dead, who wanted Li Tao under his control.

Li Tao's fingers flexed at his side. It was going to happen.

'Governor Li.' Louder. 'Tao, I'm here.'

He swung around and glared at her with black eyes devoid of light. Her heart skipped dangerously.

'Ling *Guifei*?' Gao sputtered.

The old warlord was startled. His guards, confused. And Li Tao was angry, angrier than she'd ever seen him. The muscles in his jaw wrenched tight.

Of all of them, Gao recovered first. 'Please join us.' His smile was welcoming, his gaze keen.

'You have no place here,' Li Tao growled.

He angled himself to shield her from Gao as she stepped forwards. The fluidity of the movement shocked her.

'But Lady Ling must stay! We need something more engaging to look at than our own frightful faces.'

All the smooth charm that Li Tao didn't possess. Gao looked at the two of them with growing amusement. He didn't know how close he'd come, how close he still was, to death. All three of them dangled preciously close to it.

Lao Sou had his men take her to the meeting place. They'd left her to disappear into the forest, but they would be waiting. The leader of the assassinations would demand her obedience now, as well as Li Tao's. But she couldn't think of that now. The immediate danger was before her, gesturing politely for her to sit.

She brushed past Li Tao to take one of the chairs at the table. He had no choice but to seat himself rigidly beside her. He was there. He was alive. Her heart ached at the sight of him and she wanted so much to touch him, but there was no opportunity. Gao was watching.

'The last time I saw Ling *Guifei* was at the banquet hall in the imperial palace. These old eyes still remember the sight.'

'It has been a long time, Governor Gao.'

He nodded warmly, as if they were co-conspirators, but they had never been anything of the sort. He had held all the power and she had feared him. Gao pinned her with his gaze. He was assessing her, planning for this sudden change.

Her old fear remained, but it had grown like a wound that had festered over time. She was no longer in the palace and no longer the expendable concubine, but she had so much more to lose. A child grew inside her, a tiny thing that held more power over her than Gao Shiming ever had.

Li Tao remained tense, ready to strike. She was here beside him, unharmed, yet he still refused to back down. If he murdered Gao, there would be no escape for any of them. Li Tao would be denounced and executed. Her stomach lurched and she forced out a breath. She knew what had to be done.

Gao Shiming had used her and tried to kill her, but now she had to keep him alive.

She lifted the ewer to pour with poised hands, supple wrists, practised grace. Courtesans were brought to such dealings to be beautiful diversions. It was akin to being a mediator used to keep the peace.

'You do look very well, Lady Ling.'

'The governor is kind. I am well.' She glanced to Li Tao as she handed him his wine. 'Well and safe.'

His hand paused on the cup for a heartbeat, his fingers just shy of hers.

'It's been a long time since I've poured for such illustrious company,' she said.

'An art form,' Gao acknowledged appreciatively.

Li Tao scowled. Everyone was playing the part but him.

'The rule of the August Emperor was a different time, wasn't it, Governor Li?' Gao lifted his wine cup in tribute.

'It was.'

'A great time, blessed by Heaven,' Gao remarked.

Li Tao finished his wine and set his cup down. 'Say what you came to say.'

A low rumble hid beneath those words. The old warlord laughed. Showing impatience was a sign of weakness. Someone else was in control and you were not.

'I forget who I'm dealing with,' Gao crowed.

'I doubt that.'

Gao took his time sipping from his cup, enjoying the game too much. Her heart pounded, and she could feel her palms going damp. Gao was oblivious, overconfident in his advantage. His guards wouldn't be able to stop Li Tao.

'Don't be so impatient, Tao,' she scolded with a sweetness she'd never affected for him.

Li Tao stared directly at Gao. 'I don't think anything said here will change my mind.'

'But one must always consider alternatives,' she argued hastily.

If Li Tao would only look at her. She was no longer hostage. Yet he still believed killing Gao was the best solution. Nothing could sway him. She groped for his hand beneath the table and brought it to her midsection. To the place where a tiny part of them rested, innocent and unknowing of any turmoil beyond its haven. She was shaking inside and out as she closed her hand over his.

Li Tao grew deathly still.

Would this child mean anything to him? Or had he already resigned himself to death? The knot at his throat lifted as he swallowed. His gaze was still pointed at Gao, but his hand tensed beneath hers.

'One must always think of the future,' she went on. Her throat was suddenly parched, but she didn't dare drink. She didn't dare to do anything but wait for Li Tao's response. If one soul could ever cry out to another in silence, she did it now with all her being.

Please, Tao. Please.

Endless heartbeats passed between them. She willed him to choose the right path. Only a slight sharpening of the lines around his mouth told her anything. Her true adversary wasn't Gao or Lao Sou. It was Li Tao and he was more difficult to negotiate with than either of those scheming old men.

Gao chuckled. 'Why, Lady Ling, you should do all my negotiation for me!'

She shot the elder warlord a warning glance. His presence was as welcome as a disease. 'Perhaps you should speak quickly, Governor,' she said.

Her challenge brought back the Gao Shiming she had feared all those years ago. He shed all civility and charm and fixed his attention intently on Li Tao. She became nothing. She was below nothing. An instinctive shudder slid down her spine.

She held her breath and prayed.

* * *

The earth stood still. The heavens revolved around it and he was nothing but a speck beneath the sky. Suyin's fingers twined gently over his.

He knew. He knew deep in his flesh and blood what she was telling him. On the heels of the knowledge came true fear.

Across the table, Old Gao stared at them with a shrewd look. Li Tao never felt anything when he was asked to kill, but this time— this one time, he wanted nothing more than to remove this smiling demon from the world. A quick sword through the tangled weeds and Gao would no longer be able to threaten them. Now that he had the crafty warlord before him, Li Tao could sense the truth of the Old Man's taunt.

It would be easy. One knife, one death. This was what he was meant to do.

'You and me,' Gao proposed.

'Why would I even consider it?'

Li Tao removed his hand from Suyin. She was trembling, though her expression showed nothing but cool tranquillity.

'You and I want the same thing,' Gao continued.

'Which is?'

'To honour the memory of the August Emperor. The true imperial line. The only claim Shen holds over the empire is the strength of his army. He's a usurper and a barbarian.'

'I'm surprised that you've decided to act so openly,' Li Tao countered. 'A man who usually thrives on rules and laws and petitions before the court.'

'Times are changing.'

He regarded Gao sceptically. 'Who will rule, then? You?'

'No.' Suyin's response startled everyone. She faced her old enemy with all the poise the years in the court had given her. 'The revered governor never acts directly. He's found some puppet. Some distant relation with a blood tie to Emperor Li Ming. Your family claims imperial blood, does it not?'

Gao wanted to use Li Tao's army to face Emperor Shen on the battlefield, while Gao would continue to fight political battles in the capital. This was *shōu guān*: endgame. A time for bold moves and decisive measures.

Li Tao had come here committed to action. The bitter taste of death hovered on his tongue. After years of scheming and politics, he welcomed the quick efficiency of this solution. This was familiar. Certain.

He looked to Suyin. Grace and beauty, even now. Her poise never broke in the face of her longtime enemy. She hadn't faltered before Lao Sou either, not until he'd been threatened. He wanted to embrace her for it. Hold her fiercely to him. Hide her away from all this. He could never have peace, but she could. Their child could.

He had decided.

'You spoke of loyalty to our August Emperor and to the dynasty.' Li Tao folded his hands thoughtfully before him, the daggers beneath his sleeve easily within reach. He had a clear line to both of the guardsmen should it come to that. 'Laughable, considering that you owe Emperor Li a debt of blood.'

Gao's focus darted to Suyin.

'Don't,' Li Tao warned.

The sharp reprimand brought the older man's gaze back to him. No one was smiling now, feigned or otherwise.

'I would advise you not to look at Lady Ling. Do not do anything to convince me you have any intention of harming her. We will talk now, like civilised men as you so desired. But if I think for a moment that she's in danger, I will stop talking.'

The guards tensed, but Gao wisely held them back with a raised hand. The coldness of his gaze showed that he, too, could show no fear in the face of death.

'There was a list given to me by the August Emperor,' Li Tao began. 'The names of the men who had conspired against him. I recently learned that there was one name left off the list.'

'You're *jiedushi* now,' Gao replied smoothly. He was skilled at the art of confrontation. 'You command thousands upon thousands. I would think you would look beyond revenge.'

'It was never for revenge.' Out of the corner of his eye, he saw how Suyin shuddered at his cold words. She should know what was required to become who he was now. 'There was never any emotion to it, for me or for you. You supported the August Emperor, yet murdered his Empress after he was taken down in battle. Loyal to no one.'

'What does loyalty matter to you?' Gao sneered.

'It matters to Shen.' And it mattered to the other noblemen and warlords who revered the imperial line. The same families Gao strived to bring under his control. 'It seems that you, Shen, and I have come to the same conclusion—balance can no longer be maintained. My army, my captains and the entire Rising Guard have been sworn over to the Emperor as of this morning.'

Gao took in the blow impassively. His shrewd expression wavered, but not in defeat. Already he was reassessing and coming up with a new plan. A simple knife in Gao's chest could stop those treacherous thoughts for ever. It was the only way to ensure that Suyin would be safe. Li Tao considered it. His hands itched from considering it.

'So you must ask yourself, why did I come here when there was nothing left to say?' he posed calmly. 'Why did I come here alone to meet you?'

Gao's jaw worked silently. A drop of sweat beaded over the old warlord's brow—his first sign of fear. Suyin froze in her seat. Her knuckles were white against the edge of the table. He could see the jump of her pulse beneath the pale skin of her neck.

'It is bad form for men like us to hack at each other like butchers,' Gao said through his teeth.

Death would have been easy to accomplish. His knife would cut through the two guards. He'd wring Gao's neck with his hands if he had to. He was fast enough and more ruthless than any of the other men in the room, but Suyin's presence and the secret she'd revealed to him changed everything.

Li Tao exhaled slowly. 'I agree.'

A dark sense of peace had washed over him that morning when he'd signed the decree swearing his army over to the imperial prince. Soon he would be done.

But he'd been wrong. Murdering Gao would only send the opposition charging forth under a banner of righteous outrage. Their confrontation would come soon enough, once the battle lines had been redrawn.

'Go,' he told Gao. 'Before I remember that list.'

The old wolf stared at him before rising from the table. 'An army of thousands is easy to find.'

The bastard bowed before leaving.

Suyin held her breath beside him as they watched Gao's withdrawal through the windows of the tea house. His men helped him on to his horse to return to his troops. Gao would continue to work his schemes, but the warlord's secrets were exposed. He would have to face them out in the open.

Suyin turned to him with a gasp. Her arms curved around him, squeezing tight. Relief poured from her.

'Tao,' she whispered.

Her curves fit against him and he could smell the faint perfume in her hair.

He remained unmoving. 'You're with child?'

'I am.'

His chest tightened unbearably, and he could hear each individual beat of his heart in the silence. There would be a son or a daughter.

Wordlessly, his arm tightened around her waist to lead her from the tea house. Once outside, he kept her close. Gao had departed, but danger continued to lurk in every shadow. His bodyguards waited for them at the bridge. Somehow Suyin had been smuggled past them.

He would think of a suitable punishment for such carelessness, but he was more concerned about getting Suyin as far from there as possible. The knowledge that she was with child left him vulnerable. The feeling was new and decidedly unwelcome.

Her hand curved warm over his stiff fingers. She shouldn't look so relieved. Part of him would live on once his life was over, but that knowledge was all he could have of this dream. He would never see their child take his first breath.

'You're not happy,' Suyin said as they neared the riverbank.

'Nothing has been resolved.'

'But you've sworn allegiance to Emperor Shen.'

She didn't yet understand. The threat was still very much with them. Gao would gather his followers and attempt to denounce Emperor Shen. The Emperor would go on the offensive. He would need his strongest generals behind him. And that was only part of the danger. Li Tao could never let down his guard, not even for her. She was his one weakness and it had nearly destroyed everything.

Li Tao looked to the two guardsmen. 'Now is not the time to discuss—'

'Now *is* the time.' She shook free of him and stood her ground. Pain and anger radiated through her. She'd thrown herself between him and Gao Shiming. He owed her an explanation. He owed her more.

It took only a minute to order the guardsmen to take the horses. They moved slightly ahead on the path, just out of hearing range. These were matters that couldn't be spoken of in the open.

'How did you get free of Lao Sou?' he asked.

When she didn't answer, he knew his suspicion was correct. She had put herself in the Old Man's debt to come to him.

'What does the Old Man want from you?'

'It's not like that—'

He took hold of her arm to pull her close, speaking only in a fierce whisper. 'I've failed Lao Sou twice now and I can't protect you. I can't protect our child. Nothing means more to me than that.'

'Nothing means more to me.' Suyin tried to cradle his face in her hands.

He pulled away from her. Every touch pained him. Her words held so much hope and faith.

'You made a deal with him. Suyin, you shouldn't have.'

'You were going to your death. It was the only way.'

He'd always known that someone would come for him one day. It was useless to fear the inevitable, but everything had changed. The assassins knew that and they'd taken her to force his hand. They would never stop. Then there were the countless other enemies. Gao, even Shen himself. No one was truly an ally among the *jiedushi*. He'd already endangered her too many times. He wouldn't do it again.

'Does Lao Sou know you're with child?' he asked.

She shook her head. It was only a small mercy.

'You need to go away. Far,' he insisted. 'No one can know about the child.'

'*Our* child.'

An indescribable emotion coursed through him. Suyin seized on it.

'We may never be safe and we may never be free.' Her fingers gripped the collar of his robe. She was a fox spirit, a sorceress, a goddess. 'I don't want to hide any more. I want to live openly. I want to see your hair go grey. I'll grow old and ugly beside you.'

'You'll never be old and ugly.' His voice grew rough with emotion and he finally did hold her, running his hands from her shoulders down the length of her arms. His eyes never left her face. 'Lao Sou will never forgive this second act of defiance. You don't know what he's capable of. He'll come for my soul. He'll come for you.'

'I will die without you,' she insisted.

'You won't.'

Her eyes flashed with anger. She bit down to keep from lashing out.

'You'll survive and care for our child,' he went on. 'Tell him my name when he's grown.'

'You want me to leave? After all that has happened?'

'This is the only way.' The words were more difficult than he'd anticipated. He had to force them out. 'I am doing this—for you.'

Her nearness and everything about her tempted him, but this was not his happiness to claim.

Suyin looked ready to claw his eyes out. 'I'll tell your child his father was a coward for abandoning his own flesh and blood. And you know what it is like for a woman alone.'

The pulse in his neck throbbed. 'You can be quite wicked.'

She shoved him away with a frustrated sound. 'You already tried to send me away once. We can't hide. You should know that by now.'

He braced himself, giving her nothing to strike at. No anger, no passion, no emotion at all. It was too easy to be persuaded to take the few hours, days, or even years they could steal for themselves.

'After I join my army with Shen's, there will be war among the *jiedushi*. It is inevitable.'

'Men have lived with the threat of war for ages,' she argued.

She was right, but she didn't understand the whole of why he couldn't give in to her now.

'Death will follow me,' he said bluntly. 'In one way or another.'

That was the final truth. He was a killer who had defied the most dangerous men in the empire. From his very first night in the alleyways of Luoyang, he was never meant to have a future. Every moment since then had been stolen. Suyin needed to take their child and go far away where she would be safe. That was all he could give.

'I won't go.' Like a stubborn child, she wouldn't look at him. 'What will you do then?'

The commotion came first from the guards. He looked quickly to them, saw the movement bursting through the trees. He only had time to grab Suyin and pull her behind him.

At first he thought the attacker had punched him. Sharp pressure struck his side, knocking the breath from him. But the pain continued. It spread as he fell back with a hand clutched to his abdomen.

A stream of heated blood seeped between his fingers.

His hands had become nerveless. His sword. He was under attack and needed a weapon, but shock and pain overtook him as he reached for his sword. He staggered and crashed to the ground. Ru Shan appeared above him. Suyin cried out, but the rebel soldier held her back.

'Lady Ling, you must come with me.'

'Get away from me!'

Ru Shan's hair was unkempt, his jaw scraggly with a growth of beard. Suyin clawed at him until he let go of her. Li Tao watched each action while his heart pounded. With each beat, he bled, his strength draining quickly. His gaze narrowed as Suyin collapsed beside him. She pressed both of her hands over his, over the wound. She was trembling. Frightened. He needed to say something.

His lip curled. 'Fitting.'

All of Suyin's clever manipulations, all the deaths he'd inflicted. 'Please,' she whispered. 'What do I need to do?'

Her face was wet with tears, but he couldn't brush them away. He didn't want to get blood on her. There was blood everywhere. She was going to watch him die if he didn't do something.

His chest heaved. It took a surprising effort to speak, but he was only searching for one word.

'Suyin.'

She leaned close. With his free hand, he stretched out his fingers to touch her cheek. So soft. She always felt like an indulgence, an undeserved kindness. He didn't want to look away.

The upstart Ru Shan was careless. He'd missed the vital organs. This wound would bleed him towards a slow death. Ru Shan had swooped in on the wings of righteousness, honourable and unwavering. He'd wanted to save the beautiful consort from the tyrant. All things came around and back again, didn't they?

'Go with Ru Shan,' Li Tao said.

'No.'

He met Ru Shan's eyes briefly. 'He'll protect you,' he urged.

'This was my doing,' she cried.

It tortured him to see Suyin weeping and broken. She laid her cheek against his. Her breath fanned against his ear. 'Tell me,' she demanded through her tears. 'Tell me what you've been refusing to say.'

His mouth curved involuntarily. Imperious to the last. He couldn't help but obey.

'I love you,' he said. 'I will never love anyone else—in this life or the next.'

She sank against him, her face buried against his neck. 'I will die without you.'

'You won't.'

Her body shook with each sob. He looked up to see Ru Shan watching them. The knife lay slack in his hand, dull with blood.

'Take her,' Li Tao said.

The soldier could finish him easily, if that had been his true intent. Almost obediently, Ru Shan reached out to pull Suyin away.

She shoved him aside. 'Don't touch me!'

Footsteps padded swiftly in the distance. *An Ying*, winding like shadows and smoke through the trees.

Li Tao tried to warn her. 'They're coming.'

His eyes fell closed. His body sagged heavy against the earth. So this was how his victims must have felt: the shock of pain, this creeping numbness, the exhaustion of a lifetime pressing down on his bones. The last thing he knew was Suyin pulling him close. The enticing scent of jasmine wrapped around him.

Chapter Twenty-Four

Li Tao awoke with a start. He remembered the numbness, the blood, the salt of Suyin's tears against his cheek.

'Suyin—'

He choked out her name. A firm hand pressed against his chest to guide him back down on to the mattress.

'Slowly or your wound will open.'

He opened his eyes to the sight of a strange bedchamber, but the reproachful tone was familiar. It had grown raspy with time. His former master sat by the bedside, struggling to fix his sightless eyes on to him.

Li Tao pushed himself to sitting position. The quilt fell from his chest and he slid his hand to the dull throb in his side. His wound had been bound.

'You did this?'

'Do you think I only enlist butchers like you?' Lao Sou asked gruffly.

There were too many questions. The first of them being, how he was he still alive when the lord of assassins sat by his bedside? One thought overpowered all the others. He could still see Suyin next to him, holding on to him even as he commanded her to go. She never followed orders.

'Suyin?'

'She is safe.'

'Let me see her.'

Lao Sou reached for a cup of tea and drank slowly. 'What? No trust?'

'You have been trying to kill me for fifteen years.'

The old man slammed the cup back on to the table. 'Do you think if I was trying to kill you for fifteen years you would be alive? I took you from the streets. I taught you how to be a gentleman, a leader of men. But still you're no better than an unwashed beggar.'

The loss of blood must be making him light-headed. What was the old man talking about?

'Where is Suyin?' he demanded.

'Insolence!' Lao Sou would not be deterred from his rant. 'I gave you an order and you defy me—not once, but twice.'

What sort of game was he playing? Lao Sou had released Suyin with some greater purpose in mind. It was the only explanation.

'If you have harmed her—' The threat withered as pain snaked through his side. He sank back. 'What do you want from me?'

There could be no other reason he was left unharmed. He was weakened to the point that the Old Man could slit his throat easily, even blind as he was.

'Relax, Tao the Unreliable. Your debt is settled.'

The satisfied look on Lao Sou's face chilled his blood. He had woken up to his worst fear.

'Your wife is very clever.' Lao Sou chuckled. 'Much more intelligent than you.'

'She is not my wife,' he replied warily.

'You better marry her soon, you worthless dog.' Lao Sou shook a knobby finger at him. 'My ward will not be without a name.'

'Your ward?'

Lao Sou's smug expression broke into an outright grin. He tilted his head, angling his ear toward the door. 'Ah, there she is now.'

The door burst open and Suyin flew towards the bed in a peach-coloured blur. His heart leapt as she settled against him, soft curves and silk and perfume. He folded her into his arms, and the heavens curved inwards, shrinking to encompass the space around them.

An old wound opened up, deeper than the one in his side. This wound gaped open and raw. Suyin poured into it like an elixir.

Her lips brushed his neck. 'Tao, you're awake.'

'What have you done?' he asked her.

She wasn't listening. She fitted her warm body into his embrace and held him, eyes closed. For several heartbeats, he simply obliged her.

'Tell her she shouldn't be running like that while round with child,' Lao Sou scolded.

She pouted a little. 'I am not round.'

To his eyes, Suyin had the same willowy figure that had become so familiar to him: elegant, sensual and perfect. It was hard to believe their child was already growing within her.

'You will not touch my child,' Li Tao declared.

The Old Man sniffed. He spoke only to Suyin. 'See? Ungrateful.'

The world had turned on its end. Suyin's arms hooked around his neck as she perched on the edge of the bed. He wished they were anywhere else, far from the clan and hidden away from his former master, who hovered over them expectantly, his blank stare even more disconcerting than if he could see them.

'What have you promised this old dragon?' he asked.

'It will be fine.' She met his eyes and he saw strength there. He'd kiss her senseless if he could.

'When I found Tao, he was nothing more than a scrawny street urchin,' Lao Sou railed. 'Only I saw he could be something more.'

This was unbearable. Li Tao started to rise to demand an explanation, but Suyin placed her hand over his chest, just above the tap of his heart. A soothing warmth ran through him, despite the madness of the room. This woman had a hold over him stronger than anything he'd ever known. It was frightening. He couldn't survive without it.

'Apologise to Lao Sou,' she cooed.

He took hold of her hand. Her fingers curled naturally over his as he looked on his former master. 'Never.'

Lao Sou snorted.

'Let me speak to him.' Suyin reached out to touch Lao Sou's arm and the formidable leader of the assassins' clan begrudgingly took hold of his walking stick and stood. He gestured with the end of it.

'This is only right, since I brought the two of you together.'

'What are you talking about, Old Man?' Li Tao demanded, only to have Suyin jab him, gently this time, in the ribs. He would have to break her of that habit.

Lao Sou looked pleased. 'The letter, you fool. Would have been a shame, to lose such a talented lady.'

'You must have been the most devout of monks in a past life to deserve her,' he grumbled.

They listened to the uneven tap of his stick as he moved away. The door opened, then closed. Suyin looked back to him, drawing him in with those dark, captivating eyes. He could admit it now. He'd been caught from the first time they'd looked upon him, over fifteen years ago.

His questions could wait. He drew her close and kissed her; slow and fierce. She murmured a sound of surrender that went all the way through him.

'I was so frightened,' she whispered once their lips parted. She slid her fingertips gingerly over the bandage at his side.

'Lao Sou is a dangerous man,' he reminded her.

'So are you.'

Her bottom lip curved in a way that he knew would captivate him for the rest of his life. It was hard to ignore that he was half-undressed and in bed with the most beautiful woman in the empire.

'Tell me what you promised.'

'Nothing at all,' she said, all innocence. 'Our child will call Lao Sou "grandfather".'

He shook his head and passed a hand over his eyes. 'This is a bargain with a demon.'

'You were dying. He brought in physicians and exorcists.'

'Exorcists?'

'He wanted to hunt Ru Shan down and have him executed, but

I stopped him. Don't you understand?' She took hold of his chin and levelled his gaze to hers.

He loved this fire in her. She would always challenge him like this.

'Lao Sou always wanted you as his successor,' she explained. 'When he sent you to assassinate the August Emperor, it would have elevated you to immortal status among *An Ying*. That was why he was always so angry you defied him. He was fond of you.'

'Fond? This man has dreamt of countless ways to kill me. I won't be his puppet and I won't allow you or our child to be under his control.'

'That's not the way of things any more.' She ran her hand along his chest and there was not a thing in the world he could deny her. 'He's old and lonely.'

'You believe the master of the assassins simply wants a grandson?'

'Yes.'

He rebelled at the absurdity of it. All the attempts on his life, the constant threat. Lao Sou had sent him once again to his death merely days ago.

Then Li Tao realised what he had wanted from the moment he woke up, surprised to still be breathing. He wanted life. He wanted sons and daughters with Suyin. Grandchildren after that if he was fortunate enough. As much as he didn't deserve a moment of happiness, he longed for those sunset days she spoke of. They would be slow and grey-haired beside each other.

His former master had indeed wanted his revenge in the past, but he could have changed. Lao Sou did seem to scold him as if berating—it was unfathomable to even think it—a son.

Suyin had negotiated a crafty deal. The empire was on the brink of civil war and he still had too many enemies to count. But they would have Lao Sou's protection. There was still danger hanging over them, but there had always been danger.

'This is madness,' he muttered.

'I know.'

But perhaps it was the only way for their debts to be paid. Suyin curled closer to him and something fierce and demanding inside him reached out for her. He suddenly felt as if he could fight off an entire legion if he needed to. This wasn't weakness. This was strength.

For no reason he could understand, he thought of Luoyang. Running the streets at night, hiding from the city guards who watched from the walls. He had been waiting all this time for the arrow to pierce him. It was no way to live.

'No more talk of hiding or going away.' Suyin wrapped her arms around him and glanced up at him uncertainly. 'Stop fighting me. I am round with child, you know. I tire very easily— What is it?' she demanded.

He was grinning. It surprised him as well. Suyin was drawing from all her skill, doing everything in her power to coax and charm him, when she didn't need to. Yet he wanted her to do so anyway. She was a wonder to behold.

'Is tomorrow a favourable day?' he asked, sinking his hand into her hair. She was soft, warm, perfect.

She frowned at him. 'I don't know. I suppose I would have to ask Auntie.'

'If not tomorrow, then the next day. I won't wait any longer than that for us to be wed.'

'Scoundrel.' She swatted his chest, but he could see the smile tugging at the corners of her mouth. 'What about the engagement ceremony? We need our fortunes read. And Cook will need a whole day to roast a pig.'

'Who are we to obey custom?' he asked in all seriousness.

'Well, we have no ancestors to appease.' She sighed. 'We don't even have our birthdates for the fortune teller or true names.'

There was no sadness in it. It was who they were. Who they had created themselves to be. He didn't need astrologers to bless their union. He only needed one thing.

'What we have is between us,' he said. 'Only us.'

She settled obligingly into his lap and he found himself wondering how much activity he could manage with the threads sewn into his side. If he simply lay still…

He ran his palm gently down her back and the look she gave him chased away any lingering doubt. This was his destiny, his path from this moment on. Life, not death. He loved her completely. He *loved*. It had taken the moment of darkness before death for him to realise it. As if death was the only language he knew, but not any more.

His arms circled her while she rested in his lap. Odd how they could fit together so perfectly like this. The pain in his side barely bothered him. It was a blessing that Ru Shan, competent soldier that he was, was a failure as an assassin. One of many blessings.

Suyin laid her head down against his shoulder and let out a long, drawn breath. 'No more negotiation this time,' she said. 'Not one night, not one month.'

The moment curled over them like a woollen blanket. He thought of long days with Suyin. Days as well as nights. Years. Hope grew inside him. It was a strange sensation, like a new skin, like a first, awkward step. But it felt right.

'Yes,' he agreed. 'Yes.'

There was no more negotiation. There were no more boundaries. Li Tao placed his hand tenderly over Suyin's stomach and imagined the tiny heartbeat there.

* * * * *

UNTAMED ROGUE, SCANDALOUS MISTRESS
Bronwyn Scott

Notorious Crispin Ramsden is captivated when faced with self-made Miss, Aurora Calhoun. She's a woman whose impetuous nature ignites a passion that is as uncontrollable as it is scandalous! Can these two wild hearts find a place to belong?

HONOURABLE DOCTOR, IMPROPER ARRANGEMENT
Mary Nichols

Dr Simon Redfern has risked his heart once before and is shocked when he longs to make the compassionate young widow Kate his wife. Faced with family disapproval, Kate must fight her growing attraction to the man she can't have but so desperately wants.

THE EARL PLAYS WITH FIRE
Isabelle Goddard

Bitter Richard Veryan was left heartbroken after beautiful Christabel Tallis jilted him before their wedding. But when he and Christabel meet again, years later, temptation hangs in the air. He wants to prove he can still command her body and soul—then *he'll* be the one to walk away...

HIS BORDER BRIDE
Blythe Gifford

Clare, daughter of a Scottish lord, can recite the laws of chivalry. She knows dark rebel Gavin, illegitimate son of an English prince, has broken every one. Clare is gripped by desire for this royal rogue. Could he be the one to unleash everything she's tried so hard to hide?

Mills & Boon® Hardback Historical

Another exciting novel available this month:

THE SCANDALOUS LORD LANCHESTER

Anne Herries

The wayward widow

With her wealth, beauty and playful nature, young widow Mariah Fanshawe is not short of suitors. Yet the only man she wants to marry is immune to her obvious charms! Upright Andrew, Lord Lanchester has always seemed determined to resist, but Mariah has a new plan to win him over…

Andrew is thrown when Mariah asks him to help her find a husband. The truth is he'd like nothing more than to make the wild Mariah his own obedient wife! But Andrew is living in the shadow of a scandal...

SECRETS AND SCANDALS
Nothing stays secret for long in Regency Society

Mills & Boon® Hardback Historical

Another exciting novel available this month:

HIS COMPROMISED COUNTESS

Deborah Hale

The scandalous wife!

When his beautiful, flirtatious wife scandalises Almack's by being caught in the arms of his enemy, Bennett Maitland, Earl of Sterling, finally ends his unsuitable marriage. He banishes Caroline to his remote childhood home— only to end up trapped there with her!

Having lost the love of her cold husband, Caroline is outwardly defiant, yet her wounded heart aches for what they once shared. If she dares, she has one last chance to break through Bennett's icy reserve—and rekindle the fiery passion that once consumed them!

Mills & Boon® Hardback
Historical

*Another exciting novel available
this month:*

THE DRAGON
AND THE PEARL

Jeannie Lin

The most beautiful courtesan of them all…

Former Emperor's consort Ling Suyin is renowned for
her beauty, the ultimate seductress. Now she lives quietly
alone—until the most ruthless warlord in the region
comes and steals her away…

Li Tao lives life by the sword, and is trapped in the treacherous
world of politics. The alluring Ling Suyin is at the centre of the
web. He must uncover her mystery without falling under her
spell—yet her innocence calls out to him. How cruel if she,
of all women, can entrance the man behind the legend…

ST0112 HB TDATP